ONCE UPON A CORPORATION

ONCE UPON A CORPORATION

❀

Leadership Insights from Short Stories

Tolly Kizilos

Writers Club Press
New York Lincoln Shanghai

Once Upon a Corporation
Leadership Insights from Short Stories

Writers Club Press
an imprint of iUniverse, Inc.

For information address:
iUniverse, Inc.
2021 Pine Lake Road, Suite 100
Lincoln, NE 68512
www.iuniverse.com

Credit for graphic: Melissa Khaira

ISBN: 0-595-25827-1 (pbk)
ISBN: 0-595-65363-4 (cloth)

Printed in the United States of America

To the memory of my father and mother
Peter and Marina Kizilos
For their love and support.

Whoever wants to be first must be last of all and servant of all.

—Jesus Christ
Gospel of Mark 9:35

A man is a little thing while he works by and for himself; but when he gives voice to the rules of love and justice, he is godlike.

—Ralph Waldo Emerson

The first responsibility of a leader is to define reality. The last is to say thank you. In between, the leader is a servant.

—Max DePree

To become one's self is man's true vocation

—Soren Kierkegard

Wonders are many, and none is more wonderful than man.

—Sophocles
Antigone

Contents

❀

LEADING WITH HEART, BRAINS AND BACKBONE

Foreword

❦

Tolly Kizilos has a rare and remarkable talent—to teach about the nature of organizations by telling stories, constructing fables, imagining Socratic dialogues, and describing composite people who seem real because they are so very much like individuals we have all known and had to deal with in real-life organizations.

There is a good deal of literature by story-tellers about administrative process—that is, about behaviors in organizations of individual human beings, which is so different from the way the same people might think and act in other contexts. Unlike most such storytellers, Tolly Kizilos is not limited to his own personal experience.

That would certainly be rich enough: he is a perceptive observer of how organizations work, and a skillful practitioner of the art and science of organizational development. But Kizilos is able to extrapolate from his own wise observations to a more generalized wisdom; he's able to imagine people and situations that typify the major problems, and the many kinds of problem-people, that constrain productivity in modern organizations.

Although his readable fables and lovely metaphors are drawn primarily from corporate experience, I am personally struck with how well they illuminate also the terrain of the public executive and educational administrator. That's been my terrain as an executive and as a writer about leadership and management (*The Future Executive*, *The Knowledge Executive*, etc), as well as a onetime teacher in the field of public administration. Tolly Kizilos' writing thus translates readily into the public, educational and non-profit sectors, which most writings on the Business bookshelf do not.

It's now clear enough that the main problems facing the U.S. industry are not the imagination of American designers or engineers. The main problems have to do with the adaptability and flexibility of American executives and managers, and with their adjustment to the two huge changes in the modern environment for getting things done: the pervasive use of information technology and the subsequent globalization of money, business, and governance.

What I long ago called the "twilight of hierarchy" shines through much of what Tolly Kizilos has written. But he gets his message across not by diagrams and explanations and admonitions; he scores with stories that will jerk tears and produce irrepressible chuckles from readers with their own deep experience of organizational life—because it is precisely those readers who will most clearly recognize the foibles and fallibilities of people working together to make something different happen.

Based on a considerable acquaintance with writings about organizational behavior, the kind of thing Tolly Kizilos is able to write is unique. His insight is in a class with Peter Drucker's (and that's first class), but it shines forth in a very different style, a more accessible style for readers who like to read, but are not motivated to *study* about people in organizations.

Many readers who are put off by books of heavy organizational analysis, yet offended by all the management-made-easy literature that overstuffs the Business shelves these days, will be grateful when they learn that it is possible for a business writer to help them understand organizational complexity by telling stories—and maintaining a lively sense of humor.

Harlan Cleveland
President Emeritus
World Academy of Art and Science
Founding Dean of the Hubert H.
Humphrey Institute of Public Affairs

Acknowledgments

❀

Many of the stories in this book have their origin in the work life of a great organization, the Systems and Research Center (SRC) of Honeywell, Inc. This organization was dedicated not only to the advancement of technology, but also to organizational, personal and professional excellence. It was consistently recognized as one of the most innovative organizations within the company and among similar organizations in the country.

I worked in this organization for many years, some of them under the leadership of Dr. William T. Sackett, whose vision of excellence and dynamic initiatives were the driving forces guiding the Center. I want to thank him for the opportunity he gave me and many other professionals at the Center to innovate and become better persons. With Dr. Sackett's guidance, SRC pioneered the introduction of many management processes such as team development, participative management with consensus decision-making, personal empowerment for leadership, conflict resolution processes, management selection by teams and career development training, just to mention a few, when these now familiar systems were just becoming known in the business world.

I hope that I, along with my now departed friends, Dr. Alan Anderson and Rev. Dr. Richard E. Byrd, both extraordinary Organization Development consultants, and a few other brave hearts in the field who worked with us, will always be members of exciting teams like those we built at SRC, forever dreaming up and implementing ways to empower people as persons and leaders in worthy organizations.

I also I want to thank the people of SRC, who were determined to solve work-related problems in enlightened ways and create a great organization. The satisfaction I derived from serving them was the most valuable reward of my organizational life.

Introduction

❀

We all learn from books; we all learn from experience; and we all learn from relationships with people; but the fact is, most of us also learn a great deal from stories. That's why the Old Testament contains so many narratives, and Jesus spoke in parables; that's why the Greeks came up with myths to talk about their culture and religion; that's why nations create legends with heroes who exemplify their most cherished values; and that's why children begin to learn about the world around them from bedtime stories.

In the thirty years that I have been in the organization development business, working with employees and teaching MBA students various aspects of management and leadership, I have learned that people pay the most attention when they read or hear stories of work life experiences. It seems that people grasp the essential meaning of a work life situation best, integrate learning faster and retain what they learn the longest when they read or hear insightful stories or anecdotes. Sometimes, attracting people's attention and tickling their curiosity requires that these stories take them beyond their everyday world to environments shaped by the imagination into metaphors, parables, parodies or satires, and populated by idiosyncratic characters doing familiar things in extraordinary ways. Management may be a science, or an art, or both; but more than anything else, management, and leadership, in particular, are complex relational experiences, and the best way to communicate knowledge gathered from such experiences—though not the only way—is to tell stories about them. We are doing a disservice to our students and employees by educating them in leadership and management using only books written for cognitive learning and excluding books of fiction, which are most suitable for experiential learning.

The twenty-seven contemporary fables, allegories and other narratives presented here are based on the realities of modern corporate work life. They offer insights into the organizational experience many of us know, and contain useful lessons on how to survive, even thrive as productive and caring human beings in spite of organizational pressures. Yes, these stories have morals; yes, they are instructive; and, yes, you'll recognize yourself and many other coworkers here; but, I hope, that you'll also have a good time reading them, and a hard time forgetting some of them. The insights you gain from reflecting upon these unusual, tongue-in-cheek stories should come, not from identifying with heroes and berating villains, but from recognizing the humanity of all the characters and discerning the many ways people in the lead can serve others as well as their own enlightened self-interest. The theme underlying many of these stories is that stewardship should be a prime value of leadership.

The first part of the book contains fifteen stories, all of them portraying "Characters with Character at Work." What these characters do is the result of who they are, and affirms their existence. Work life for them is meaningful because it is committed to values they hold dear. The kind of work that these corporate specialists do full time is what most of us do only on occasion; the way they do their work is the way many of us would like to do some aspect of our function, but seldom get a chance to do. The Reality Coordinator, for example, tries to define reality the best way he can, so that others may benefit from his knowledge and act accordingly. All of us do the same thing in momentary flashes or short reflections to understand reality and get "the lay of the land." But the Reality Coordinator works full time, according to a set of rules, and he does his job thoroughly, aggressively and with a missionary's zeal. Another thing many of us have tried to do is to cheer up a team by emphasizing the bright side of the issue being discussed; we felt good when we succeeded, and terrible when we failed. The Staff Optimist presents these optimistic views day-in-day-out, because the job he has committed to do requires it. But, how does one do that? What does failure to convince others do to him? How do we feel when no one takes our hopeful views seriously? What about a Staff Pessimist to tone down highflying sales engineers? Shouldn't we make a point of presenting all sides to any issue? I knew an executive who would become very upset, if anyone made a presentation to him and didn't cover both sides of the issue with stark realism. The Image-fixer, another one of the "characters," has a more difficult problem to deal with: he has to convince a severe critic of his that his job is worth doing; then he has to convince himself of it! Issues of substance and appearance have been dealt in philosophical treatises, but it is possible, I believe, to get a flavor of some of the arguments from a story like this one. It is possible to analyze all the characters in these stories, pondering different questions, if one wants to go a bit further than having fun from just reading the stories. Some of these characters will surprise you with their unusual skills and talents. Students of organizations may even want to speculate on what might happen if actual organizations were to adopt some of the practices of the organizations that these characters serve. A lively debate might ensue, if thoughts were shared.

But, why bother to write these tongue-in-cheek stories, many of them about imaginary jobs without much of a chance of implementation? It is certainly not to outline formal job descriptions, or to satirize the people who try to study or practice decision-making, problem-solving, interpersonal communication and so on, as their job requires. Rather, the purpose of writing these stories is to focus attention on certain interpersonal aspects of leadership, especially in the context of management, and reexamine organizational values that may have been neglected, such as forgiving mistakes, respecting intuition, discerning the facts and values beneath the sales pitches, making demand for quality a way for caring for others, assessing the costs of freedom of expression "inside the plant gates" and others. This is done in the hope that managers and non-managers alike will reflect upon these aspects of their world and, perhaps, find ways to enrich their work lives and their organization's human environment.

The second part of the book presents twelve short stories and parodies, which examine in new ways several systemic aspects of corporate work life and management. Among these are: ethical conduct, participation in decision-making, working "smart" but responsibly, dealing with fear in the workplace, power and politics up and down the management ladder, conflict, dignity, motivation and finding meaning in work life. The exploration of these topics is done by parodying Socratic dialogues, satirizing a bit of relevant fiction by the master-satirist Mark Twain, creating epistolary fiction which uses Machiavelli's work and portrays him as a character, and by parodying management memos and satirizing some organizational situations. I have used whatever literary forms seemed appropriate for communicating these complex management issues. For example, I had tried to write several "articles" on participative management, but I was never able to get my message across until I remembered the penetrating exploration afforded to the writer by the Socratic dialogue and used it for that purpose. Participative management to me is more than just "involvement in the process," and I was determined to find a way to say what it is. The dialogues, I believe, served me well: after the publications, people no longer ask me what participative management was; they told me either that they agreed with me, or didn't believe this type of participative management would work. Both dialogues on participative management were published—one of them became the only fiction I have ever seen published in the

Harvard Business Review—and are included in this set of stories by permission. The underlying theme of all the stories in this part of the book is that it takes three broad qualities of leadership to create corporate organizations that excel in fostering meaning, personal growth and business success. It takes leading with heart, brains and backbone.

"Heart" is the quality of caring for one's fellow man, and some of the characters in these stories possess it. In the context of corporate work life, caring means treating employees with dignity; it means solving problems that make life easier for them by taking present reality into account rather than "going by the book;" it means giving people a chance to do their best and empowering them to do so; and it means managing people without being or appearing to be arbitrary or self-interested. Only when organizations, through their leaders, encourage people to care for each other, can there be trust, essential for teamwork and meaningful work relationships at every level of the organization. High morale, initiative, freedom from fear to express adverse views, job satisfaction, acceptance of responsibility and creativity that comes from enjoyment of the work are all related to the degree of caring people experience in their organization. Leading with "heart" to achieve these worthy goals takes a lot of effort, using all the skills and talents one has, but more than anything else it takes the right attitude toward people and the will to care.

It also takes "brains" to care for people while, at the same time, advancing the stated goals of the organization. A caring manager must have a record of solid organizational accomplishments to avoid being called a "bleeding heart" and discredited. It seems that to do some good in this world, people have to be "street smart" and resourceful even as they care and are willing to take a risk in helping others. They must "be wise as serpents and innocent as doves" (Matthew 10:16).

"Brains" are always valued in organizations, especially when they belong to a person who also has a "heart." Intellectual power is needed not only for solving problems in technology, marketing or accounting in order to achieve organizational goals, but also in creating solutions to personal, interpersonal and organizational problems—the kind of problems that try managers' souls day in and day out. "Brains" are also needed when leaders at any level of the organization must show "backbone," either to change the minds of tough minded managers by well thought out reasoning, or to counter the machinations of wrongdoers who put up obstacles in doing the right thing. Some characters in these stories find out that their good intentions fail to yield results; they just didn't bring enough brains to bear upon the problem they were trying to solve. Finally, leaders need to use their brains to learn from experience and create new frameworks for living and grow in wisdom.

The third ingredient of leadership is "backbone"—the courage to "stand up and be counted." One of the leaders I worked with for several years had little respect for people who refused to say what was in their minds and utter contempt for people who knew that there was something wrong and didn't speak out. There were times when people fought pitched battles on a variety of business issues with this leader, and everyone watching them thought they had done themselves in, only to find out later that their display of "backbone" or "guts," supported by good reasons, was greatly appreciated and often rewarded. In that organization all people were empowered by their leaders to do their best and did it more often than in any other organization I have encountered.

People find out what "backbone" really is when they reach the "forks on the road" of work life: one road usually leads to personal gain of some kind by doing something wrong or something illegal, or by just keeping quiet when speaking out would have been the right thing to do; the other road requires action to do what one knows is right and sleep well at night, even if that has to be paid with deprivation of ill-gotten benefits, or suffering career setbacks or loss of a job. Sooner or later people stand at this "fork on the road" and find out how much they care about integrity and dignity, how much they value wealth, power or fame, and whether they have the backbone to follow their heart. People who want ill gotten gains of any kind are immoral and worse; people who cannot stand up and defend what they know is right are pathetic, because they betray their heart. People, who know the right thing to do and go ahead and do it in spite of the costs, are the builders of institutions that last and prosper to the benefit of all stakeholders. Backbone is the only safeguard against wrongheaded, superficial, unethical and illegal decisions and actions—it empowers people to speak out when others don't think well, or miss important aspects of the issue, or when others cheat, lie, break laws and trample upon other people's rights. No laws will ever be devised that can prevent all corporate fraud as effectively as the values that guide the behaviors of leaders. But, since we can never know for sure what's inside a leader's heart, tough laws are also needed.

People with backbone, like many of the protagonists in these stories, don't keep quiet when something is amiss; they defend their views against the higher ups, or in public meetings; they present solid arguments for their views; they refuse to authorize questionable expenditures; they decline favors and refuse to approve rewards that have little or no merit. People with backbone are not intimidated by rank, loud or angry voices, reputation, fame, wealth or accusations of disloyalty and sanctions. People with backbone are dangerous to autocratic managers, dictatorial leaders, to fakers of wisdom, to crooks and would-be crooks, because they are the only people who can expose them.

There is no particular order to these stories; they can be read at random without any loss of meaning. Just open the book on any story and start reading. At the end of each story, however, stop and reflect on what you just read: What is the message of the story? Is there a moral here? How does it fit into my work life experience? And most important, what does this story have to say to me? This is not a "how to" book, and nothing you'll read here is intended to guide you step-by-step to more effective management or enhance your leadership skills. But, perhaps, there are some insights here and there for you, some ideas worthy of more reflection now and then, a chuckle of recognition reading some stories, a moving gesture you'll remember and an "Aha!" here and there. These are the leadership insights, which could help you think about your profession and the corporation in a way that adds meaning to work life. This isn't a farfetched idea. After all, the corporation is the place where many of us spend most of our waking hours, the place where we achieve some of our dreams, form many important relationships that help us learn about ourselves and the world, and the place where we do a lot of our loving and hating of our neighbor.

Once Upon a Corporation is a book of fictions written for the purpose of sneaking up on the real world of work and seeing it anew again and again.

Characters with
Character at Work

CHAPTER 1

❀

A Reality Coordinator's Lament[1]

When people at social gatherings ask me what kind of work I do, I—a person normally skillful at answering personal questions and often welcoming them—I become clumsy and want to flee to escape embarrassment. I wish my answer was easily understood and didn't require a lengthy explanation. I wish I could say: "I am a plumber." It would be comforting to be able to give the answers such people as carpenters, chemists, or firemen can give rather than have to say: "I am a reality coordinator for a large industrial organization."

A response of this kind, as you can imagine, is always followed by questions and comments that distress me. "What exactly does a reality coordinator do?" Or, "Is this some kind of a joke?" And, with a dismissive knitting of eyebrows, "It must be hell working in a place where reality needs coordination." I am thankful when the responses are not accompanied by snickering or, worse yet, by outbursts of sarcastic laughter. I try to describe what I do without revealing my dis-

---

1.   First published in *Personnel, 2/1990,* with the title "A 'Reality Coor-
      dinator's' Lament," by Tolly Kizilos, and printed here by permission.

comfort, but the sensation of sinking in quicksand is inescapable. Reality coordinators are people with considerable understanding of how things are done in the organization—people whose job is to gather whatever information is available at the time, and piece together the shape of reality that others may find useful in performing their work or improving their circumstances.

To construct these ever-shifting shapes of reality, I observe the behavior of everyone around me. Also, I ask questions and probe others for thoughts, intentions, plans, schemes, hidden desires, undisclosed hopes and feelings. With every new morsel of information I am able to gather, I revise the shape of reality I have constructed and pass on the latest version to anyone who asks me.

My policy is as follows:

- I have only one version of reality at a time.

- I am the only person responsible for my version of reality.

- People do not have to subscribe to my version of reality, but if they do and act accordingly, they are entirely responsible for the consequences.

- All employees in the organization have an equal right to my reality.

- My performance as a reality coordinator must be judged on the results that people achieve when they make use of the reality I offer, rather than on the preferences of my boss.

But these general explanations are rarely satisfactory to the people who probe me. Most of them mutter a devastating "interesting" or declare their boredom non-verbally with a blank stare, and move away. A few people are genuinely intrigued and press on with more questions, and the occasional sadistic cynic ridicules me with a remark such as, "Sounds like you are a professional gossipmonger. Can you actually make a living at this?"

What can I say, then? How can I make people understand that reality coordination is a profession of great complexity worthy of respect? It involves not only skill, knowledge and experience, but also the character of its practitioner. You don't ask whether a plumber is quarrelsome or a chemist is a philanderer before entrusting them with assignments; but reality coordinators have to be even-tempered and trustworthy, and possess an impeccable character.

And that isn't all: reality coordinators must also have a merciless conscience so they can detect and prevent the slightest attempts at confusing their own self-serving or cowardly views with the facts of reality. They must be capable of probing the world of other people, sometimes at great risk and with very unpleasant consequences for themselves. They must be as transparent as glass, so that others can see inside them as much as they attempt to see inside others.

Is this an easy job? Don't you think that a person who has these attributes deserves to make a living? People shake their heads in disbelief, look at me as if I were a preacher of some weird cult, and drift away. I am left alone, wishing that I could lie, make small talk, give evasive answers to personal questions and avoid these ordeals. But this is something reality coordinators can never afford to do and still be true to their profession.

Perhaps, ten years from now, reality coordination will be an established profession, and no large organization with aspirations for excellence will be without its full complement of such professionals. Then people at social gatherings will not be so cruel to those who try to give honest accounts of the human environments they experience. But until that time comes, I must resign myself to going through the ordeal, as I am sure accountants, cosmetologists, and proctologists must have had to go through in times past.

I think that amateurs have started every profession, and reality coordination is no exception. Of course people are their own reality coordinators; but in a pinch, they are also plumbers. People are professionals when the quality of their work is superior to that of most amateurs, and others are willing to let them do what they can only do poorly or with great difficulty by themselves.

If my versions of reality were based on gossip, rumors, unchecked impressions and other such dubious data, I'm sure no one would want to know what I think about reality. But this is not the case. My data are gathered painstakingly with every skill and talent I possess, and with the fearlessness of a man who can afford to be seen for what he is rather than what he chooses to show to the world. Every chance I get, I observe what is happening around me and ask the questions most people want to ask but never will. I am a connoisseur of defense mechanisms, facades and plots that conceal self-interest. When I happen to provoke a violent response from someone, I know how to stand my ground and absorb the emotional blows.

But I wouldn't want anyone to think that I do these things because I am curious about people's thoughts and feelings, or because I derive any pleasure from confrontations and the occasional crumbling of some towering egos. Since I have no power to reward or punish anyone, I am neither a rich uncle nor a judge. I am also not a sadist, because my work gives me agony and sadness rather than pleasure. No, I am a reality coordinator because it is the only thing I can do better than most people, and it is of some value to others.

My services are in such high demand during times of change and transition that people who want my opinion, have to make appointments two or three weeks in advance. I am always invited to meetings to help managers define reality and make better decisions. In executive conference rooms, motels, retreats deep into woods, and even occasionally on the company plane, I follow discussions that affect the lives of dozens, hundreds, sometimes thousands of the company's employees. I listen, observe, analyze and formulate hypotheses about the situation before me, and fire away questions that cause the participants to take stock of themselves. They search beyond formulas, finances and worn-out clichés, until they touch the core of their existence.

When executives set profit goals, I ask whether or not these goals will adversely affect their employees, and what effect higher or lower goals would have on themselves and their families. When plant closings are being contemplated, I ask the most vocal advocates whether or not they accept the responsibility of putting people out of work to cut costs. Are they cutting costs to help the company survive or to maximize profits? In strategy sessions prior to union-management negotiations, I ask whether the participants would be willing to reveal their strategy to everyone, and if not, why not. Is it because the strategy they have in mind is based on deceit? Is it because they don't trust others enough to study the facts and act responsibly? Is it because, in spite of many assertions that all employees are members of the corporate family, managers and union leaders see each other as adversaries and want to beat each other down?

A couple of weeks ago, during a planning session for the introduction of a new product into the market, I asked the director of quality assurance whether he was personally satisfied that a new company product was safe and would perform its intended function. "Based on what I have seen," he started, but I didn't give him a chance to finish. He was hedging; he was shirking responsibility; he wasn't comfortable with my questions.

I continued, "Based on your humanity, your caring for your fellow human beings, your honesty, your intellect, on everything that is you, is it safe? And will it do well the job it is supposed to do?"

The director of marketing, who is in charge of advertising, tried to come to the rescue of his colleague, but I stopped him. The director of engineering tried to say something about functionality, but I asked him to wait. I didn't know at that moment whether the director of quality assurance would question my right to ask such questions and ask for my removal from the room, or break down and admit to himself and everyone else that he should have never yielded to pressure and given his blessing and approval to that product.

Actually, he admitted that he didn't like the product and didn't believe that it was either safe or functional. But he had checked and double-checked the test results, specifications, laws, rules and regulations, and could find no basis for rejecting it. At that point, all hell broke loose in the room, and after a two-hour discussion, the product was shelved.

After that meeting, people who asked me what I thought of the organization's management, its products, and its decision-making processes received a more hopeful answer than if the management team had approved the product. Recruits and employees who wanted to transfer to the department of quality assurance were informed that it was a vital organization headed by an honest, bright and caring man. Those interested in marketing were cautioned to not let their ambition get the best of their judgment, especially because a "success-oriented" director was in charge of the department.

Sometimes, when business is slow, I visit factories, executive offices, plants, warehouses, sales offices, any building where working human beings may be found, looking for false images, illusions and evidence of conditions, practices, behaviors or policies that are unhealthy. Greed, manipulation, ignorance, insensitivity and ineptitude—these are my enemies. The questions I ask hold individuals responsible. They cannot answer them with statistics, surveys or anecdotes; my questions require answers that commit the responsible individual to the answer. I am filled with sorrow if managers tell me that the way they run organizations is based on fear, intimidation and deceit because people are greedy, fickle or lazy. I can tell no one about the specifics of any response, and I can do nothing to change these managers' values and ways. But my version of reality in such an organization is bleak.

Fortunately, years of experience in this job convince me that most people are decent and mean well. Though I have encountered a handful of mean-spirited characters, most people who do something wrong are ignorant, or inept, or blind to the reality around them. So my questions are designed to define the work environment, by inducing self-reflection in the person I question, and nurturing any urge the person may have for improving the world around him or her.

I am really nothing more than an echo of that person's conscience, and whatever success I enjoy in describing reality comes from the strange effect that is produced when a human voice echoes precisely the thoughts within another human being's mind. Since I have no power to order how things must be done, my success depends on producing echoes rather than voicing views. In all the years of practice I have had, I can recall no occasion when I brought about any improvement without someone else wanting to make the world better. My failures, as anyone can see, are due to the occasional mismatch between what I voice and what the other people hear within themselves. Being a voice in the wilderness is the nightmare that haunts me, and will haunt reality coordinators forever.

I realize that I am a bit too verbose here, but I rarely get a chance to explain in detail what I do to people outside work. Besides, I am always so busy working with others, that I hardly ever have time to reflect upon my own reality. I used to do that a lot in earlier times, but I have neither the time nor the energy to do it now. I am always so drained after a day's work that I crave escape into illusions. I sit in my favorite armchair eating my TV dinner, with my eyes, my attention, my very soul glued to the tube. I am like the cooks who are glad when they can escape from their kitchens, and like physicians who have no stomach for diagnosing their own ulcers. In short, when I am off duty, I have absolutely no desire to know how people think or feel, or what is true or false around me.

Perhaps this dedication to my profession explains why I have no family, no lover and no friends, not even acquaintances. I am pleasant and sociable at gatherings or parties, and content to keep a low profile. People who don't know me at work think that I am superficial and unable to form meaningful relationships. I go through life being either totally involved or totally aloof.

My mother, who used to visit me on my birthday every year before she died, told me that when I was a boy, the other kids avoided me or beat me up because I was disruptive to the group. Now that I think of those times, I remember that my troubles were always related to my unwillingness to follow the leader, my penchant for questioning the rules of any games we were about to play, and my refusal to accept that the world was as it appeared to be.

I was a misfit then and I would be a misfit now, if adults were as accepting of myths and fantasies as children are. Yet, none of this explains why I do what I do. But is this so strange? Do people really know why they are bus drivers, or stockbrokers, or TV repairmen? All I know is that people want to know what my version of reality is, and as long as the company wants me to provide it for a decent salary, I'll go on offering my services and be content that I perform a useful function.

❀

CHAPTER 2

The Goldie Decides

When Constantine Saroyannis completed his Ph.D. in solid-state physics at the Massachusetts Institute of Technology, he received several offers for the position of assistant professor from some of the most prestigious Universities in the country, but to the surprise of all academics who knew him, he declined all of them. The rigorous regime of melting down a doctoral candidate's personality and remolding it to fit the dreams and rewards of academic life hadn't worked its magic in his case. Saroyannis was made out of a metal too hard to soften easily, let alone melt down and reshape. Instead, he accepted an offer for a job from a small company in the Boston area that was interested in his field of work and set out to put into practice some of the ideas he had conceived, while researching his thesis. He wanted to create useful products, rather than spend his time fashioning theories that would further his academic standing, but would make no dent on people's lives for decades, if ever.

Two of his ideas on integrated circuits were turned into products, and would have made the company prosper, if people had been able to work together and capitalize on Saroyannis' creative genius. But, conflicts, confusion, lack of commitment to common goals and absence of leadership caused delays and failures, and eventually the collapse of the company.

It is said that one of the characteristics of wise men is that they learn from their mistakes. If this is true, then Saroyannis was on the fast track to wisdom, having learned plenty from his failure as a technological innovator. He realized that the key to innovation was not so much a great idea, or the availability of superior intellectual powers, but the ability of people to work together effectively and efficiently toward shared goals. Doing his own informal survey on this issue, he found out that just about everyone of the experts he asked, told him that the key element needed for success in the technology business was people's ability to work together well. He became convinced that there would always be some people around to come up with technical ideas and solutions to problems, but he had no idea how people could solve the organizational problems that plague so many efforts to turn ideas into products. He examined many of the courses offered by the top universities on leadership, teamwork, conflict resolution, trust-building, and other relevant human relations topics, and wondered why all the knowledge that was available to everyone didn't help. This wasn't a technical question, and Saroyannis knew the boundaries of his expertise. He knew that, if he was going to solve the problem he had uncovered, he needed to learn much more about people at work. It seemed to him that the best way to expand his awareness on this subject was to find workplaces, which had few or no problems, and study how they were doing it. Clearly, no successful organization was about to open its doors to the scrutiny of a genius bent on discovering its secret of success, so he could compete more effectively. Also, Saroyannis was an unconventional thinker, and he wanted to find a way of learning first hand the fundamentals of successful workplaces, rather than rely on other people's research reports. After much thought and reflection, he decided to search for answers in distant lands; he resolved to become an anthropologist of sorts, and study how primitive people went about organizing their work. The advice of one of the wise old professors he had at MIT, also helped him decide to take this unusual approach: "If you want to innovate in a given field of knowledge, don't study that field the way everyone is trained to do. Study something else and then apply that knowledge to it. There is a reason why a naval engineer is head of the Mechanical Engineering Department here, and a chemist heads the Machine Tool Laboratory."

He wanted to find out what made people select ruthless or unenlightened leaders; how hunting parties enforced discipline in the bush of Africa; how responsibility was developed among the seal-hunting Eskimos of Alaska; and how decisions were made and conflicts were resolved in the Sahara and in Borneo.

After two years of travel and study, Saroyannis returned to the Boston area, and with the backing of some wealthy friends, who knew his extraordinary abilities, started his own high tech company, to manufacture computer memory devices for special applications, based on his own patents. Within ten years, Mindworks, Inc., had become one of the five largest companies in the field, and Saroyannis was a very wealthy man. His success was attributed to his inventiveness and the fun he had in taking risks. But, this wasn't really the case. Though not widely known, his ability to create a highly effective organization, which could prevail against cutthroat competition, could be traced to his understanding of people and the way they can work together as a group in a culture. While others studied the Japanese and tried to transplant their successful methods to the American workplace, or admired the "lean and mean" philosophy of some American CEOs, who boosted quarterly profits by slashing workforces and starving research departments, Saroyannis was studying the Ibos of West Africa, the Gruah tribe of Mozambique, the Shans of Mongolia, and the Roro-speaking people of Melanesia, for clues to their effectiveness. Whenever he discovered a process, a ritual, a belief or a technique, which had allowed them to do their work more effectively, he would consider its adaptability to the American workplace and, if it seemed promising to him, he would experiment with it at Mindworks Inc.

Though Saroyannis introduced many innovations to the American work place, for better or worse, his name will always be associated with the function of the Goldie. This was a prime example of a successful transplantation of a primitive work-facilitating system. Having the Goldie decide, boosted productivity and gave Mindworks the winning edge in the marketplace.

Saroyannis was traveling in Johore and the South Pahang islands of Malaysia, ostensibly exploring the feasibility of building a small assembly plant for some of the simpler components made by Mindworks, but in fact studying the Jakun tribesmen. He had discovered that the Jakun, who inhabit the west end of South Pahang and a strip of central Johore, had been known for many years by ethnologists for their hard work and a peculiar custom of using an otherwise taboo language while working. The *pengulu*, as their leader is called, and the *sakai*, his workers, communicate in this language only at work. Apparently, this was their way of maintaining a sense of identity, going back many generations, when they had been indentured to foreign masters for the purpose of collecting camphor in the jungle. Saroyannis was intrigued by this language, which is only partly Malay, and is known as *bahasa-kapor*. He was intent on finding its role in their work habits, which were revealed to be conducive to phenomenally high productivity, compared to other groups and tribes he had studied.

In his characteristic way, he insisted that discovery is unpredictable, and research is only the context within which one can get lucky—"research buys you a ticket to the lottery, but doesn't win it for you," he used to say—he stumbled upon the concept of the Goldie quite by accident, while engaged in the study of the Jakun. The taboo language, he discovered, was nowadays used to cement the relationship between the *pengulu* and his *sakai*, but had nothing to do with work efficiency. That was due to the function of the *moganu,* a cross between an arbitrator, a facilitator of disputes and a judge, who told people how to proceed when they couldn't agree among themselves, or refused to follow the directions of the *pengulu.* Since no one could foresee when a mere difference of opinion would escalate into a full blown labor dispute and waste time and energy better spent on production, anyone could shout *"pokena-moganu"* and immediately all discussion would cease and the matter would be referred to the *moganu* for resolution. The *moganu's* decision would be carried out, though people who didn't get their way would be furious with him; but, the relationship between the *pengulu* and his *sakai* was always congenial, and team work was never disrupted.

Though there are countless examples of ways that various cultures have devised to facilitate not only work but also other necessary or desirable functions, not many can be transplanted whole cloth, as it were, from one culture to another. The American organization theorists' attempts to apply Japanese team work norms to the American workplace didn't always take into account the resistance of American individualism *vis a vis* the Japanese communal mentality. When Japanese methods of high productivity teams were introduced in the American work place, for example, it was decided not to reward the top performers with bonuses, to avoid interfering with the team's cohesion. Japanese workers were known to feel shame if they were ever singled out and rewarded with bonuses for their top performance. It goes without saying that this particular aspect of team recognition was a disaster for the motivation of individual American workers, and had to be discarded in a hurry. The genius of Saroyannis was his ability to discern which of all the new ways he discovered could be fully implemented at Mindworks and the American work place more broadly, and which should be left alone.

"Freedom, has allowed us to pursue our dreams without encumbrances, but has fragmented consensus to the point where it is rare even for two people to agree on anything under the sun," he used to say, with a style formed by high school training in ancient Greek polysyllables and a New England businessman's directness. "And when they disagree, it is considered cowardly to yield for the purpose of agreement, since freedom has made everyone a fearless defender of his opinion, which is based these days upon sacrosanct principles, unalienable rights, values, beliefs and experiences that feed the greedy self. No longer can a manager issue orders, give directions, or even tell workers nicely what to do and have them do it, without endless discussions and countless disagreements. And, even when he manages to get their consent, there is resentment lurking in their gut, which chokes their initiative, their creativity and every other quality needed for high productivity in the fast-changing, complex world we live in. Somehow, we have twisted the meaning of freedom so that when the boss' way goes against our way, we feel wronged, diminished, alienated and demotivated."

With his penchant for using polysyllabic words where short snappy Anglo-Saxon ones might have done the job as well or even better, he would become philosophical: "Once upon a time we were accustomed to perceive what was expected of us and go do it. We used common sense and trust, the consensus view and averages, the rulebook and the law to set aside fringe opinions, esoteric interpretations, and downright muddled thinking. Now the boss has to sweat or to shout to get his people to get anything done. Herodotus, in 500 B.C., called this kind of individualistic thinking "idiotic," and all but dismissed it before the community's will that produced what was perceived to be the truth. Now, however, there is no common sense, no middle ground, no communal consensus and no respect for knowledge, or rules, or even laws. Now, the average is encountered as frequently as the preposterous. We no longer have Gaussian, bell-shaped distributions of accepted and expected opinions, principles and values; rather, we have a flat, spread-out spectrum of these, where anything is as meritorious and valid as anything else, and deciding on a course of action is a hazardous activity. We lose time and energy sorting out what in the past would have been obviously worthless. And, ironically, sometimes it is precisely the obviously worthless alternative that can save us, give us the edge, lead us to new understandings and improve our lot. So, who is to say what should be done?"

"The *moganu*, that's who!" Saroyannis would blare out with child-ish enthusiasm, and pound the table, or podium, or any surface he could find near him. And, he would go on to explain that the job of the *moganu* was transformed into the function of the Goldie, i.e. the person who applies the Golden Mean to resolve conflicts by deciding which of the various views held by the disputants should prevail.

Just as the *moganu* was the least of the *sakai* among the Jakun, so was the Goldie reduced to mere survival and confined to the work place. Unlike the *moganu*, however, who held his position for life, the Goldie occupied his only for a year. This was long enough to master the skills required for the job, and short enough to attract to the position many worthy candidates and make the selection of one of the most talented people in the company quite likely.

In spite of the rigors of the work and the absence of personal gain during the year of service, there were always several people who wanted to have the power and responsibility of the Goldie. For, who, among the many ambitious people in the company, wouldn't want to be the final arbiter of disputed issues among one's co-workers and bosses? And, who wouldn't forego immediate gratification for the privilege of stating at some future time in his resume that he was the Goldie of Mindworks when one of the great decisions was made, and knew first hand the burdens and the exhilaration of deciding crucial matters with even greater freedom of action than most CEOs?

After several small scale experiments with the function of the Goldie, a job description was written and a policy was issued, giving all employees the right to call upon the Goldie, and requiring that they follow his or her advice, without appeal to anyone else. Prospec-tive employees had to agree with this policy, if they wanted to be employed by Mindworks, Inc. The existing work force was asked to pass on it soon after the trial period was completed. An overwhelming majority gave the Goldie's function its support and, after that, defended it as one of its cherished rights. The few employees who initially opposed it were persuaded to give it a try and, in time, most of them were convinced of its value, based on the results. The handful, which could not accept "the arbitrary and dictatorial character of the system," as they put it, left the company, to the relief of their fellow employees and the good wishes of their superiors.

The first Goldie was selected by a blue ribbon team of managers and non-managers, using a clearly spelled out selection process, and the system was up and running with total support from the workforce. Whenever people disagreed on an issue, they'd call out, "I've had enough of this; let's take it to the Goldie!" All discussion would end, and the group or its representatives would head for the Goldie's office, which was part of his or her living quarters. After explaining to the Goldie the issue, with questions of fact unresolved, the values of the disputants still tangled, and the diverse opinions often unsupported by any thorough analysis, they would give him the view of each disputant as an item, and ask him to choose the alternative they should all follow. The Goldie's only restriction was that he could not create a new alternative, but had to choose one of those they gave him. When the Goldie gave them an answer, they would leave and proceed with its execution, knowing that it was one of them who proposed this course of action, and that the Goldie chose it from those they had given him.

Before the Goldie, the humblest and the mightiest employees were equal, and his "advice" was never challenged. To avoid the possibility that the Goldie might advise a course of action that could harm irreparably an individual or the company, Saroyannis was persuaded to accept a modification to the *moganu* function. This modification allowed Saroyannis himself to overrule or even dismiss the Goldie from the company, with no questions asked, if he determined that the Goldie was acting with malice, or wanton irresponsibility. He was reluctant to agree, but yielded to the request of his legal department, believing that their fears would never materialize and his power would never be needed. Clearly, Saroyannis believed that even the lowest level employees, when finally empowered, were transformed into responsible people, who could decide issues as wisely as anyone else or, at least, let others with greater knowledge decide. He believed that the choice of a course of action was not the determinant of high performance; rather, what mattered most, was the willingness of people from the highest to the lowest ranking employee to move in unison, and attack the work with the same purpose in mind. Saroyannis never thought of himself as a dictator. He called himself "a believer in elitist democracy."

These unorthodox beliefs of Constantine Saroyannis were proven correct, judging by the success of Mindworks in the marketplace. The Goldie made it possible for the work force to come together and produce with efficiency, which was the envy of the competition. After some time had gone by and every one got used to the new state of affairs, the Goldie's advice was followed not because the employees had agreed to follow it, but because they knew that the Goldie had nothing to gain from what he advised; because his or her period of advising, wisely or foolishly, would eventually end in a year, and he or she would be just another employee after that; because the Goldie had available before him or her all the views any manager or interested non-manager could possibly have, since all views were expressed openly and without fear of intimidation; and, because they had experienced the way decisions were made before Goldies existed and had no more confidence in the wisdom of those who were supposedly experts in deciding than they came to have in the Goldie. "He has nothing to gain," people would say after receiving his advice. "She did her best with the information we gave her, and now *we* have to give it our best."

The occasional dissenter who proclaimed his readiness to suffer any consequences rather than take orders from someone he called ignoramus or a dilettante or "shamanoid" or whatever, would usually come to his senses and follow the Goldie's advice however grudgingly, knowing that if he didn't and the function was abolished, the organization would revert to its old ways, with a multitude of self-interested managers, entrenched in authority, protecting their fiefdoms, issuing orders, sometimes better, sometimes worse, but always biased toward one viewpoint, their own, for endless years to come. "After all," the Goldie's defenders would remind everyone, "who really knows which is the best decision on any one issue, until actions follow and prove it right or wrong?"

The function of the Goldie was Saroyannis' baby, and under his caring presence and coaching it became a thriving institution and set the tone for a collaborative organization. Even after he relinquished control of the company, Saroyannis continued to devote time to the selection and training of Goldies. He was in his late sixties when he retired, but he still came to work once a week to spend some time with the Goldie and give him encouragement and advice based on whatever insights he had gathered following the work of the Goldie's predecessors and the wisdom of the primitives. He had made arrangements to have a man by the name of Carlton, one of the most successful Goldies, take over from him, when he could no longer oversee the Goldie's work.

Everyone agreed that the function of the Goldie was a success at Mindworks. Other companies with leaders of lower risk-taking ability than Saroyannis' were reluctant to adopt the function, but there was general agreement among organizational experts that, in time, some variant form of such a valuable innovation would be widely adopted by organizations everywhere. And, it might have been, if the secret of the Goldie's decision-making process had not been revealed shortly after Saroyannis' death.

Saroyannis had taken the company public just before he retired, and had picked his successor carefully for his understanding of people and technology. But, after his death, and at the first signs of trouble, the board of directors, canned Saroyannis' hand picked successor, and brought a whiz accountant, who had been CFO for a successful competitor, to run Mindworks. Daryl Teigren was a tough boss, and demanded to know all the facts about everything, including the process of the Goldie's function. Carlton had no choice but to tell him exactly how the Goldie made his decisions. Carlton was a true believer and had no doubt he could sell the function to Teigren, however primitive its origin and modus operandi might be, since it had been one of the key elements of the company's success. Unfortunately, he was dead wrong. When Teigren heard the particulars of the Goldie's decision-making method he said he found it offensive, and abolished the function on the spot. The official reason given to the employees of Mindworks for doing away with one of their most cherished institutions was "a desire to develop teamwork and decision making skills among all employees, by working through problems, however painful this might be at times."

Carlton left Mindworks as soon as Teigren's memo on the Goldie came out. He felt that he had let Saroyannis down, and saw himself as the person responsible for the loss that the people had suffered. Just before he left, however, he published a memo of his own, laying out the method of Goldie's decision making for all to see, as Saroyannis had outlined it, and Goldies had practiced it for twenty-three years. This is what the memo stated:

"The *moganu* of the primitive Jakun tribe chooses one of the disputed issues brought before him, not by assessing facts, analyzing issues or weighing the pros and cons of various viewpoints; he decides purely by chance. He throws the knee bone of the *kamassa*, "the wild boar that kills the very cautious hunter." The bone having four surfaces upon which it can land, allows the *moganu* to select one of up to four alternatives, views, opinions or issues brought to him. This way he is certain that no bias can enter his selection, and that, in time, everybody's view will be selected as often as everybody else's. The Jakun, apparently, do not believe that the tribe's survival requires that work-related decisions should be made by the *kingulu* who gives the group cohesion, or anyone else for that matter, who may have some expertise or a trait relevant to the work.

"I and all those who served you as Goldies over the years, used a similar method to choose among the alternatives brought to us by various groups. Instead of the knee bone of the *kamassa*, we used electronic random number calculators, setting the size of the sample equal to the number of alternatives presented to us. We assigned a number to each alternative, view, opinion, or whatever was at issue, and chose the one displayed by the calculator. Our decision to use chance rather than rational methods for decision-making wasn't forced upon us. We gave the matter considerable thought and argued with Saroyannis for endless hours, before we could become convinced that this approach had at least as much to recommend it as any other approach we were familiar with. I remember that we never had any difficulty in agreeing that dictators, autocrats and other know-it-all operators would run into trouble as they have usually done in history, but we needed very good reasons for rejecting the virtues of true workplace democracy and other forms of rational decision-making with worker participation. Saroyannis, ever the patient and learned teacher, loved to explain why such a radical approach made sense. How often do our most thoughtful decisions turn out to produce ridiculous or tragic outcomes? Didn't the Athenians use reason and free debate to find Socrates guilty and put him to death? Wasn't Christ judged by the wisest men of Israel and put to death? Didn't the German people elect Hitler freely as their leader with an overwhelming majority and watch him lead their country to disaster? Didn't the United States Senate pass the Gulf of Tonquin Resolution by a vote of 98 to 2 after proper rational deliberation, and give President Johnson all the power he needed to escalate the disastrous Vietnam War? Reason is useful as a guide for the individual mind, but doesn't seem to be the decisive factor for group decisions. Is it reasoning that determines our decisions really, or the loudest voice, the most frequently voiced view, the handsomest face, the sexiest body, the cleverest presentation of one's views, or the voice feared the most? Are the wise people heard, or those who offer solutions for immediate gain, regardless of the pain these may inflict later upon others? And, how often are some of the most qualified people neutralized or left out of the decision making processes for reasons that have nothing to do with qualifications but everything to do with political maneuvers or outright deception? Surely over the thousands of years that important decisions have been made for the survival of a group, its women had little or no say in them; neither did people who had been enslaved and others who were kept at the margins of society for various reasons. Were there no women, no slaves, no people with disabilities and no other outsiders who had better thoughts, at least some of the time, than the decision-makers of the group?

"The fact that a group or a society survived without benefit of all its resources, sometimes without its best minds and talents being used, shows that quality of decisions is not the most essential element for the survival of a group; rather, it is concerted actions and solidarity in implementation which are the critical elements for success. Our reliance on chance in deciding which among several reasonable alternatives should be implemented, was much less daring and arbitrary than oracles of old giving advice by chewing laurel leaves, or diviners reading the bones of dead birds, or seers interpreting dreams. Let's not forget that we never advised anything which wasn't espoused by someone in the work group, and that we relied on the ironclad laws of chance rather than the hocus-pocus methods people have used over the millennia. It may require some time for reflection, but it is not difficult to see that what often passes for reason and is revered as the ultimate human instrumentality, is a murky mixture of emotions, habits, and selfish motives sprinkled with reason. At least, that's how we saw things, as we advanced in our training and became qualified to be your Managers of the Golden Mean, or "Goldies," as you affectionately called us. Even if we admit that reason sometimes prevails in a group and good decisions are made as often as they are by the Goldie, the advantages of the Goldie's decision-making method in terms of speed, conflict elimination, and empowerment of all individuals fully justify its use.

"I have described the decision-making process we used, not because it was the most rigorous part of our training, but because Mr. Teigren found our reliance on chance most distasteful during his discussions with me. I suspect, however, that there are other reasons which he dislikes much more about the Goldie's function—reasons, which have more to do with power and control than decision-making philosophy.

"I want to add for the record, that besides studying decision making processes, free will versus fate, epistemology and anthropology with special attention to the influence of technological reductionism in our culture, we spent a lot of time learning how to respond to people with humility and concern for their needs. Counseling those whose alternatives didn't prevail became one of the main concerns of all the Goldies around the Company. I can recall many discussions about the strange and exciting world Constantine Saroyannis described to us, but the one thing that sticks in my mind above all else is his urging us to remember that all employees are persons, entitled to all our skills and abilities, no matter what positions they occupy, no matter what their qualifications or opinions. He hated the word "loser" and all but banned its use in the culture. He was a lover of all individual human beings, and this produced the best working teams we know of. As he used to say: 'If it isn't paradoxical, it probably won't work!'

"There will be no Goldies anymore, but the concept will live on in the hearts and minds of those who had the chance to experience the function and use it. Good chances to all of you."

Teigren denounced Carlton's memo through his managers, many of whom had been staunch defenders of the Goldie's function when

Saroyannis was the boss. They insisted they had no idea that decisions had been made by chance and business had been, as they put it, "nothing more than a crap shoot." Even people, who had scored notable business successes by following the advice of the Goldie, now were incensed, and ridiculed the primitive methods of an obviously deranged mind.

Carlton tried to interest other companies in the function of the Goldie, offering to train people in the practice, but the adverse publicity surrounding the function made it impossible for him to find anyone who cared to try it. The experts in organization development who had attributed the business success of Mindworks to the Goldie, acknowledged the genius of Saroyannis as an entrepreneur who managed to succeed, as they put it, "in spite of his eccentricities, most notably the introduction of myth, magic and the irrational in what became known as the 'Goldie affair.'"

The employees of Mindworks gradually forgot about the Goldie and remembered Saroyannis only as a winner, who built the company up with the sheer force of his entrepreneurial risk taking and his technological innovations. They thought of him often, especially after Teigren took over, because the company kept losing market share, its new products couldn't stir enthusiasm, and quality in its manufacturing facilities could not be maintained as it had been in the old days. Teigren gave up after two years of trying to restore profitability through market focusing, restructuring, reductions in force, reorganizations and strategic repositioning. The new CEO has a lot of energy, but everybody can see the writing on the wall.

The only people who are doing well are the former Goldies of Mindworks: unbeknownst to anyone, Saroyannis' will contained a codicil which provided that, if the function of the Goldie was ever abolished, all former Goldies would receive a generous stipend for life, which they could use to further the study of other cultures and apply relevant knowledge to what he characterized as "our supra-rationalistic expert-noxious culture." They formed the Goldies' Society, and have been presenting their findings regularly every year to highly receptive audiences.

The only Goldie who didn't fare well was Carlton. He was never able to recover from the abolition of the Goldie. When all his efforts to spread the Goldie's function failed, he went to Johore of Malaysia and lived among the Jakun, trying to institute the function of the dispute arbitrator in their tribal society. According to the report of one Reverend Truax, a missionary in the area, who wrote to the Goldies' Society about Carlton's life and work there, Carlton called the person in this function "the Tin Man." Little is known of Carlton's state of mind at the time, but Truax thought that he desperately wanted the tribe to expand the number of its problem solving techniques by utilizing a sophisticated process for conflict resolution. Apparently, the Jakun were offended by a stranger introducing among them alien ways for deciding on how to deal with work related disputes. To them it was insanity to reason with people who were mad at one another at the time. Besides, they had no urgent need to learn about conflict resolution, since conflicts were very rare events, thanks to their *moganu*. Not even Reverend Truax possessed such missionary zeal as to try and reconcile totally irrational or disinterested natives, if or when they started fighting among themselves.

Reverend Truax believed that the Jakun did learn from Carlton how to use reason to make decisions and resolve conflicts in a group. But, this wasn't their preferred method. Carlton was never popular among them. Resenting his interference, the Jakun reasoned together that the stranger with his dangerous new ways had to go. They tied him, gagged him and left him in the jungle alone, where a *kamassa* mauled him to death. For whatever interest it was to the Society, the Reverend Truax added that the present *moganu* uses Carlton's knee bone in his decision making craft, claiming that now he can decide from among six rather than four different alternatives, since there are six more or less flat edges on the human knee bone. One might say that the advancement of technology is relentless.

CHAPTER 3

❊

The Oracle of Metrimax

After the fall of the Berlin Wall and the dissolution of the Soviet Union, Metrimax Inc. was attempting to establish business relationships with small, newly constituted companies in Russia, to take advantage of their high talent professional people, whose wages were much lower than they would have been in the US. Some of the professionals employed by these companies were so exceptionally qualified for the work our company was doing that we wanted to hire them on the spot as regular employees. This however was done only in rare cases because of the many time-consuming and energy-intensive steps one had to follow in the immigration procedure. One such case, in which we did make the effort, was that of Dr. Irena Maistrova, a professional with superior mathematical ability and computer expertise, working for one such small company in Omsk.

Dr. Irena Maistrova was mute, but her disability presented no serious problem in her work. The employees of Metrimax Inc. didn't know how or why a mute mathematician from Omsk had been hired to work in the Strategic Planning Department of the company, but I, as a human resources employee representative with the responsibility for processing her intricate paperwork, knew that she had suffered in a Siberian prison for activities against the communist state and was given priority to immigrate to the US and a job with us at the intercession of several religious groups. Rumor had it that she had provided valuable services to the CIA, but this story could not be verified by any data that I had seen in her personnel file. There was a lot of admiration for her because she had opposed the soviet regime and survived the brutal penal system. Everybody was anxious to show her that she was more than welcome in our midst, and we were indeed indebted to her for whatever services she had provided to our country. One might have guessed that the outcome of such excessive solicitude, which was often patronizing, might make her withdraw. But, Irena wasn't the kind of person who would hold the well-meant unawareness or clumsiness of others against them. She couldn't talk, but her smile and the myriad expressions she could communicate with her eyes were reassuring and made people feel at ease. If anyone called her Dr. Maistrova, or Ms. Maistrova, or anything else, Irena would shake her head to indicate disapproval, and would flash a button she had pinned behind her lapel with her name in bold red letters "Irena" on a gold background and tap on it with her index finger until the person said her name. When that happened, a beautiful smile would grace her face. The recipient of such impromptu training could never forget either the stimulus or the reward of the interaction. Within a few months Irena was able to change the feelings of pity and the attitudes of excessive helpfulness everybody had toward her to feelings of healthy camaraderie and even respect for her as a professional. For who could have such disdain for formality and titles but a person who is sure of her own self worth?

After she had been with us for a year, it was clear to everyone who was familiar with her work that the results she produced were not only very useful but also exceptionally accurate. People who worked with her agreed that she was a top-notch mathematician and a wizard with computers. Her *forte* was forecasting, the front end of the planning process, which takes in all the available data and by means of complex statistical methods gives reasonable extrapolations about future events that are significant to the company's business. Others would use these forecasts to make plans for action. The better the forecasts, the better the plans and the actions, which implemented them. Forecasters are, after all, our modern day oracles, and their results can make the difference between success and failure in the fortunes of individuals, corporations, even the nation. They are much more influential than the readers of tea leaves and the psychics one sees on TV, or those who attract ignorant or desperate people for an answer to some personal problem.

Irena's co-workers were in awe of her ingenuity in constructing mathematical models into which to feed data, and of her ability in manipulating data with mathematical formulas. Whereas others used only packaged software for all their work, Irena would often find flaws or inadequacies in the existing software and would thrust herself into a frenzied effort to write her own and come up with more accurate predictions. Rumors of these feats of virtuosity began to circulate in the company and Irena's reputation as "a math wiz" began to grow. Even the title "Oracle" started to follow her name affectionately in chats and friendly talks about her. People no longer thought that she was a poor, needy immigrant who begged her way to the land of milk and honey; they started to think that Irena's coming to Metrimax was another coup, scored by our shrewd managers in the personnel wars that are forever raging in prosperous times. A few said that she was a godsend, destined to do work on bigger and better things than Metrimax could possibly offer. In just a couple of years, the basis of friendship with Irena had shifted from pity, to respect, to admiration. I thought it would be helpful to Irena and the company to have an article about her published in the company newspaper, but Irena said she wanted no publicity, and we called it off. Nevertheless, she no longer had to flash her name button and try to put people at ease; now, most people around recognized her immediately and welcomed a chance to be with her. Though she was unable to speak, she participated in any group she found herself in by expressing her opinions with her eyes, her face, her hands, on the board, or by typing on a new laptop she had acquired with what sounded like a more human voice output than the one that communicates Stephen Hawking's deep thoughts.

As I have already mentioned, I had met Irena when she came to Metrimax and took care of all the paperwork for her hiring. I had been impressed by her quiet, I would say, peaceful, even otherworldly demeanor. From the start, I offered to help her with any matters that had to do not only with employment but also with problems that might arise while trying to fit in our culture.

"Do you know good Russian supermarket and restaurant to give me address?" I remember her writing on a piece of paper and smiling. When I said that I could find out and let her know, she shook her head. "Just joke," she wrote. "I have more friends than to know I have," she wrote, and laughed gregariously. It was hard not to enjoy such moments with her.

When she first got her laptop, she stopped by my office, placed her new toy on my desk, sat down beside me and typed a message on it. "I came to chat here," her machine spewed out the words in its monotonous, vaguely masculine voice. Immediately I relaxed and had a delightful conversation with her about friendships in Russia. "We meet in friend's apartment, maybe five or ten peoples, and talk the last law the politicians made or the how Dostoyevsky, or Melville, or Lagerkvist talk about evil in world—you know the Lagerkvist? We drink little wine, eat little cheese and sardines and after sing songs. You know balalaika? I had a friend who make big music in that." And I would tell her about our gatherings around barbecues on backyards, or some Super Bowl TV party with the best ads money can buy, or a spaghetti dinner at a church fund-raising social, where heated discussions about homosexuals and baseball and the NFL standings, the stock market and other such life-and-death issues would rage for hours on end. "No jokes on work days," she would say, translating literally some Russian expression, I thought, and plead with me to be serious so she could learn more about the social life of Americans.

I saw her from time to time in the course of my work and had a chance to answer a few questions about benefits and immigration matters for her sister, who was getting ready to leave Russia, fed up as much with the life after the fall of communism as she had been with the life under communism. That's when I found out that Irena's husband had been an army officer, and she had been a protester against the government's war in Afghanistan. She said that he was "the sun and the stars in my world" and loved him more than anyone in the world. Later, she told me that her husband was killed in that war, while she was in prison, and *that*, she thought, was the reason they gave her back her freedom. "But, I made freedom make ring with other free peoples," she wrote. I didn't press her for any details. I was surprised that even when she spoke of sad experiences in her life, she was at peace, conveying only acceptance. Every time I met with her was an occasion for learning how to communicate with another person without worrying about the ulterior motive of every utterance, or about saying something offensive or stupid and regretting it the rest of the day. In time, I came to see her more as a friend than an employee.

As she was leaving I asked how things were going with her work. She had already packed her laptop, so she went by the small easel that was a permanent fixture in my office, ready for any presentation I might be called to make, and wrote in slow deliberate movement, "My boss ask many questions how I do things but I no like." I wanted to know whether her performance evaluations were as good as they had been from the start, because that's where the first official sign of trouble in the employment relationship would show up. "Grades is good," she wrote, and with a smile, "Irena is good pupil," she added. When I smiled at what she said and told her that her English was getting better, she gave me a disapproving teacher's head-shaking with a face full of pursed lips and frowns, topped, however, by a smile that wiped out any disapproval of my behavior she might have conveyed. She pointed to me, then to herself, and locking her index fingers together, she shook both hands up and down. "You and I friends?" she wrote, and the question lingered on her large bright blue eyes. I took the marker from her hand and wrote on the easel, "Always!" She waved goodbye and left. But, I wasn't sure what all these questions her boss was asking were about.

Sometime after that I was promoted to management and started working long hours to prove that I could handle the new job as well as I had handled my employee representative's job. I forgot about the questions I had after my meeting with Irena, until I happened to bump into her boss, Foss Mandrick, months later, at one of the company's expanded management meetings. He congratulated me for my promotion and offered help, if I ever needed accurate projections in the employment market, or any other aspect of forecasting in human resources for that matter. "If you have data, we can give you the future," he said with a reassuring smile.

I thanked him for the offer, but cautioned that predictions were never very good when it came to people. "We are the unpredictable creatures of God," I joked.

"It doesn't much matter what we are," he said and let the words hang in their mysterious meaning for a while. "It seems that the lady wonder from Omsk can use any data you give her to come up with accurate results."

"So, Irena is doing a good job?" I asked, trying to elicit from him a definitive evaluation of her work.

Foss was no greenhorn manager, and knew better than to commit himself on such a weighty matter as a subordinate's performance appraisal at an accidental meeting with a personnel man. "Oh, Irena has many skills that produce results, but we don't always know what these skills are, or how she uses them" he said, apparently pleased with his cryptic response.

"That's what you'll get from a sharp mathematician who looks at facts and makes stories out of them," I said in a humorous tone.

"She refuses to disclose the steps she goes through to get to her final projections. She makes forecasts of sales, operating expenses, earnings, turnover, you name it, and they are all very damn close to what they end up being, but we don't know how she does it," Mandrick said with frustration. "What are we going to do if down the pike she forecasts some disastrous situation? There is no way we can tell corporate officers that we're headed for disaster on this venture or that product decision, without telling them how we know that. Are we going to lay off people, if she forecasts a bust next time? We need explanations and documentation. If we don't get some answers soon, we're going to have to do some serious thinking about Irena's situation."

"Are we headed for some kind of disaster?" I asked with concern.

"No; but one of these days Irena may come up with some such news from her 'statistical integration process,' as she calls what she's doing, and we're going to face a serious problem. I just don't want to find myself there," he said with determination.

"But, if the results are accurate, I'm sure that her methodology must be good," I said, trying to show both understanding for his predicament and present a credible defense for an employee I liked and respected. "Perhaps, she has some serious communication problems…"

"Communication problems my eye!" Mandrick burst out. "That lady is smart and has no problems getting her way. No! She probably has come up with some new computer algorithms and she is not disclosing them to anyone. Job security, I think. She is afraid that, if we find out, we'll have no further need of her, and we'll can her. I cannot get through to her that this is not the Soviet Union, and we are not the KGB."

We couldn't continue the discussion because someone called the management meeting to order, and we had to break it up. "I'll talk to her, if you want me to," I offered to Mandrick as we parted.

"I'll let you know if I need any help," were Mandrick's last words.

I wanted to call Irena right away and try to make her understand that she had nothing to worry about in disclosing her methodology, but I held back. One of the early lessons that a personnel man learns is to be very reluctant to get himself in between a boss and a subordinate, without having secured the boss' invitation, or the subordinate's cry for help. The reason is that after he leaves the scene, the subordinate remains at the mercy of the boss. And, a boss who feels that his authority has been compromised by a subordinate's appeal to other power centers is not a person any subordinate would want to take orders from.

I didn't hear from Mandrick for a couple of weeks, but when he called me, he didn't want me to just talk to Irena; he wanted her to disclose her methodology or get out of Metrimax. "We don't hide things from each other in this company," he declared with irritation. "We are a team and one is either in it, or out of it."

I told him that I should first talk to Irena and find out her side of the story. "After all," I said with as much objectivity as I could muster, "if we ever have to move against her, we'll need to know where she's coming from as well as we can." He must have liked this conspiratorial-sounding thinking because he agreed without objection.

I called her number right away to set up an appointment for the next day. The department secretary informed me that she couldn't answer the phone because the voice software of her laptop was on the blink. I set up the appointment anyway, and told her to inform Dr. Maistrova and call me as soon as possible with her answer. Ten minutes later the secretary called and told me that Dr. Maistrova would be at my office as I had asked.

Next day Irena stood at my office door with a smile, holding the doorknob. She wore a beige suit with a white blouse, and waited for me to invite her in. Sunshine glazed the golden hair of her ponytail.

She lifted up her laptop, pointed to it, then placed her hand in front of her mouth and made the motion of talking lips, ending up her signs with an abrupt thumb down. I told her that I knew about her laptop problem, and she could use the easel board to write on. Instead of doing that, she placed her laptop on my desk and moved a chair next to me so I could read whatever she wrote. When she was all set up she glanced at me as if she wanted to signal me that I could begin telling her whatever I had to tell her.

"Your projections of future bookings, sales, workforce needs, overhead increases, production costs, revenues, earnings and all things of great interest to your management and the company are absolutely on the mark," I said, expressing the gratitude of the company with the right attitude. Then, I paused and waited for her response.

She placed her hand on her chest and moving her head ever so slightly she smiled with an unmistakable "Thanks from the heart."

"The reason I asked you to meet with me is to discuss with you a concern that your management has regarding your methodology for obtaining such accurate predictions. It seems that they have employed many planners over the years, but no one has demonstrated the kind of consistent accuracy that you have shown. They would like to understand your methods so that they can use you for even more important decisions, perhaps in acquisitions, market competition and so on at corporate headquarters." The idea that corporate headquarters could use her was entirely mine, and as I said it, I hoped that Mandrick wouldn't get wind of it, or if he did, he wouldn't mind anymore. Anyway, I didn't think it was such a far-fetched idea for her career development.

She looked at me enigmatically, as if she was trying to figure out the real reason for the request of her management.

"This has to do with the questions you told me that your boss was asking. Is it possible for you to explain to your management the methodology you use?" I asked, choosing to go to the heart of the problem without further delay.

"Why?" she signaled to me by raising her hand with spread out fingers to the level of her face and giving it a twist.

"You will have greater career opportunities for advancement."

She turned to her laptop and typed, "I am very happy at my job. No need in advance."

I thought I detected a tinge of defensiveness and spoke with as much calmness as I could muster. "OK; but you, as a technologist, can understand that a number representing some important fact has to be justified before it can be believed. Your management has to justify the numbers it presents to top executives. They cannot just say, 'these are the numbers we pulled out of a hat' and expect to be taken seriously."

She shook her head, looking very calm but very attentive. Her gaze rested on me, and I had the feeling that she was trying to fathom my deepest convictions about the world, about the essence of reality.

"You have nothing to fear. Your job is secure, if you just disclose your methods and algorithms. Can you give your management all the steps you use to get your results?"

Now she looked at me with profound sadness clouding her face. Then, she shook her head slowly from side to side, signifying "No."

I was taken aback by her refusal. After all, it isn't everyday that an employee refuses to give up her work product to her superiors. This is what the salary is supposed to buy! "Is there any reason why you refuse to do that?" I asked trying to recover my balance.

She was silent for what seemed to me to be a long time, as if she had to make a very hard decision. "Suppose you ask what is product of two big numbers," she started to type, "say 1234 by 5678, and suppose I tell you the answer is some big number, maybe 'Numero Big-

Biggo' and that is correct number. Can you make my result use?" She
stopped typing and waited for me to respond.

"That's not the same thing, Irena," I protested.

She pointed at me, her eyes relentlessly demanding a response.

"I would ask you to tell me how you got your answer."

She bent back down on her laptop. "You live within 1909. You are
banker. You have no computers, no machine calculators, nothing,
only pencil and paper. You have make much calculations. Somebody
say can do calculations in head correct. No machine. 1909. Do you
hire not her for job?"

"I suppose you have to give her a chance," I said, not without
some difficulty.

"Even as you no know how she do it?"

"In such a clear cut case where there is a right and wrong answer,
and you can know the result right away, I suppose, you take advantage of the result, even though the process isn't known," I said, hating
every word I spat out.

No sooner had I said that than she started typing again. "Pick 4
digit number you like," she wrote and pushed the laptop closer to
me.

"No need to play games now," I said reluctant to string along anymore. She was in control of the discussion, and I knew it, and didn't
like it one bit. I was prepared for a demand, which I was ready to
turn down, but it didn't come. Instead, Irena, joined her hands and
pleaded with me. "Anyone number!" she wrote.

"Six seven eight two," I typed out the numbers.

"Another long number, please, to multiply," she typed.

"Five seven nine eight," I typed below it.

She studied the two numbers on the screen, straightened up,
leaned back on her chair, closed her eyes and was silent for a few sec-
onds.

"39322036," she typed, and then looked at me with a smile that
had a smidgeon of mockery in it. "Get calculator," she typed and

pointed to my desk. I opened my center drawer, dug into it and pulled out a pocket calculator I used mostly to figure out percentages of salary increases of unhappy employees who came to me with complaints. I punched in the numbers I had given her. I had a hunch that her answer would be correct, but there was no way of avoiding the actual process of verification. With a motion of her hand she asked me what I had come up with.

"You're right," I mumbled after comparing my calculated number with the number she had typed on the laptop. "Are you some kind of an idiot savant?" I teased her.

"We all know things for certain times. I just know some things more often, better consistent. Multiply numbers is trick with very very good memory. Forecasts is different. Like doctors make prognosis—you know prognosis?—and some is right, some is wrong. Mine is good prognosis many many times. I no oracle. I am good prognostical person, is all. I have showed my calculations to boss, but cannot show him rest of process because in my head, in my heart. How can I tell you how answer came in me with numbers you gave? I cannot! It came!" She looked at me as if to gauge my response. "We know things, but do not know how we know. Trust is that kind. And love. No algorithm, but you know. Everything is not formula, not explain."

"Did you always have this ability?" I asked, suddenly realizing that I might be in the presence of a miracle worker of some kind and struggling to come out of my confusion. Calling her "the oracle" affectionately wouldn't sound like a cute metaphor anymore.

As if she knew my thoughts, she relaxed and leaned back again, and shook her head. She stared at me very intently for a long time, as if weighing the pros and cons of her possible answers. Then she sprung forward and started typing on her laptop again. "The answers come after I have took all the possible data," she typed on her computer. She banged the last key hard, and the machine started using the voice software again. We stared at each other for a moment, totally baffled, and then burst out into laughter.

"It seems that you scared the machine into behaving properly," I said in jest.

"Machine should do what woman wants, no what machine wants," she typed, and the machine pronounced it obediently. For just a fraction of a second, I thought I detected a note of discontent in the machine's sound. "I understand trends, factors critical, environment conditions to impact the issues, and I make good algorithms like everybody do, maybe better, but in end I extend result from use of inside me. I no know exact relation in data and algorithms and results. I not know future. Nobody know future, but I know what people want, what is important, where events go probable. It is no easy explain. My mind take mathematical answer, process it and give me better result. Is it a wrong to have better from the heart than only the mathematics? That is all I say. I no hide. I no afraid."

I heard the words coming out of the laptop while wondering how a trained mathematician could assert so blatantly that she was using gut feeling to make forecasts. Was she pulling my leg? I had heard about the genius of Russian mathematicians, and I was in awe of them. Russians weren't all that great in technology applications, but they knew theory, all right. Was she trying to protect some valuable statistical method she had developed? Did she have some quick mathematics trick for multiplying numbers? I had heard something called Mathemagic—was that relevant? Could she predict the stock market better than all the Wall Street money managers? Had she been lucky in her projections, and her managers were exaggerating her achievements? Or, did she, perhaps, have supernatural powers to see the future? And, how does one see the future, which cannot exist until we create it? Even if God sees the past, the present and the future spread out before him in the eternal now that Augustine imagined, even if that is true, human beings have no such eye view, no right to such knowledge. These thoughts came to me as I tried to digest Irena's answer.

Finally, unable to settle on an answer, I smiled and leaned back on my chair. "Irena, you are a strange one!" I said, not without added admiration for her poise and quiet strength. "I don't think one needs to know how everything works, when it works. I'm not one of those guys who have to have everything explained to them before they can believe it. But, this is not the way things are done in the business world."

"Are you not rationalist?" the machine cranked out the words.

"Yes and no," I said with a chuckle. "I ride the train of reason as far as it can take me and then I put on the wings of faith and fly further," I said enjoying the exchange. After all, she could have told me it was rude of me to tell her, out of the blue, that she was "a strange one." She was becoming a more intriguing person as she revealed her beliefs.

"Good!" She said approvingly. "You can understand. I work very hard, but my work is facts not only. I train mind and the soul like I trained brain. I will do my excellent for the company, if manager accept truth is some from facts and some from some other place, maybe heart."

"I understand. We call it gut-feeling, intuition. If you have a special gift, as your management says that you do, I'm sure we can use it without pressing for answers that do not exist," I said and stood up.

Still in front of her laptop, Irena worked for an answer. "I will my excellent for company, if they not ask me how I do," she wrote, and looked at me expectantly.

"Let me talk with them and see what they say," I said and offered her my hand to seal our agreement.

After the meeting with Irena, I called Mandrick and went to see him at his office. I explained to him that Irena wasn't hiding anything from him or anybody else. I told him that her methodology consisted of taking the data as far as she could take it with statistics and then adding her own intuitive sense of what the forecasts should be, to come up with the final results.

"You mean to tell me that all this time we've been giving the management of this company the opinions of a Russian immigrant lady, instead of respectable and rationally supportable statistical answers?" he said quite upset with my response.

"Well, in a way, yes. But, we do know that her forecasts have been exceptionally accurate," I said in Irena's defense. "And, please, don't forget that this lady is a top notch statistician with a PhD from one of the best Universities in the world, Moscow University. She is no more guessing than a top notch doctor is guessing when she makes a prognosis for a patient's illness."

"We just can't use her," he said with stubborn finality. "I certainly cannot stand up in front of a top management group and tell them that these numbers are the best guesses of somebody. It just won't happen!"

"You cannot fire a person for doing a great job, just because they do it in ways that they cannot explain in detail," I said with authority. "We have employment law here, and it isn't going to support any move to fire an employee who's done nothing wrong. Besides, she is a valuable resource—you just don't waste resources like this. It's just plain stupid," I shouted quite angry at his bullheadedness.

"I'm unable to use the lady in the work of this department," he repeated with the steely determination of a person who is convinced of the correctness of his position. "You figure a way to get rid of her, or someone else will do it for you," he said and went back to examining a stack of computer printouts that were on top of his desk.

I was about to turn and walk out when an answer I hadn't thought of before flashed in my mind. "I understand your situation, if you ever had to present results that were too far off the expectations and you couldn't support them with hard data and algorithms," I said in a conciliatory tone. "Our problem is that this very sharp lady mathematician comes up with terrific results, which, however, are not only mathematical but also intuitive, right?" Mandrick raised his head and stared at me as if he were watching a bug crawling up at the ceiling. "Our problem is that she does more than she should, not less," I said and let the words hang in the air for a while. I thought I saw a glimmer of agreement in his eyes. "So, if we tell her that she must stop just before she adds her intuitive twist to the mathematics, we could have exactly what we want. Good mathematical, algorithmic answers, supported by solid data and, produced by a crackerjack mathematician. Doesn't this make sense to you?"

"I have no idea how good her mathematical results are. She has to disclose her algorithms, so we can find out," Mandrick said, obviously considering the solution I proposed.

"I'm sure she'll have no problem doing that. Her results must be justified by the mathematics—no question about that," I agreed. "Even if the results she comes up with are not as good as she has been coming up with, I'm sure they'll be as good or better than other forecasters can come up with. She is a good mathematician, right?"

"Damn good," he agreed. "Go tell her and find out if she wants to play straight. No guessing; no hocus-pocus; just the math with good algorithms!"

Before going up to my office, I stopped by Irena's office. She knew that I had been talking with her boss and had guessed that I might be stopping by to tell her what was her fate. I knocked and opened the door. She was leaning up against her desk, one leg planted firmly to the ground and the other bent up and dangling. An empty hardboard box was on top of her desk, and her laptop was slung over her shoulder. She smiled when she saw me and held up a yellow notepad in front of me on which was written, "Thanks you for help, but it is not good thing. I must to leave company now. I did my job excellent, but is no good."

I smiled and sat down. "This time you guessed wrong, Irena," I said smiling, not without glee. I pointed to her chair, and she sat down across from me. I proceeded without introduction. "You are a very valued professional, and we want you to continue your good work with Metrimax," I began my message. "But, from now on your management wants you to present to them only the results you derive from your algorithms. They just want the mathematics, not the final things you add from the heart. No gut feeling; no intuition; just the math and only the math." I paused to gauge her reaction to the proposal. I thought she was weighing the pros and cons, so I waited for her to make the necessary calculations and come to a decision.

"The results no so good this way. I am no do my best for company. I cannot so good professional," she said with sadness.

"Your boss is willing to accept whatever results you come up with from your algorithms. Even occasionally flawed results. He wants to make sure that when he presents the results to top management there are exact algorithmic solutions to which he can point and justify these results. Everybody can accept the flawed nature of statistical predictions, but no one in management will accept perfect predictions from the heart."

She stared at me intently for some time. "He only wants results from algorithms—no interpretation?"

"That's right. Nothing but math."

"I do that. It is no best, but is good some," she acquiesced.

"I know you feel that they want worse answers than you can provide them with, but they pay your salary and that's what they want. But, make sure you show them all your methodology. Anything you cannot show is no good. Don't use it. Take it out. Forget it. If you don't, it's bye-bye Metrimax."

"You know Dickens in *Hard Times*? They want me be Thomas Gradgrind. No intuition, just facts. But, I must needs earn money for good caviar, no?"

"Right on! I don't know this Gradgrind fellow, but you are learning fast the values of our business world, maybe even our society," I agreed with some discomfort.

"O.K. algorithms only, Mr. Zeeth. How you say here: new ball-game, right?"

"Just Nick," I corrected her.

"O.K. just Nick. But, tell, you feel I do right? You feel you win?"

I stared at this strange woman unable to decide whether I should feel offended or just answer the question. "Always!" I remembered writing on the board affirming my friendship with her. She was a friend, wasn't she? This was just the kind of question that a friend would ask; a question that a friend *should* ask. "I have mixed feelings," I said, feeling miserable. "It seems that I'm always in the middle. I'm glad that we won't have to deal with some future blowup of having to justify to top management that we make decisions by intuition down here, and I'm sorry that the gift, I believe, you have will go to waste, and that the rationalists have scored a decisive victory here."

She set her laptop on top of her desk. She grabbed the empty box and hurled it up against one of the corners of the room. She crossed her legs and wrote on her pad, "It is good. I agree. The mute have last word!"

We laughed, but I wanted to make sure she understood. I asked her again, and again she promised to stick to algorithms. She told me that her sister had not yet received a visa but she was hoping that it would be approved in about a year. I told her to see one of "my people," if she wanted any help and I wasn't available. I left her office sure that I had earned my keep that day.

I didn't hear from Irena for a long time after that meeting. Mandrick told me that she was doing a fantastic job and was already up for a promotion to the level of Master Planner. "Now, I think, she realizes that all that stuff about tweaking the algorithmic results with intuition was nonsense, because her results are as good as they've ever been," he boasted, and we laughed.

When Irena's sister arrived in this country a year later, Irena came to see me about a job for her. She was an administrator for the

Department of Agriculture in Russia, and Metrimax had nothing to do with agriculture, so I couldn't help her get a job with us. I gave Irena some ideas to explore, and she left smiling as always. I wanted to find out more about her work and the relationship with her boss, but I had a full schedule, and the only thing she said through her laptop was that "all is swell." I teased her about her mastery of English and we parted.

Three months later, she came to my office to tell me that she was leaving the company. She was going to tell her boss on that same day. She said that her sister had been unable to find any suitable position in town, and they both had decided to look for work in Washington D.C. "I'm sorry to leave Metrimax, because I like my work here really much," her laptop announced. "We go work for government now," she typed. "Maybe forecast end of conflict for real war and peace, not novel," she typed, and then smiled playfully at me.

I noticed that she wasn't taking as much time as she used to for typing, and teased her about her virtuosity in typing.

"New program I made," she typed quite pleased with her accomplishment. "I do steno, no typing. Much faster."

It was hard not to admire such talent. I told her how sorry I was to hear that she was leaving us, and wished her good luck in whatever new job she chose to take. "I'm sorry also that you didn't get to use your intuition as much as you wanted to, and get the best results for us. But, I understand that your results have been as good as ever."

She was about to zip her laptop's case, but she stopped. She looked at me, examining me, trying to read me. Then, she tossed back her head and her ponytail spun around. Her laughter filled the room. "I never stop using my intuition," the machine announced. "I just made new algorithms for take account of my heart. I not cheat. Only algorithms. Only math and nothing but math. Just like Gradgrind, almost."

My mouth fell open and stayed open while she typed. "But, they must have known that when they examined your results, no?" I asked lamely.

"Algorithms is complex thing. People saw, they not go inside, take apart. They say all is good. They say they understand but I know they not understand. It is good. Good for company. Good for Department. Good for Mandrick. Good for me. Good for you, Nick! You make the winning contract, right? Nothing but algorithm. All decisions of life are algorithms and we fix with facts, opinion, heart, how you say it—hodgepodge? I told you, 'the mute have last word.'"

For a minute I was unable to put any coherent thoughts together and take action. I wasn't sure who had won. I was sure however that I could never be either a winner or a loser in this life, since I was always in the middle of all issues. I was a worker. I looked at Irena with her laptop slung around her shoulder, ready to get going. She knew where she stood. She knew what was the right thing to do, as well as Mandrick did, and she had managed to make things right for everybody except for me. Only I could do that, but it wasn't very likely. I thought that she might want some assurance from me about keeping this conversation strictly between us, but she didn't. She considered me her friend, and she trusted me. Irena knew what it was to go by her gut.

She pointed to me, then to herself, and locking her index fingers together, she shook both hands up and down. I knew she meant "You and I are friends." Then, on her way out of my office, she waved goodbye.

I waved goodbye to Irena. "Friends," I said and went back to work. I never heard from her again, but somebody told me that she was doing great working for the Department of Defense, somewhere in Washington D.C. I wondered whether we might find ourselves at war with some country out there because Irena forecast a quick victory for us and smiled to myself.

CHAPTER 4

❁

An Artist of Sorts

Many people, when talking to another person, use the word "you" without any particular differentiation among the countless people they address. The "you" for A is no different from the "you" for B. But, if A is "you" and B is also "you," how can one distinguish A from B? "I" is always personal; "he" is always impersonal; but "you"—"you" is always somewhere between these, which is really nowhere without some additional qualification. People who use "you" without any qualifier blur the differences between people.

But, there was one man who became known as the Artist of You, because, when he addressed you, you knew that he meant you and only you, and the "you" he used for you was never the same "you" he used for anyone else. When he addressed you, you came to understand the person that you were. The artist of "you" could sort out one "you" from another by the special relation he had with each "you."

Some people said that the Artist of You was very skilled in the art of communication and others attributed his gift to his pleasant manner, his melodious voice and the well-chosen words that preceded and followed every "you" he wove into his sentences. Most of them also reported that the Artist looked into your eyes so intensely that you knew he would receive with joy whatever response you chose to offer him. Implicit in his gaze and words that followed it was the desire to support you and offer you his help without ulterior motive. You felt that he did it because of you. The Artist himself could offer no explanation for the effect he had on others because he was never aware that he was doing anything different than anyone else. To all praise, compliments and expressions of gratitude that people expressed to him on occasion, the Artist responded with a smile and a sincere, "Thank you for your kindness."

Many people tried to learn the Artist's way and practiced long and hard, because it was clear that his way produced results in dealing with other people. They analyzed his style, examined his words for patterns and studied him for hours on videotapes, trying to decipher his way with "you." But all attempts were doomed to failure: when they said "you," it was the same old "you" for A and B and C, and nothing could distinguish one person from the other.

One day, the Artist of You said to someone the word "I" in talking about himself. It was an unprecedented occasion and gave a clue to the mystery of the Artist's way. For it became clear to the man who heard that single, solitary "I" who the Artist of You really was. The man said that he perceived the Artist with the same clarity that he had perceived himself when the Artist said "you" to him. He knew then that the Artist achieved his effect not by *how* he said "you," but rather by the life he led. He felt that he knew the Artist as he knew himself, because that "I" was a window into the Artist's soul, and only a man with such a soul could say "you" to you and mean all that made you a unique person.

When pressed to describe in greater detail what exactly he had perceived in the Artist of You the man was at a loss. He could only talk about the effect in general terms, but had nothing useful to say about the cause. That's why the people who had hopes of explaining the Artist's behavior and producing a series of videotapes with manuals and other aids to train salesmen in "the Art of You-ing" their customers, as they put it, had to give up the effort. Everyone concluded that the Artist's "you" was a mystery, and his way could not be communicated effectively by anything other than the word "you" and the life he led.

CHAPTER 5

❀

The Image Fixer

No one in our organization doubts that having the right image is a necessary condition for success. Even Novas, a relic among managers who believes that appearance should not be tampered with so that it can honestly reflect a person's substance—even he admits that the wrong image is a stumbling block to getting ahead. Yet, he and a few others cling to the notion that improving one's image consciously and systematically is, somehow, wrong and repugnant.

But, why should anyone want to be stuck with the wrong image? If Novas could project the image of an executive who is in control of his emotions rather than one who misses no opportunity to express his "gut feelings," as he calls the strong stands he takes, or to reveal his earthiness with his roaring laughter, his tears and his anger, all of which are disruptive—if Novas could see that it is undignified to go around the executive offices with crumpled pants and ties spotted with spaghetti sauce, he might have become a Vice President and be in a position to help "the little guy," as he likes to call everyone who does what he's told, without ever uttering a word of protest. Isn't his opposition to image fixing the very thing that keeps him from fighting image fixing effectively?

Fortunately, our organization is enlightened and has created the Department of Image Rectification to help people adjust to our culture. We don't have many people in the Department yet, but we are committed to the profession and have already established a little ladder for career advancement, which we hope to expand as our contributions to the business attain wider recognition. I, for example, have already received praise for my efforts, and I am on the way to better and bigger things. After three years as an Image Diagnostician, I was promoted to an Image Fixer, and in a couple of years, if I continue the good work I'm doing, I have no doubt that I will be promoted again, this time to the position of Image Maker.

As a Diagnostician, I could only study people's images and identify flaws without the responsibility or the skill to do anything about them. Now, as a Fixer, I can proceed from diagnosis to the rectification of particular blemishes. There is a lot to learn, and the responsibility weighs heavily on my shoulders, but I am progressing nicely and, I'm sure, that when I have made my mistakes and learned from them, I will want the freedom of the Maker, which allows him not only to straighten out wrinkles, but also to revamp the entire image of a human being.

One of the essential skills I have to master in my present position is the art and craft of persuasion. I have to learn various techniques and use them to persuade people who have been diagnosed to have an image flaw to do something about it. That's not an easy task. It doesn't cost a person anything to go to a diagnostician and find out that he needs to change his appearance, or that she must do something about being perceived to be a negativist, or that he could go farther and faster, if people thought of him as a team player rather than a lone wolf. But, to get someone to fix the behaviors, which betray these flaws, is a task of much higher degree of difficulty.

Though people who begin to worry about their image are generally on their way to doing something about it, they often have to overcome their scruples and their fears. So, my job is to put them in the right frame of mind so that they believe deep down to the core of their being that the change they are about to undertake is a worthy project, a noble adventure. No one will sustain the rigors of the process without being convinced that he or she will be a more honest and a better person during the climb to the top. People, after all, always want to have their cake and eat it too!

If a client has been exposed to the kind of doubts about Image Rectification that Novas and his kind spread around, I have to respond with a rationale that builds faith in the process where doubts exist. So, before we even begin to discuss what to fix first and how, I spend a considerable amount of time wearing down the client's resistance to change. This is a laborious process, but I will outline its essential features here.

First of all, I say, nobody really cares what you believe, or what you feel, or what you think. You are free now and will always be to hold any beliefs you choose, feel whatever you like, and think the most bizarre, the most humdrum or the noblest thoughts you want to think. These things are your business. No one cares what your beliefs and values are, and no one would waste a minute trying to change them, even if it could be done. This bold, unequivocal expression of freedom I convey, immediately gives my client room to maneuver. No longer does he feel that coming to me and following my suggestions will bring about fundamental changes in his own private, inner self. He is willing to listen to what else I have to say, believing himself to be in control. The few times I didn't bother to go through this little reassurance drill, I sensed a lot of hostility in my clients, as if coming to me, at who knows whose suggestion or advice, meant being fitted for a straight jacket. Now, I can see before me a person who wants to proceed of his or her own free will, because I have limited the extent of the changes and the consequences of any image fixing we may undertake. I can almost see the glimmer of a little "Aha," a small, but I believe, most crucial insight.

"What people care about is what you and only you choose to show them from the multitude of beliefs, feelings and thoughts you have," I say in conclusion. Again, as you see, I give the clients control of their destiny. Actually, it's the bait around the hook I use to reel the clients in, so that I can help them. I don't deny that there is an element of manipulation here, but show me an educator who doesn't manipulate and I'll show you a lousy teacher! Novas—I can almost hear him sometimes, as I say these things—would say that teachers manipulate students into learning openly and with their consent by virtue of their relationship, but I do so covertly, because my clients don't see themselves as students or me as a teacher. It's a detail we can argue and have argued, as a matter of fact, endlessly. You just don't walk into the Image Fixer's office with a lousy image, without expecting him to use his skills to change you! Besides, manipulation of one kind or another is part and parcel of management. Look it up in the dictionary, if you don't believe me. Sanctions, incentives, promises, pressure, carrots and sticks, alliances and the gamut of political maneuvering—all these ideas and actions are fundamentally manipulative. Anyone who denies it lives in La-La Land, not the organization I know, and is due for a rude awakening. So, I manipulate my clients because I want to help them. I make them feel in control, and they really are, though more often than not, they don't choose to exercise any.

Then, I embark upon an examination of the reasons for fixing the particular client's image. He is a capable person needed by the organization, right? He has a vision about our business, the way our employees and customers should be treated, the strategy we should follow to succeed; but his flaw doesn't allow him to acquire the power he needs to make all these things happen. Is that good? Does he want to remain forever limited, or does he want to overcome? Expand? Succeed? Of course he does. Of course he wants to change, fix whatever is wrong, and reach the top. The point of this little discourse is to align his energy with change, because change, i.e. the repaired image, embodies what he perceives to be the goodness that lives within him.

"And, what if there is no such goodness inside your client?" Novas would say. "What if greed, dishonesty, desire for domination and other such snakes lurk inside your client's gut?"

This is another set of doubts he hurls at me and at whoever else will listen. What if there is a dove inside him that wants to fly and bring hope and enlightenment, but is trapped inside the man by his inadequacies? I say. Who is to know what wonders live inside any human being? And, why should I assume evil rather than good inside this or that person?

"You miss the point, he retorts. The point is that when you fix the flaw in the image, you make the man opaque, and no one can get to know who he really is. You make him appear joyous when he feels hurt; you make him able to appear kind and caring when he may be greedy, consumed by envy and a desire for the other's destruction."

In short, Novas claims that I am teaching people how to deceive and get away with it. All I do, I protest, is teach people how to control the appearance of negativity in themselves. Besides, some people can do all these things without any coaching from our Department. They do it, and nobody knows anything about it. Doesn't this put people without guile at an unfair disadvantage when it comes to promotions? And, isn't therefore my function a defense against the whims of nature's random giving of gifts and flaws? And on, and on, *ad nauseam*, in our *tete-a-tetes*...

I always assume that the client wants to do what he believes to be the right thing: to be good, to help himself, yes, but others as well. My argument gives him a reason to do just that. And he begins to think that image fixing may be a noble adventure, after all, to which he should commit energy and time. Most clients, unlike Novas, are gradually persuaded that not only can they be different inside than they are outside, but that they can also bring their image into harmony with their inner goodness.

But, I don't want to move too fast. I want my clients to hear all the arguments against tampering with their image from me, not Novas and his friends. I want to be present in their awareness when doubts about their actions arise. So, just as they start to feel ready for the great undertaking, I torpedo their ship of hope and collaboration with another doubt. You know, I say, that there is a risk in all change. The risk with fixing flaws in your image is that you will appear to everyone else as someone who may be different from the person you know yourself to be. For example, you may appear to be knowledgeable and wise, when, in fact, you feel stupid and foolish. And, if you do this over and over again, you may start to feel that you *are* knowledgeable and wise. This is a trap, a delusion, which you must avoid at all costs, because you run the risk of being exposed and discredited as a phony, not to mention the risk of becoming emotionally sick.

Coming from me, one of the foremost proponents and a resident expert of image fixing, the argument stops the clients dead on their blissful tracks. Doubts about such a risky undertaking swarm in their heads, swoop down like vultures in front of their troubled eyes, leaving claw marks on their wrinkled foreheads. I can see fear in the clients' worried eyes. All seems lost, as it was calculated to be. Wow! Am I glad that *I* was the one to surface this internal mess! If Novas had buttonholed these innocents and fired such doubts at them, I wouldn't stand a chance to do them any good because they would have never set foot in my office.

And, just when all seems lost, I begin the great salvage operation that will produce the commitment needed to proceed. Fixing flaws in one's image, I say, is not for everyone. It takes a person of great awareness to keep the image and the substance straight. If you don't know yourself very well, if you cannot keep straight what belongs inside and what belongs outside, then, you'd be better off hobbling along with the flaws you have and accepting your limitations. There is nothing really wrong with admitting to yourself that you are terminal in your present position. Happiness, after all, can be found in other pursuits besides the executive suite. Our janitor on this floor is one of the happiest people that I have ever met. It's not happiness that image fixing promotes—it is success. And, the two should never be confused.

The client is about to jump ship and is already looking for a lifeline. I can see it. I wonder if there are people who have ever admitted that they are limited and have chosen to remain limited, nevertheless. If there are any such individuals, I haven't met them in our organization yet. Anyway, the choice of whether one will admit such a thing or not is still his or hers. But, pride is the most abundant resource people have, let alone people with ambition to rise up the corporate ladder. And pride is always blind to any limitations. Of course the client can keep substance and image straight! What do I take him for? What could possibly make me think that she wouldn't do exactly that? Why am I even talking about these things? Did I think he is some confused underling that can't manage his affairs? She is a leader, who gives direction, sets an example for others, takes all kinds of risks every day in business…He has found strength by tapping into his greatness, his "firstness", as I like to call this trait. And, she is committed to prove it to one and all, by embarking upon the arduous journey of image fixing, which I have already planned for her.

Novas: you lose! Now, try and convince this client that we are all flawed; that we all have strengths and weaknesses; that we should not be afraid to show our warts and ask for acceptance, as we work toward change from within. The client now knows he is in control, believes in his basic goodness and, if there are limitations he feels—he's not sure of this, but "if", I say—then, he feels quite strong in managing to keep them to himself. Some of you will say that now she is corrupted, but I say that now she is ready to begin fixing the flaws in her image, that's all.

I reassure the client's ruffled conscience—this is a tricky entity, and should never be neglected in such heavy-duty maneuvers—by saying that if you change your image, so that people feel comfortable in your presence, if you appear caring and accepting and stop doing whatever you do that limits you, then, you may feel inclined to start working on your substance.

Most people believe that the image is the puppet of substance, and if you want to change your image and be honest about it, you must first change your substance, i.e. your beliefs, your feelings and your thoughts. I say—and I emphasize this—I say that this is bunk! One can just as easily say that, if you want to change your inner self, start acting as if it was already changed, i.e. change your image, and before you know it, substantive changes begin to take place. It's not a bad argument, after all! Why not? I have to believe that change can proceed from the image to the substance just as well as the other way around, or I may find myself out of a job.

Take me, for example: by the time I'm ready for promotion to Image Maker, I expect to have become oblivious to Novas' doubts. I act as if everything I tell my clients is exactly what I believe, when in fact I am plagued by doubts, and I expend a lot of energy to keep up the appearance of self confidence and faith in the value of my work. Novas is never far away from my thoughts. I think I am a fraud; I feel rotten to the core; and I believe that I am doomed to hell. But, I hope that I can overcome this despair and, in good time, align myself to the image I have chosen, an image that has given my career a much-needed boost. I believe that the time will come when Novas' voice in me will fall silent and will not break my concentration at work or trouble my dreams, as it does now. But, what kind of a person will I be then?

CHAPTER 6

❀

The Do-Gooder's Challenge

Some people work hard to provide for their families, others because they want to get ahead, and others yet because they derive satisfaction from what they do. Aloysius Applebaum worked for the well being of others. He was a personnel man, and nobody appointed him to be the protector of others, not even those in trouble with the System. But, Aloysius had no need for a specific goal in his job description, or the granting of a charter to do what he thought was the right thing to do. He performed his mission so matter-of-factly that it seemed part of the routine of any personnel man's work, taking no credit for his many kindnesses, shying away from any praise, and rejecting any suggestion that he was in any way more caring than anybody else in the Division. As far as he was concerned, anyone with a similar commitment to the business and in possession of the same facts would do the very same things that he did in that situation. Of course, no one else went out of his way to get the facts, or stuck his neck out as far as Aloysius often did.

This is what Aloysius did when he found out that Morton was planning to fire an engineer who wasn't performing according to the standards Morton had set. Aloysius knew all about Morton: he was a manager who cared only about outputs, and ruled his fiefdom with an iron fist. Aloysius had no respect for this kind of a manager, but when he found out that the engineer lived in mortal fear of Morton and was paralyzed every time he was given an assignment, he became incensed. His heart went out to that unfortunate engineer when he found out how hard he had tried to please Morton, only to be rebuffed and put down every time.

The first thing Aloysius did was to go to Morton's office, close the door and start talking to him about that engineer. He explained to him how a little kindness, a little encouragement might work wonders with this particular man. But he just got a cold, harsh response from Morton. He had no authority to countermand a manager's orders, but Aloysius had never given up trying for lack of authority. He told Morton that he was a cruel boss and was destroying a human being. Morton was offended and, in a fit of anger, told Aloysius that as of that instant he was no longer responsible for providing a job to that engineer. "If you want to be in the welfare business," Morton growled, "that's your business, not mine. So, take your damn lemon and find a place where they can squeeze some juice out of him and make lemonade. I've had it with incompetents like him and do-gooders like you!" he said, and shoved the employee's file in front of Aloysius' face.

Aloysius, caught up in the whirlwind of his own emotions, blurted out instinctively a totally unauthorized, completely out of line, ridiculously quixotic, "Done!" and walked out of Morton's office, holding in his hands the engineer's file and career.

It took him a few minutes to realize that he may have actually ruined the career of an employee. A personnel man had no way to employ anyone and certainly not an engineer. Yet, this engineer had to be given a job to do, or he'd be out in the street for a long time. There was no way he could find a job with another company with the kind of recommendation Morton would give him. What would happen to this man of crumbling self-esteem under the barrage of rejections he was likely to get? And, how would his family survive? In his helplessness, he decided to see Bill Bergman, the general manager of the division, and ask him to find a job for the engineer he had inherited from Morton.

Bergman listened to him explain the situation, and let him know, in no uncertain terms, that he couldn't possibly go against one of his managers to protect an employee who wasn't performing his job well. As gently as he could, he tried to make Aloysius understand that he had to reign in his philanthropic tendencies and do the job he was supposed to be doing as a human resource professional. Aloysius bit his tongue.

Aloysius never thought that he was doing a job; he had a mission that gave him power far beyond his position and expertise allowed. So, he pleaded with Bergman for some training funds for the engineer to learn new skills and perform useful work in another department. He assured Bergman that the engineer's low performance was the result of Morton's style rather than the man's incompetence.

Bergman looked at him with pity, as if he was suffering from a strange affliction. "The budget is already overrun; but, even if it wasn't, we wouldn't expend precious resources to fix what clearly is broken beyond repair," he said with finality.

At this point, anyone with any organizational sense at all would have thanked the boss for listening to him and beat it out of his office. Instead, Aloysius stayed put, and stared at Bergman for a long while, as if he was about to take a plunge into the unknown. Then, he made his move with decisiveness. "This is 1995," he began with a soft but firm voice. "Tell me, Bill, in a few years, after you have retired and are enjoying a quiet evening in the backyard of your new home in Arizona, or some other nice place in the Sunbelt, which memory will make you happier: the memory of balancing the division's budget in 1995, or the memory of saving a human being's life? Because this is exactly the choice you have right now. This engineer cannot make it on his own out there in the demoralized state he's in. He may take to drink, or sink into depression, or bump himself off, if he's fired."

Bill Bergman stared at him in disbelief, not sure whether he was dealing with a fanatic of some strange cult, or a personnel man run amuck.

"I'd like to know where you stand," Aloysius pressed on in his quiet but determined tone of voice.

"You want me to give a job to a guy who can't cut it?" Bergman shouted now, betraying the despair of a cornered animal.

"Take a chance on this guy, Bill. If he still isn't making it in six months from now while working for another manager, we'll know for sure he can't cut it, and you can fire him then. Find a job for him now, and give him something that makes him feel useful, needed. Give him some training funds, to get him started. We'll survive. I'm sure others will approve, and will feel more commitment to this place, because you care." Almost prayerfully, he added: "And, you'll have done a good deed, and have your conscience at peace."

"Damn you, Applebaum!" Bergman burst out. He was angry because he felt that he had to choose between doing the right thing for one person and supporting decisions made by his managers according to the chain of command. "Go and talk to Jackson," he finally said throwing the words out like a man tossing a towel after a vigorous workout. "Tell him to come and see me. I don't know why I'm doing this, but somehow…I'm doing it."

"You won't regret it," Aloysius said, already at the door.

Perhaps, no one would have found out what happened, if Jackson hadn't spread the news among his fellow managers. Morton raised a stink with Aloysius' boss, but got nowhere with his protest, because Bergman held fast. There was nothing left for Morton to do but give in and declare himself the sworn enemy of Aloysius Applebaum. "You and I are worlds apart," he fumed. "You've done a lot of harm to this company with your tricks, and if there's one thing I'm going to do is stop you once and for all."

Aloysius didn't want to argue with him. "You are a hard man," he said, and went about his business.

"I don't know how, but I do know I'll find a way," Morton railed at him. "Keep looking over your shoulder, because I'm going to be after you every step of the way, watching you."

And, true to his word, Morton watched his every move, as if that could prevent Aloysius from carrying out his mission.

Time after time, Aloysius found ways to make life more tolerable at work, pleading cases, creating solutions, playing whatever politics his meager organizational power allowed him to play, even threatening to quit and go pump gas for living, if a safety hazard wasn't disclosed to the workers and the authorities, or some unfair practice was instituted. He did these things because he was trying to create a community, to save jobs, redress grievances, change the organization so that people could show their better selves and perform their work with some joy.

After some years of such service to those who didn't have the power or the skill to defend themselves, everyone in trouble thought of Aloysius and asked for his help. He would go to work, finding out what had really happened, developing arguments, devising alternatives, gathering support, and advocating causes that many couldn't understand but nevertheless supported. Most people were not in trouble, so they paid little attention to what he did and why, but all people knew that there was "some Applebaum guy to go to, if you're ever in deep yogurt."

That's how Corina knew about him, and why she showed up at his office, and told him what trouble she was in. He found out that Corina, a secretary in the marketing department, was being investigated for theft of some petty cash that was missing. She said she wanted his help because she had three kids to take care at home and, if she lost her job, she would be out in the streets.

Aloysius looked her straight in the eye and told her that if she were innocent he would do his best to make sure that nothing bad happened to her; and, if she had taken the money, the best thing for her was to tell the truth, pay back the money, and ask for a second chance. Corina was like a frightened kitten as she defended her innocence. He told her not to worry. "This is a division with a heart," he said. "We don't toss people out in the streets on a mere suspicion, or even the first time they do something wrong." Corina cried on.

Aloysius went immediately to work on Corina's problem. He discussed her problem with the chief accountant, and was assured by her that even if it were proven that she had taken the money, which wasn't certain at all, even then, they wouldn't have to fire her. If she was a good worker and would admit her guilt, and agree to make restitution, the problem could be taken care of without reporting it to headquarters and making a federal case out of it, because the amount of funds involved was below one thousand dollars. Aloysius was heartened by the news and went to his boss, the personnel manager, for further support. After explaining to him the situation, he got him to agree as well that there would be no need to make an example out of a low-paid secretary with three little kids at home.

Aloysius went home in a hopeful mood, planning to meet with Corina's boss first thing next morning, and straighten out the whole thing.

But, first thing in the morning, Corina appeared in his office and told him that she had thought over what he said, and had decided to take his advice and do the right thing. She had already seen her boss, and confessed that she had taken the money over a period of a year to make ends meet at home. She was in tears, because her boss had told her that this admission of guilt was grounds for dismissal. Aloysius felt his guts churning. He wished that he had been more careful with his advice. But, what else could he do? Tell her to keep her mouth shut? Lie, and compound her mistake? He tried to console her as best he could, and told her not to despair, because there were many options left to explore. He was determined not to leave a stone unturned to save her job. Besides, he thought, honesty must count for something!

He went to see Larry Conti, Corina's boss, and tried to persuade him to forgive her.

"Let me understand you," Larry said in disbelief. "You want me to continue working with a person who is an admitted thief? How's that going to look to all the other people who do their work with honesty? What kind of justice will they think we've got here? And, most of all, how can I ever trust her again?"

"She made a mistake," Aloysius persisted. "Everybody makes mistakes. At least, she admitted she did wrong. Punish her with a fine. Hold back part of her wages for a period of time. But, for God's sake, don't sack her this first time. She has no place to go. She has three little kids at home."

"I'm sorry," Conti said, without the slightest indication that he felt anything other than right, and justified, and fair.

Aloysius tried to think of something that would threaten Conti, some indiscretion he might be guilty of, some impropriety with customers, anything at all he could leverage his pleas with. But, he had nothing on him, nothing at all. Unfortunately for Corina, Conti was an honest man, a good man, a man guided by clear principles of right and wrong. "You are a Christian, aren't you?" Aloysius asked out of the blue.

Conti was taken aback. "Sure, I am," he said angrily, "but what has that got to do with anything?"

"Forgive her," Aloysius said quietly.

"I do, and I wish her all the luck in the world," he said with impatience, "but she's got to go. Forgiveness is one thing, punishment for wrongdoing another. She's got to go. That's all."

Aloysius was at a loss. Conti was now beyond his reach, and he knew it. He knew he had pushed him too far. He didn't like himself. "I'm sorry for this," he said with regret. "I had no business…"

"I'd heard about your tricks, Applebaum…Morton is one of the people who talks a lot about you…but, I never knew what people meant until now. You're good, damn good, in what you do. But, this is one of those times when you really are fighting for the wrong side."

He left empty-handed, thinking of the uphill battle he'd have to wage. He needed to marshal support from the chief accountant, his boss, Bergman himself, if that's what was needed to change Conti's decision.

The chief accountant stuck to her previous position, but said that she could do nothing, if the employee's boss insisted on firing her. That was his prerogative. Next, Aloysius went to see his boss. Without the personnel manager's approval, Conti might change his mind and leave Corina alone.

"You've got to talk to Conti," Aloysius began. "I think he could be convinced not to fire her, if he was sure he wouldn't be blamed for doing something against company policy." He knew he was stretching the truth a little too far, but he had decided that a lie without a selfish motive might be justified to save Corina's job.

"The problem is that headquarters has several cases like this one on litigation…" he began.

"Headquarters doesn't have to know," Aloysius interjected. "The chief accountant assured me that we don't have to report it, because the amount is small."

"I checked with them this morning," his boss said in a businesslike manner, "and they told me…"

"How could you? I told you yesterday we didn't have to report it, and you agreed," Aloysius burst out in anger.

"I'm sorry, but that's not the way I like to do business," his boss said curtly.

"You're sorry? You're a hell of a lot more than sorry!" he shouted, and started to leave.

"You know Al, this time you've gone too far. We can't keep thieves and lemons and other deadwood around this place," his boss countered. "Besides, I can't hide things like that from headquarters and live in fear of the Contis and Mortons of this world to spill the beans; just can't, OK?"

Aloysius' anger subsided. Of course, there was always Morton stalking him. "I'm sorry," he said. "I should have guessed…" Thinking aloud, he said, "I'm going to see Bergman."

"You can go wherever the hell you like; but remember, this time you don't have a leg to stand on. A thief is a thief!" his boss shouted, fuming.

By the time Aloysius got to see the general manager, Corina had been escorted summarily out of the plant. Bergman said the case was out of his hands, but even if it wasn't, there was no way he could take the side of a thief, if the case was brought officially before him for a decision.

Aloysius left the general manager's office a broken man. All of a sudden, the world didn't make sense to him. He felt alone, as if the people he had trusted and served all these years had never really existed. They were strangers who decided and acted according to rules he couldn't understand, let alone obey. He felt lost in the hallways he had crossed countless times every day at work; his office was a cold, confining enclosure that made him afraid. He knew what he had to do. He had no doubts. He put on his coat, stuffed the picture of his wife and son in his pocket and left the building without saying a word to anyone. He knew that he would never return.

No one protested publicly his loss, even though people found out the circumstances of his leaving and talked about it in hushed, sad voices. Not a single employee of the dozens he had helped over the years took the risk of telling any manager that Applebaum's loss was a blow to the organization.

When Morton heard that Aloysius was gone, he smiled knowingly and said with glee, "Good riddance," feeling vindicated at last.

Talking over the "Applebaum situation" some managers tended to believe that, on the whole, Applebaum had been a disruptive influence in the organization. "He alienated those who could help him, and befriended those who were powerless," said one of the people who had never known him, but had heard of his gutsy moves. "That's always a dumb thing to do!" someone else agreed.

The engineer whose job Aloysius had saved some years back from Morton's firing squad, having just been promoted by Jackson but knowing nothing of the battle Aloysius had fought and won on his behalf, said quite philosophically, "That kind of do-gooding activity always gets you in trouble. You just cannot win."

CHAPTER 7

❀

The Boss Reader Interprets

Everyone knows that if you want to get ahead, or even just survive in our organization, you have to learn how to read your boss. He's never going to be an easy read, but neither is he going to be a treatise in Logical Positivism. People who really want to know and are willing to take Beno's advice will find a way.

Anastasia Burke, called Beno by everyone, is the most avid boss reader in the company. She knows everybody who is anybody in a way that is useful to those who have to work with them. She has studied bosses for twenty-three years and can translate every word, move and mood of your boss into consequences for you. So, listen when she guides you through the story that defines your boss. She hates to reread the same boss for the same employee, so don't go to sleep on her.

Take our boss, Bart Hoch, for example. She has read him loud and clear for most of us, and there's no way we could go wrong, unless we dismiss her reports, which, of course, we have no intention of doing.

When Hoch comes to your office excited and asks you to "look into" an idea he had for sometime, or an idea that came to him while shaving that morning, listen, take notes, and after he leaves, forget the request was ever made. Hoch never remembers anything he asks you to do for the first time. According to Beno, if you read him wrong and go to work on his idea, you'll regret it. Hoch will have had second thoughts about it, his attention will have been focused on some other idea and he'll think less of you, because you expend your energy impulsively. Listen to Beno: forget that first encounter and proceed with whatever you were doing before he showed up.

Besides, Hoch doesn't like people obeying him like puppets. Only if he mentions the same thing to you for the third time do you need to spring into action, to avoid trouble. This "Rule of Three," as Beno calls the behavior, has been in existence ever since Hoch took over our group, four years ago, and is well tested.

While Hoch discusses an issue with you, he'll listen attentively, saying very little. Sometimes he'll grunt contentedly, which is a sign to you that he accepts as fact whatever you are saying and you have a green light to go on. But, if he crosses his legs, gets hold of his left shoe with the palm of his right hand, and begins to twist his foot, as if doing an exercise prescribed to him by a physical therapist for strengthening his ankle, proceed with caution. Beno says that these are sure signs that you have begun to bore him. Do whatever you can to stop "the Twist", because the next thing you'll hear is his staccato voice spitting out, "Fine, fine…sounds good," which means that he is approaching the limits of his tolerance for listening to trivia. The yellow is about to turn to red, and you'll have to slam on the brakes. Beno insists that you offer a nugget of wisdom at this point. It may be your only hope to stop your slide toward disaster. At the first sign of a pithy comment, Hoch will straighten out his sagging shoulders and, with a face pleasantly surprised, will pronounce some of the nicest words he knows, showing his restored faith in you and his approval of your ideas: "Really? That sounds terrific!" he'll burst out, releasing his captive foot and uncrossing his legs. If, however, your nugget is fool's gold, or if you didn't read Hoch correctly and you go on with facts and ideas which he finds boring, or unacceptable, or plain wrong, he'll stand up and pace the floor, his face turning a hue of orange red. Beno states in no uncertain terms that when Hoch reaches this stage of discomfort it is too late to prevent an outburst, which, one way or another will include one or more of the following three words: "inconceivable," "precipitous," or, most devastating of all, "moronic." Nobody else would dare use any of these three words owned by Hoch, lock stock and barrel, though many admit that these words make their way into their consciousness when they reach a similar point of explosive disagreement with others. Some even reported dreams in which hostile rowdies spat saliva and these dreaded words at them.

Beno's studies show that in meetings with several managers, Hoch doesn't reach his boiling point as quickly. Instead, he goes through two different stages to warn those in the meeting of his mounting discomfort, thinking, perhaps, that frequent displays of impatience in public are counterproductive. He'll say, instead, "I was rather thinking..." or, "It seems we have a bit of a problem here with..." or, if these expressions are not properly read and don't cause a change in the direction of the discussion, he'll proceed to the next rung up his discomfort ladder, with a sad, one might say, forlorn, "This makes me very uncomfortable," or, he'll pull out a penknife he always carries with him in his pants pocket, and begin cleaning his fingernails which, I must say, are always spotlessly clean and the only thing that a penknife can do to them is ruin the manicure. "It is unwise for anyone to persist when Hoch begins this 'Manicuring Maneuver'," Beno advises.

All these expressions of negativity, discontent and discomfort are naturally studied more extensively, but by no means imply that Hoch doesn't have just as many, or even more ways of expressing support, delight and enthusiasm. A rapid fire burst of "Splendid, splendid", never once, never three times, always two rapidly fired "Pair of Splendids" (or just "the Pair", for short, as in "I got the Pair today") expresses approval, a happy and productive state of affairs. Better yet, if Hoch leans back on his chair, looks up at the ceiling and thrusts both arms straight upward, like a prisoner ordered to keep his hands up, and utters a single protracted cry, which sounds like "Wow!" or "Awe!" or "Yeah!"—no one has been able to decipher it with authority yet—if Hoch goes through this "Mini Ecstasy Drill" (MED, for short) because of something you proposed, or in response to an idea you had that morning while staring at your face in the mirror, then you have won your battle and you'll get your way.

The few behaviors of Hoch, which have been described thus far, are well documented, and their interpretations are accurate by all accounts. But, Beno would be the first to admit that, as it often happens with reading anything, Hoch exhibits some behaviors, which afford a variety of interpretations. These constitute Beno's works in progress. Take, for example, Hoch's posture of standing up against the wall of some conference room, with hands akimbo, surveying the meeting with the Sphinx's expression of amusement and sadness on his face. What does this mean? Some say that this happens when he has formed no opinion about what is being discussed; others insist that he knows very well where he stands, but is trying to figure out the best way of expressing his thoughts without interfering with the process. And, there are some who believe that "the Akimbo" has nothing whatsoever to do with the meeting, but is rather the symbolic gesture of a bird flexing its wings before a flight, an outward manifestation of the boss' inner desire to escape from the meeting, the building, the whole world of his stupid job.

Beno tends to think that this last group of people who, contrary to all logic, believe that the boss wants, in effect, to abdicate his position and lead a simpler life, are romantics. "They want him out, but are way off the mark," she said, when I asked her recently. "It is more likely that Hoch knows that he is being widely read and dislikes most explanations of his actions," she went on. Beno's aging face softened, and her bright eyes focused far into the distance. "I'm afraid," she said dreamily, "that Hoch longs for the freedom of a character in a book. Someone who stands up and tells those who are reading him to stop attributing deep meanings to every little thing a character does, and accepts him, as he appears to be. Perhaps, 'the Akimbo' means nothing at all; perhaps…I don't know…"

"Of course, you know," I said with conviction. I thought that she was so tentative because she wanted reassurance. Boss readers, like everybody else, need to be told that they perform a valuable function and that they are contributing something useful to the organization.

"I guess you're right," she agreed, with what I believed was a thankful smile.

I was sure I had read her correctly, and felt good with what I said. It isn't every day one gets a chance to see an expert in doubt, and have a chance to reassure her. But, later that night, when I went over this encounter, trying to get the full measure of my smugness, it occurred to me that Beno might have been trying to make me look beyond appearances in gauging a person's character. She wasn't wavering; she was instructing me. Had I behaved like a fool? I threw the paper I was reading against the wall. She needed my support like a bird needs flying lessons.

A real expert, I guess, never forgets the limits of her expertise. It took me awhile to see how astute she was. I sure had a long way to go in reading Anastasia "Beno" Burke. She doesn't know it yet, but she'll be my boss one of these days, if I have anything to say about my future.

CHAPTER 8

❁

The Self-Appointed Scapegoat

They can unearth no reason to explain why, or even if Beck hates Cooper, yet not a day goes by without Beck shouting angrily at him. Every week, as if planned in advance, Cooper gets a full dressing down in Beck's office, complete with put downs, foul language, and all manner of abuse.

"Cooper can take it," his co-workers say, when you ask for explanations. They give no reasons, no cause and no history of the conflict. It seems that Cooper has been Beck's scapegoat forever. They say Cooper is a grown man and knows what he's doing. They add, "What right do we have to interfere?"

And, it is true that Cooper comes out of these ordeals in hell apparently unscathed. His face doesn't change color; his voice is calm as always; he loses none of his composure. He smiles, and utters vague references to "the poor man." A strange, peaceful light lingers in his eyes.

But, why does Cooper take it like that?

People wonder, but offer only conjectures. "The boss has many troubles," they say, "and since Cooper can take it…"

Beck finds many reasons to lash out at Cooper. He accuses him for things he does, which he shouldn't do; for things he does wrong; for things he doesn't do, but should; even for things he doesn't do, but, for sure, would do wrong in Beck's opinion, if he ever did do them. And, when he runs out of things to run him down for, he accuses him of things that others did wrong because of him, or for things that others did right in spite of him. When the list of possible wrong moves is exhausted, the boss finds fault with Cooper's attitude, his intentions, the way he looks at other people, the way he looks, the way he talks, how he walks, "drummer-boy-like," he says, or how he sits, "like a man bound up, it would appear…"

On more than one occasion, Beck has accused Cooper of being "a pig, insensitive to the needs of others," even though Cooper's magnetic soul attracts every sorrow and every joy his co-workers harbor inside them. People say that, even if nothing was wrong with what Cooper does, or what he is, or what he appears to be, the boss would accuse him of breathing his air, just to get things off his chest.

And, how does Cooper feel?

"Cooper can take it," people say with relief. "Cooper isn't as sensitive, when it comes to his own pain, as other people are. He's got thick skin. He doesn't lose any sleep over Beck's antics. He's got nerves of steel, and a titanium belly. Nobody can get to him. Besides, Cooper never does anything he doesn't want to do. No one need feel sorry for him. He is no scapegoat. He is Cooper, that's all."

One day Cooper retired, and Beck came out of his cage, looking for people to harass. Ever since that day, Beck preys upon the hard working and the lazy, the excitable and the stolid, berating the guilty as much as the innocent. There are a lot of people hurting, and no one who can really take it. "If only Cooper was around," people mutter, remembering the good old days.

CHAPTER 9

❀

A Wheeler-Dealer's Dreams and Schemes

Matheson set his half empty beer mug on the table and wiped the froth left on his lips, rubbing them on the short sleeve of his khaki shirt. "You don't understand," he said with his condescending grin. He was in his fifties and there should be things he understood that I didn't, but I didn't care to be told as often as he had been telling me.

"What is there to understand?" I responded irritably. The hot humid air and the man's patronizing attitude had made me impatient. I wanted to get to the point of my visit to this hellhole. "Kohl wants to sell his factory and I'm here to make him an offer on behalf of our board of directors. What we do with each particular employee after we assume ownership is our business. We'll do what we have to do to turn a decent profit, but we're not going to toss people out in the streets, if they perform and there's work for them. We're not stupid!" I paused, and as an afterthought, I added, "But neither are we a Global Welfare Agency."

"No, of course not; but Kohl has made a promise to the tribe that none of the nine Buru will ever be laid off, fired, or otherwise removed from the company, except, of course, for illegal acts. He's given his word on this and won't go back on it." Matheson gave an audible sigh of relief as he laid out the condition for the deal.

"What the hell do these nine Burus do, anyway?" I said attacking Matheson. He was the lawyer Kohl and our team had found to draw up the acquisition papers, and wasn't really responsible for any deception that might have been going on. But, I was frustrated by the strange ways of the people in this entire region and, more than that, I was furious with Kohl, because he had mentioned nothing about special conditions to the people we had sent to assess the plant. He had built a superb electronics assembly plant at the edge of the jungle, and we wanted to buy him out and increase our low cost production. But, there were limits to what we were prepared to put up with.

"When we visit the plant tomorrow, you'll get a chance to see for yourself." He leaned back and blew smoke at the ceiling, avoiding my gaze. "I'd rather not get into a discussion on operations right now," he said as if he was asking for a favor. "Kohl will explain everything to you tomorrow. Ask me any legal question you like about the acquisition and I'll do my best to answer. The only reason I brought this matter up is that it will be part of the deal."

"I don't call this negotiating in good faith," I said expressing my disdain for secrets, mysteries, cabals and whatever else isn't open and above board.

Matheson shifted on his chair with discomfort. "Kohl asked me to mention it to you so that you can keep an open mind." Then, as if troubled by my attitude toward him, "I'm just a middle man, Thornton," he defended himself. "Don't take it out on me."

"You're right," I said grudgingly. "I hate not having all the facts, but I'll survive overnight."

Matheson ordered another beer and with renewed enthusiasm tried to focus my attention on the good aspects of the deal. "The main thing to keep in mind is that Kohl has put together the most efficient little plant in Southeast Asia, perhaps, anywhere in the world. You wouldn't be putting up with all the squalid accommodations of Tikopia, the heat, the bugs and our ways, if it weren't for the goodies you expect to get from Rakma Inc., right? If he wanted to stay on and grow the company, in five years he could become a force to reckon with. As it is, he wants out. He says he wants time to find out what else is real in the world besides making circuit boards. And, his change of heart is an opportunity for your company to expand and dominate this market. You'll get a terrific little company, if you can accept this little offbeat condition. Nine out of a hundred people or so shouldn't be an insuperable obstacle, right? The Kogala, you'll see, are industrious to a fault. They work like dogs, don't complain, don't demand anything more than they need to survive, have little need for supervision, and none for a union. Work for them is part of their religion: they believe that a human being must be a good worker before he can be a good person." He paused to let all these advantages of Rakma Inc. sink in.

"We are aware of these facts," I said with the usual disinterest of the buyer for the seller's wares. "Kohl's got a smooth running operation, and we'll make him a good offer."

"Kohl and the Kogala," he corrected me. "These people act as if the company belongs to them. They put the extra effort to save time and materials; they have a positive, "can do" attitude; they never said that the work was too hard or too much. And, whenever Kohl has brought in a trainer to introduce a new process or explain the workings of a new machine, they have picked his brains clean, working on their own time to learn every detail there is. They are fantastic workers, Thornton. But they must have the Buru around them."

I had heard enough about Kohl and his miracle workers. I needed to get up to my room and charge my batteries after the seven-hour flight and the Matheson treatment. "I'm bushed," I said. "Besides, I need some quiet time to open up my mind for tomorrow's revelations."

Matheson laughed as if he had no care in the world. "I'll draw up the papers with that little condition inserted, and I'll have them ready for you to sign, if all goes well."

"You do what you got to do, and I'll do the same," was my boorish response as I got up.

"I'll pick you up at the lobby, eight o'clock sharp." He gave no sign of wanting to leave. It seemed to me that the hotel bar was an alternative place of business for him, and his dog eared briefcase, bulging with papers and propped up against his armchair, was at the niche it had occupied countless times before. "We have an hour's drive to get to the plant," he warned, as if I had stood him up repeatedly in the past and he wasn't going to put up with such treatment anymore. "Travel in the jungle after nine is hell."

"I'll be ready to go," I reassured him and left. From the corner of my eye I saw a couple of men leave their table and join Matheson. I assumed they were natives, because of their bronze colored skin and their colorful shirts. I wandered if they were with the Kogala tribe, trying to find out how their future was shaping up. This was no easy matter to decide. I needed help.

I got up to my room and called Howard "Bobbo" Barkan, our CEO, at his home, in California. I told him what I had learned about "the condition" and asked for guidance. "We need Kohl's plant to meet our orders. He's the best supplier we've got around there and if we don't buy him out, the Clan will gobble him up and have our lunch." He meant that Discomatics, our most fierce competitor, run by the Horton family, would move in and close the deal, if we didn't. "But," he added, "if you find out that these Buru yokels don't pull their weight, cut down the offer to even things out."

My stomach started churning. It seemed to me that we were headed for another round of negotiations just as I thought we were all done with that.

"What if he doesn't go for that?" As soon as the words came out of my mouth, I realized that I had made a mistake.

"What the hell am I paying you for, Thornton?" he growled. "Are you gonna wheel and deal, or are you gonna play pinochle? You chisel him down, you negotiate, you do your thing and close the deal for the greatest advantage to your company, right?"

"Right," I said. I hated it when he called me by my last name to show me that he is boss.

"I want to know what the hell these nine jokers do. And, I don't want to play *What's My Line*, OK?"

"I understand," I piped off, and thought of Matheson trying his line with the likes of Bobbo Barkan.

"By the way, try to find out why Kohl is selling. I met the guy a few years back, and he didn't strike me like the contemplative type. He was peddling his wares every chance he got. He wanted more contracts, more deals, greater reach. Business's in his blood—why is he chucking it all off? I want to know what he's got up his sleeve. What am I missing here, Thornton?"

"I'll do my best to find out," I reassured my boss with the deference that a VP of Business Acquisitions owes the CEO of his company. And, I meant it. But, I didn't promise only because he wanted to know. I was just as curious myself.

Matheson was waiting for me in front of the hotel entrance next morning, cheery and ready to go. I greeted him politely and we took off in his jeep. Less than five minutes later we were bouncing in the ruts of a dirt road, brushing past the drooping branches of broad-leafed trees. I had been visiting the tropics of Southeast Asia for the better part of four years, looking over promising companies, closing deals, discovering frauds, taking advantage of circumstances, and even being taken for a ride a couple of times, but never before had I been called upon to do business in the jungle; never before had I found myself involved with tribes and relations between tribes. Were we biting more than we could chew? The vegetation was thick, vibrant, engulfing. It would absorb the road into its fold, if people didn't keep imposing upon it with the power of their machines. I wondered whether I should have gone directly to the plant by sea and avoided this tortuous ride, but Kohl had insisted that I meet Matheson first and "get the paperwork ready," as he put it. I was sure by now that there was more than paperwork he was supposed to get ready. I felt that he was behaving with solicitude more appropriate for dealing with a sales prospect than a client. He was selling, all right, but why? Was I a client or a pigeon? I let the doubts drift away. I could take care of my company and myself no matter what role he chose to play. Matheson didn't seem bothered by the tumbling ride, or the humid air that glued your skin to your clothes and made your lungs labor for each breath. The bugs refused to land on Matheson's pink skin, finding mine, apparently, delectable.

"I don't know if you know this, Dan, but the Hortons made an offer to Kohl recently," Matheson said, casting quick glances at me.

"No; I didn't know," I said feeling the bite of the salesman once again. "Call me Daniel, please," I added.

"Sure; Daniel it is. As for me, I'm Mathesen to everybody. About the Hortons…They had even picked one of the nephews to come here and stay for a few months until the changeover was complete."

"Kohl didn't trust the Hortons? Is that why he didn't sell?" I fired a shot in the dark, but in the general direction of the target.

Matheson laughed. "No-no-no; Kohl didn't have a chance to say what he thought. It was the Kogala who put their foot down. The day after they met this Lenny Horton they made a beeline for Kohl's office and told him they'd rather go back to fishing than work for that man."

"So much then for the compliant work force," I pounced on my host. "It sounds to me like these guys want to run the company."

He caught a glimpse of me and must have seen the glee I had in my eyes. I wasn't trying to hide anything. I got a kick out of scoring a point against the opposition and wanted him to know it. He could also pick up my wincing or my reeling when he scored a good point.

That was the game, and if he didn't like it he shouldn't be selling. But, why did I care what this guy thought? Why did I have to justify my behavior to myself? I felt stifled in the bottom of the hot green ocean we were traversing. This wasn't a proper state of mind for a master wheeler-dealer. Matheson gunned the engine whenever we approached a puddle, and it howled in torment. You couldn't know how deep these mud traps were; you just hoped that if you did your best you wouldn't sink in and stay sunk.

"You don't understand," he began. "The Kogala talked it over with the Buru and figured out in a hurry that Lenny Horton wouldn't accept the condition about the Buru being part of the work force. And, in fact, when Kohl put it to Lenny about the nine Buru being part of the deal, Lenny laughed at him and told him there was no way the Hortons would accept such a perpetual employment contract. He said that even he couldn't get such a sweet deal, and if Kohl ever found a buyer, he would appreciate knowing his name, so he could find something to peddle to *him*. The deal was off right there and then."

"Perpetual, you said?" I asked, feeling another rumble in my gut. And, should we have to worry about our reputation in the market, because of Lenny's potential foul mouthing us? I felt the complications coming like waves upon me.

"As long as the Kogala work for you, the Buru must be there also."

"I don't know about 'perpetual.' The more I hear about this Buru condition, the less I like it," I protested, restraining myself with difficulty.

"Wait till you see how the Kogala work, before you make up your mind. It won't be hard to understand why Kohl feels so strong about this." He paused as if a thought had entered his mind that he didn't know what to do with. "Kohl wants to be totally above board with this," he said with conviction. "Suppose he didn't insist on the Buru condition, and you closed the deal without knowing about it. Do you know what you would have bought? Nothing! Zilch! The plant would be shut down before you could blink your eyes. He doesn't want to take anyone for a ride, no sir!"

"If these Kogala can shut down the plant because they have a monopoly on the labor supply, the whole thing looks hopeless. All of a sudden I have the feeling you're selling Kohl down the river."

"Facts are facts, and hiding them won't change them. But, keep one thing in mind all the time: if the Buru condition is satisfied and adhered to, you got nothing more to worry about. The Kogala and the Buru are the most loyal and agreeable people you'd ever want to employ." He stopped talking, as if he realized that any further argument could do nothing but undermine the deal. He didn't seem to be happy with himself. And, I wasn't sure whether I had scored a point or not, so I didn't gloat. We rode in silence for what seemed like hours. I wanted no further discussion with a man who refused to answer the most troubling questions I had.

We made a sharp left turn and, the green parapet of the jungle was drawn back, and Kohl's plant appeared. It was a long white, one story concrete building with its flat roof on the same level as the parking lot. The sea was afire below us, bubbling hot lava poured out of the sky. We parked, walked a few paces, and stood on the balcony surrounding the roof of the building. A couple of bare-chested natives were loading boxes on a small ship down below. They moved slowly, as if trudging underwater.

Matheson smiled. "Primitives make our most sophisticated products," he said. I clutched the railing and watched. "After you've been around these people for a while you wonder how primitive we really are. You get the feeling they know things none of us knows. You might say they are strong in software—feelings, imagination, dreams, spirit."

"I wonder how long this will last, now that they are so deep into electronic assembly."

"The Buru will keep them pointed in the right direction."

"Is that what the Buru do?" I tried one last time, but he was already starting down a stairway, headed for the plant entrance and just gave me a smile.

We headed for Kohl's office down a deserted corridor. Air conditioning here was like heaven. I was struck by the quiet of the place. Silence isn't what one expects to find in a plant, even an assembly plant.

"Kohl has a very small staff, an accountant, a sales manager, a British engineer, a couple of paper pushers, but only one manager to supervise the entire operation and take care of personnel matters as well. Most of them live in town."

"Only one manager to supervise a hundred workers?" I asked.

"They do that mostly by themselves. They're really more than workers…You'll see."

Kohl must have seen us arrive and rushed out of his office to meet us in the corridor. He was a mountain of a man, but moved with agility and vigor I wouldn't have expected from a man his size. He took my hand and shook it as if it was a thing he could take and run away with. "Call me Wolf and I'll call you Daniel, OK?" I nodded my consent, and we exchanged the usual pleasantries. He apologized for any inconveniences I had endured, as if he was personally responsible for them. He told me that he had met Bobbo Barkan, admired his business savvy, and asked me how he was doing these days and how I liked working for such a successful man. I answered politely, looking for an opportunity to change the topic and get down to business. But, Kohl had got down to business the moment he saw us. He had his own way of how to proceed and wasn't going to let me change it. "Before we talk, I want you to see," he finally said. "'One look is worth ten good reasons,' as the Buru say." Seeing that I wasn't jumping up and down with excitement for the wisdom of the Buru, he added, "You don't want to buy a pig in a poke, Daniel, do you?"

I was going to tell him that our plant engineers who had visited his operation had given us their report, and everything appeared to be just fine, but I held back. I was sure that it wouldn't spare me the tour. He knew that I wouldn't be there if the report wasn't just fine, so what did he have in mind? But, I'm the guy who makes deals, a paper pusher, what do I know about electronic assembly processes and work efficiency? On the other hand, I thought, what do plant engineers know about symbiotic tribal relationships, special conditions for perpetual employment and other such details? I decided to submit to Kohl's forceful guidance for the time being. Let him have his way, I thought; I am the buyer, and my turn will come.

We were ready to begin our tour when Matheson, who had been gone for a few minutes, escorted an aristocratic looking woman and introduced her to me as Krista, "the personnel manager and operations supervisor." She smiled imperceptibly, and said she was glad to meet an executive from "the big leagues."

She was in her fifties, I guessed. Her hair was silver white, but her face was young, the skin smooth, the lips full, and the eyes clear and playful. I was just beginning to project on her all the love for a mother of noble birth, great wisdom, and boundless love, when Matheson, sensing, perhaps, my soul's inner yearning, added a further characterization to Krista's introduction: "My wife and partner in all affairs, foolish and wise," he said, and with his arm firmly around her waist, squeezed her close to him. No one could have missed the quick darting of my eyes from one of them to the other and back again, as if I couldn't believe their union. "Now, I suppose, you understand better my more than professional interest in the affairs of this little outfit, right Thornton? It has partly to do with family well being!"

I said that I was sure there had to be something more than signing a contract that caused him to extol the company's virtues so vigorously, and we all laughed. Kohl was now ready to show me his stuff and led the way like an explorer who returns to a great discovery he's made.

"This is my baby," Kohl crowed as we started our tour of the production facility. About a hundred men and women in colorful clothes were working in front of instruments and computer screens, tending to various tasks. On one side of the large workspace there were several clean rooms, and people in bright airtight suits were working under hoods. "I knew when I found the Kogala that I had discovered a gold mine," he whispered to my ear. "They are the most dedicated workers I have ever seen, and I've worked with a lot of people in a lot of places. Look at how intent they are. They don't waste a move; they don't let a moment go by without effect; they make no mistakes, working eight hours a day."

I had, of course, visited many production facilities over the years, and had some idea of what to expect. Here, however, there was an atmosphere of reverence that I had never encountered before. I had the feeling that we had entered a church rather than a production facility. The workers were absorbed in their work, and Kohl's presence was acknowledged politely but didn't seem to alter a single move they made. Occasionally, one of them would catch a glimpse of the four of us, but there was no effort to show the big boss that he counted more than anyone else, no indication that his presence might justify even a momentary pause in the flow of their work. It seemed that whatever they were doing was part of a rite they had chosen to do for their own benefit. Yet, they knew that I was there, and I was aware of being observed by their darting glances toward me and among themselves.

I noticed one of the workers taking a circuit board out of the assembly line and handing it to another worker slightly behind and to his side, without turning his head. The receiver didn't turn to see the hand that held the board but, somehow, knew where it was, found it exactly where it was supposed to be, and the exchange was performed flawlessly, as if they were trained athletes passing the baton in a relay race. Levers were pulled by one of them to help another with his or her task, buttons were pushed to stop a conveyor belt just as a hand was lowered to pick up a part from a particular location on the belt, and no word was spoken, just knowing glances were exchanged between them and an occasional nod or a momentary smile. It seemed to me that the Kogala were performing like one organism, their motions guided by a single brain. I waited for somebody to drop a tool or a board on the floor, or at least miss a cue and curse out of frustration, but nothing was out of order, nothing out of place. And, a belief took hold of me that nothing had ever gone wrong here, and nothing ever would.

We moved slowly, Kohl occasionally placing his huge hand gently on the shoulder of a worker and whispering something to the person, as if he too didn't want to raise his voice here, as if there was something sacrilegious about speech. They acknowledged him with nods and smiles, but never with words. Now and then one of the workers would get up and move around the assembly line, stopping for a moment next to one of his or her fellow workers as if offering to take his or her place. On one of these occasions, a young man sitting in front of a large console got up and went out of the room, while the roving worker took his place and continued performing the task without interruption. I waited to see what would happen. A short stocky woman got up next, looked around, saw the place vacated by the previous worker and immediately went to it and started testing the boards that were neatly stacked in front of her. The man who had left the room returned after three or four minutes, but didn't reclaim his seat. Instead, he spotted the place vacated by the short stocky woman and went directly to it, sat down, and started placing circuit boards on a fixture and lowering a lid to make the connections apparently needed for measurements. His eyes were fixed on a computer screen, while his hands worked knowingly, like those of a virtuoso pianist, unaided by sight.

A man and a woman got up as if on cue and took Krista Matheson to the side of the room and talked with her in whispers.

Kohl moved his huge head next to mine and spoke softly to my ear. "Whenever anyone gets a little ahead on his work, he gets up and goes around, offering to relieve anybody who wants a time out for a few minutes. Everybody knows everybody else's job, so there is no problem with the changeovers. Besides, they like to move around. And, there's no time lost, even for bio-brakes." He paused. "Aren't they wonderful?"

"Did you train them to do that?" I didn't want to become Kohl's booster, but it was hard to hide my admiration.

"Hell, no!" Kohl burst out. Several heads turned toward us. There was no disapproval, no scowling, just a look of mild surprise, which faded as Kohl resumed his whispering. "They figured out everything by themselves. Working efficiently is for them like doing good deeds might be for some of the more religious of us. Can you believe that?"

"I don't know what to believe…yet," I said, and I started drifting into speculations. People do things because they want to gain something for themselves—something material, psychological, spiritual, something important to their lives. What do these Kogala want so bad that they are willing to work so hard for it? I might have gone on speculating for quite awhile, but I felt Krista's presence next to me and I stopped.

"Mister Thornton," she said, her calm soothing voice putting me at ease, "the Kogala want to know if you have any suggestions on how they could improve their work efficiency."

I didn't know whether they were serious, or they wanted to have some fun with me. If the latter, I thought they had a good sense of humor. Krista's eyes told me that this was no joke. "They're always pestering visitors to give them new ideas; though, I must say, seldom has anybody succeeded in improving upon their ways."

"Please, tell them that they know best what needs to be done, and from everything I've seen so far, they are doing it very well. Of course, I don't know much about production efficiency," I said, hedging as always my statements, "but, if they become our employees, there will be plenty of opportunities to consult with our experts."

"They'll like that," she said. Her approval made me feel that I had done a good deed. She gave them a sign that all was well, but alas, no help could come from me.

We were at the end of our tour of the assembly area, when a young woman left her post and approached us. She stood in front of me, one hand spread out on her chest, as if to steady a thumping heart, and a smile like the sun breaking through clouds of anxiety on her face. "The Kogala and the Buru like you visit us," she said softly but with conviction, and handed me a wooden carving of a man in repose.

"Thank you very much," I said, caught by surprise. "I have never seen people more de-di-ca-ted to their work. It's been a pleasure to watch you work," I said, articulating my English slowly so that she might get the meaning of the words.

She stared at me for a long moment, searching, I felt, for feelings I held secret from the world. "Kogala and Buru work good together. We do good for you," she said with that sunshine of a smile touching my very soul.

"Yes, of course you do," I heard myself say.

"She got her point across, didn't she?" Matheson joked as soon as the door to the assembly room swung shut behind us.

I didn't find his remark amusing, but it brought me back to the business at hand. I wasn't in a mood to bargain, but it was my responsibility to do what I was being paid to do. "So, what's this symbiotic thing about Buru and Kogala?" I forced myself to ask, looking boldly into Kohl's gray eyes.

"Come and see," Kohl said playfully, like a child about to share a secret treasure with a friend. "The Buru have their own schedule, you understand, but we can look in on them."

Fifty yards down the hall we stopped, and Kohl opened a door gently. "The Buru go to bed late and should be still asleep," he said confidentially to me as he stood aside to let me peek into the dormitory.

The room was dark, the air was sweet with incense but the Buru were not asleep. They were sitting on the floor, forming a circle at the center of the room surrounded by their beds. Kohl was surprised and said something to them in their native tongue. An old, frail woman answered. He turned to me and said that they got up early because they wanted to meet me. I felt their examining eyes upon me, and wasn't sure what to say or do. I didn't know whether I should give them a piece of my mind for goldbricking while the Kogala were busting their butts, or just acknowledge their existence with a polite good morning and move on. But, the Kogala maiden's wish was fixed in my mind, and I greeted them with warmth that surprised even myself.

Kohl was pleased with me and introduced me in English as the acquisitions VP responsible for the acquisition of Rakma. They responded with approval, though I had no idea why. I couldn't resist the question: "How do you know you'd like working for my company?" I asked.

"We see you ride shark on waves, but then it change to dolphin and you still on top," the old woman spoke for the group.

I turned my head and stared at Kohl. He understood my consternation and lost no time explaining. "The Buru place great value on dreams," he said, as if I was supposed to understand what he meant. "They dream mostly about things that are important to the two tribes. Apparently they've had a good dream about you."

The old Buru woman raised her frail arm and pointed a finger at me. "Thornton, you better man from you think you are," she said.

I was taken aback, but thanked her, feeling embarrassed. Her praise could have been a shrewd way to disarm me, but it wasn't; rather, it struck me as a genuine expression of hope. What else could a "better man" think? Krista thanked them for the kind words and told them the Kogala were working wonderfully well together.

"Thank you. Kogala the best," the old woman said proudly, as if her *own* work had just been praised.

I said nothing until we went back in Kohl's office. What could I say? The idea that a corporation would pay people for sleeping and dreaming was too preposterous to explain even to myself, let alone to Bobbo Barkan. And, what about the stockholders? A shiver ran down my spine.

"They sleep at the plant?" I said finally, just to make sure I hadn't misunderstood.

Kohl grimaced as if I had inflicted pain on him. "Like I said, they have their own schedule."

"But, I was given to understand that the plant works on one shift only. Have you changed that?"

"No, no," he said impatiently. "Not possible to get people to do that here."

I shook my head to express my inability to comprehend the situation. I stared at the wood carving of the sleeper in my hand and tried to order my thoughts. I could only fall back on my wheeler-dealer thinking: ten percent reduction in the price Kohl was asking seemed in order. One of the natives brought a pitcher of fruit juice with plenty of ice and set it on the coffee table. He must be ahead on his work and is using the extra time to be a waiter, I thought. Krista took out four glasses from a cupboard and placed them next to the pitcher. Matheson proceeded to serve us. The room was cool, but the sun was blazing hot outside, and the dockworkers, dripping wet, were still loading boxes on the ship.

"You probably think that I must be touched in the head to have employees who do nothing but sleep, right?" Kohl asked. "Well, it may be crazy, but makes a lot of sense in our context. You saw how the Kogala put out. Have you ever seen teamwork like that? Have you ever in your life even thought that workers would want to race ahead of the schedule so they can help others take a break? Tell me, if you have, and I'll shut up."

"Yes, but…" I started to object.

"But, we have some people on the payroll who sleep, right?"

"It seems to me that this extra unproductive work force has to be prorated in our offer. There has been no mention of paying people forever just for sleeping."

"The price I asked takes everything into account," Kohl asserted with finality. "These nine Buru work as hard as the Kogala, but they have a different job to do, that's all. The output per employee is what counts—Kogala, Buru and the rest of us here. And you know by now that our total cost is less than what you pay just for benefits."

"What exactly is their job?"

He became pensive for a moment, as if he wanted to arrange his thoughts. "To put it simply, the Buru set up the dreams that the Kogala dream. As soon as the Buru wake up, around lunchtime, they meet with the Kogala and find out what's in their hearts and minds. Then, they go to work, figuring out who will dream what, and why. It takes them a few hours of discussion in groups, coming up with ideas, fitting them together, modifying them, arguing for or against requests and wishes they have received and so on, until they get everybody's dreaming plan finalized." Certain that he had my attention he went on with the job description of the dreamers. "After the shift ends they all go back to their families at the village and go about their life. But, around midnight, while the Kogala are asleep, the Buru go out and roam the jungle and the beach, lining up the spirits they need and urging them to bring to the Kogala dreams that will respond to their requests, problems and wishes. They don't get to bed until four or so in the morning. They sleep at the plant, to be close to the people they work with and catch them just as they take their lunch break to listen to their previous night's dreams, to give new dream ideas and get new requests. We don't know exactly what the process is, but that's the rough outline we've been able to piece together from various discussions with them. It takes a while to get all this done, so we give the Kogala a generous lunch break, but they work out most of it later."

I didn't want to put anyone down, but I must say, I didn't want to give anyone the impression that I was some kind of new age enthusiast, ready to buy anything anybody sells. Disbelief was imperative. "Are the most productive workers in the world too lazy to dream their own dreams without any help?" I said, with more than a hint of sarcasm, partly in jest and partly in defense of my intelligence and sophistication.

Kohl's eyes flashed, but before he could form a word, Krista put out her hand and stopped him. She set her glass gently on the coffee table and turned to me. "These two tribes, as far as I have been able to find out, have had this symbiotic relationship for at least a hundred years," she began in a patient, tutorial tone of voice. If Kohl had started out this lecture I would have cut him short, but there was no way I could do that to Krista Matheson. Somehow I had the feeling that all she was concerned about was my education, not selling, not winning an argument, just my own growth. "It seems that the Buru lost a war to the Kogala and most of them were slaughtered. The Kogala looted the village they had conquered, raped the women, and threw a wild party to celebrate their victory. After that they fell asleep. In the morning, so the legend goes, they woke up terrified by their haunting dreams. They found out that they had all dreamt more or less the same dream, and felt great remorse for their brutality. I have tried to find out what exactly they dreamt, but no one will tell me. They just call it 'The Sight of Horror' and leave it at that. Anyway, it is said that they asked their shaman what to do to find peace, and he told them that their dreams were no longer of their own making. They were 'dispossessed,' is the way they put it. Their mindless deeds had to be atoned by dreaming whatever dreams the Buru chose to give them. And, since that time the Kogala have been providing the few Buru that were left all the necessities of life, and the Buru, in exchange, make up their dreams based on the Kogala input and their spirits' help. Living without their Buru, or with their Buru unhappy, would be unthinkable to the Kogala. They are convinced that their dreams will drive them crazy, if the Buru are not involved in shaping them. Their victory, it seems, cost them their freedom to dream by themselves. But, they are happy with their lives, and any attempt to change it has been perceived as a hostile act." Krista paused, and fixed her eyes on me, searching for my reaction.

All right, I thought, if they are going to be serious about these tales, I'll play along. "And, how do the Kogala know that they got a dream that was planned for them?" I asked feeling a little smug.

Matheson cut in. "You don't understand," he started to say.

I had enough of his standard put down, and told him that I understood everything that made sense. He didn't seem to mind being put down as much as I did, and went on undeterred. "You should hear them tell their dream designers what happened in their dreams. They thank them and hug them for their good dreams, they plead for happier dreams and argue with them all the time from more propitious interpretations."

"There's a lot of complaining and protesting when somebody has a nightmare or some other unpleasant dream," Krista said in support of her husband, "but the Buru always have good reasons that explain what happened from the actions and thoughts of the dreamer. Besides, there's really nothing the Kogala can do when it comes down to it, but try to be more generous, kinder and more sensitive to the wishes of their dream-makers."

"They don't just explain, though," Matheson said, determined to stay in the discussion. "Sometimes they urge the dreamer to think or act in a different way than he has been acting, and on rare occasions, when all else fails, they explain that the dream they had planned for this dreamer was switched with that for another person by Dambara, that's the Trickster of the Jungle, who is forever robbing people of the best efforts the Buru make."

I stared at my woodcarving, admiring the serene expression of the sleeper. Was he a Buru or a Kogala? Was she a provider or a consumer of dreams? Why were these hard working people extolling a sleeping person? I was getting a funny feeling that there was some serious wheeling and dealing going on right under my nose. But, the feeling that I was being entrusted with knowledge that was quite genuine wouldn't leave me. I was in the "Vise," that's my description for the place where no wheeler-dealer worth his salt likes to be. "Sounds like these Buru have got everything under control," I said.

"You bet your ass they do," Kohl burst in. "That's what I've been trying to tell you. No Buru, no dreams. And, no dreams, means no labor peace and no production."

"I guess you might think of the Buru as the managers of the operation," Matheson added, just as the thought started to hatch in my mind.

"Are there only nine of them? Has their population been going up or down? How can one assure…" The questions came to me rapidly, and I delivered them in the businesslike manner they deserved.

Kohl's eyes grew dark and darted from Matheson to Krista. They also glanced at one another, and I knew I had struck a nerve. But I had no idea which, where, or whose. "Now you're in tune with the problems I'm concerned about. We've got nine Buru up here, that's minimum for the job, and there are some more in the village, who serve the rest of the Kogala. They are not exactly anxious to shackle themselves to the plant, but as long as the Kogala want them here, and you know how much they want them by now, you'll get replacements."

It occurred to me that, if these Buru were a critical and scarce resource, we should have a couple of extras on tap for security. But, I said nothing. I didn't want to weaken my negotiating position, which was that we were paying for workers, not dreamers, and if we had to pay for dreamers, the fewer of them, the better. "You think they can get them to work at the plant?"

"Listen," Kohl said with impatience, "I didn't build this business without thinking of the future. You'll get the people you need to run the plant one way or another. It's a model operation and I want it to go on long after I'm gone." He scratched his head, and went on. "As a matter of fact, I would like to put it in the contract that you'll allow a certain number of visits to the plant by people who may want to come and see for themselves what teamwork can really achieve. This is my discovery, and I don't mind saying that I want to be remembered for it."

"I suppose so," I said, finding no pressing business reason to refuse. "But, you must admit that all these additions to our contract make me wonder whether we're buying an electronic assembly plant or some anthropology research institute." Bobbo will have a fit when he hears the details, I thought, but said nothing about it.

"You are buying more than you thought, aren't you?" Krista reassured me.

I didn't like negotiating with her in the room, but I had no choice in the matter. I had to do the best for my corporation. "I really think that all these added conditions of the sale should have been brought up before," I said looking straight into Kohl's eyes, with more than a tinge of accusation in my voice.

"The plant engineers you sent us were not the appropriate people to talk of such matters," Kohl said. "We answered every question they asked with honesty, and told them that we'd finalize the deal when you arrived. That's what we are trying to do now. None of the new facts we've just disclosed to you change the value of Rakma. This is still a superbly run operation with plenty of margin for profit." He paused, as if he might have said enough, but he must have liked what he was saying and went on to conclude: "If you want it, you can have it; if not, no harm done. I'll look elsewhere. In any case, the plant will be sold. I'm getting out of the business."

"We were wondering why," I said, remembering Bobbo's instructions to me.

Kohl turned his chair toward the window and stared far into the distance. "I've got some dreams to dream too, but I can't do it here anymore," he said pensively. Then, he swung around and looked at me, as if he wanted to know how much he could trust me with his thoughts. "You probably think all this stuff we've been telling you about dreaming dreams someone else makes up for you is crap. Well, you've seen the people work, and that's no crap. The dreams one has can change his reality. I know. I've been dreaming dreams made for me too…" His voice trailed off into silence.

I was still for a long time, unable to take my eyes off him. I had no doubt the man believed what he had just said.

"What has happened here is a miracle, Daniel. Face it! The world has a lot to learn from our experience here, and I'm going to let it know."

"You're going to give lectures?"

A slow, cryptic smile spread on his face. "Perhaps…Who can tell…First, I have a lot more learning to do myself…then we'll see."

Matheson rubbed his hands together. "Do we have an agreement then?" Matheson cut into this diversion, pulling a sheaf of papers out of his briefcase.

Scooping up every ounce of my negotiating soul's stubbornness I could find, I made one more attempt. "I really would like to offer you at least five percent less than was previously mentioned, to account for all the new factors we've been discussing," I said, and felt a weight being lifted off my shoulders. I felt free. I had done my job. It was the best I could do under the circumstances. Then, I felt like a barbarian trampling down sacred covenants entrusted to me. I steeled myself. I was dealing in business, not religion. Perhaps, we were buying a miracle. Why not?

It wasn't exactly contempt that I saw in Kohl's eyes, but, perhaps, pity, for my inability to appreciate his life's work. I hated myself for that, but I didn't regret having asked. "I should be asking you for *more*, now that you know the secrets of my operation's success," he said quite matter-of-factly.

"There's considerable uncertainty involved here…"

"You should try to understand what we've got here and use it in your other plants. You could achieve a quantum leap in productivity. My price is fair," he said and folded his hands on top of his desk.

"I'll leave this up to you," I said stubbornly.

"Well, what do you say, Danny boy? Is it a deal?" Matheson said, tapping the papers on the table.

I gave him a very harsh look, but, somehow, the edge of it was blunted by his nonchalant attitude. The last person who called me "Danny boy" was my buddy Frank. He was shot by the VC, a day after he saved my life during the Tet Offensive, in Vietnam. Krista had been observing me all along. I was sure she was tracking my thoughts. The only leverage I had on her was that if she wanted to go on working here she better not make me look foolish. "I'm sure that you'll be able to sell your deal to your boss and all the interested parties, without getting into all the details we've been discussing here," she said. "You are making an excellent acquisition that stands on its merits. Consider everything else as background information, which it really is." I knew all that, of course, but the fact that she had said it, made it more believable.

I was about to consent when Kohl stopped me. "Hold that for a while," he said. "We can sign up at the house. My wife wants to meet you." I replaced the fountain pen I had taken out of my pocket. What now? "We'll relax a bit and have some lunch." He glanced at his watch. "In a few minutes our people will be breaking for lunch. I would ask you to come and observe how they deal with each other, but you wouldn't understand their language. It gets pretty chaotic at times."

A few minutes later, as the plant came to life with loud voices and shouts and laughter, Kohl led the way to his villa perched above the plant and tucked behind a jutting finger of the jungle. It stood like a sentinel watching over its master's creation. The ocean had become a mirror stretched out behind us as far as the imagination could travel. I felt the sticky air wrapped around my skin, sapping resistance, loosening the moorings of control, whispering that no action is worth the effort. The uphill walk was exhausting.

We had just sat down and taken a few cool breaths of air, when a woman of rare beauty appeared before us. She was slim and her body was all gentle curves and graceful movement. Her long black hair flowed down her back close to her body like a pelt of some exotic animal. Her eyes slid from face to face as if they were conferring a blessing upon us.

"My wife, Bendyra," Kohl introduced her to me. "This is Daniel Thornton, dear."

"Delighted to meet you, Dan," she said in carefully measured English. It was the first time I could recall that I liked the sound of my nickname in its short, snappy ring. Her eyes were asking questions I couldn't translate. "Has Wolf been nice to you?"

"Not only nice, but also patient and informative."

"And, do you like our plant?"

"Very efficient; very innovative," I said hugging my managerese language for dear life, since spouting it requires little thinking.

"But, you don't believe all this stuff about the dreams, I suppose?"

"It doesn't much matter what I believe, if productivity remains high."

She smiled and took my arm and led me to the dinning room where lunch was laid out. "Perhaps, you'd like to believe in our secrets, but you cannot. Not yet, but in time, I believe, you will. There are many realities to explore."

I'm not sure what we discussed at that luncheon, but I remember that I felt content with the world. All my concerns about the deal I was about to conclude evaporated as she explained the many other customs and beliefs of the Kogala and the Buru. I felt envious of Kohl for having such a wonderful companion in life. As I imagined him traveling around the world and sharing experiences with this woman, I knew why he wanted to leave the business.

When we were done with lunch, Kohl excused himself and escorted his wife out of the room. The Mathesons wanted to know if we planned to make any changes in the staff and whether Krista would be able to continue serving the company. They had some additional questions about the manager who would be sent to head the operation and other work details, which I answered as openly as I could. I told Krista that whatever contributions she was making had to be good, judging by the results I had seen. Her husband was about to explain the legal and administrative services he was providing, when Kohl reappeared. He looked straight at me and asked in a loud cheery voice: "Now, then, Daniel, do we have a deal?"

"Deal," I heard myself say. The word seemed to hover in space for a long time.

Matheson had added all the special conditions, including the right of five visits per year by people Kohl could send, and asked me to initial it. It seemed reasonable, and I did without haggling. We signed the contract, and shook hands. Bendyra brought a bottle of champagne and we toasted each other's success. And then, Kohl gave me a cryptic smile, and said without taking his eyes off me, "By the way, my wife believes that you can be trusted. And, she knows what she's talking about, because she's a Buru herself."

My mouth dropped.

"I've got my dreams all planned out, Daniel," he bellowed, and his laughter roared throughout the house, a victorious, wild call that echoes in my mind whenever I think of that day.

Bobbo Barkan is a shrewd businessman and took everything I told him about symbiotic tribes, dream-makers and teamwork by psychic connection very seriously. He thought I had struck a good bargain, even before the superior productivity figures of the plant started rolling in. When I told him that Kohl's wife was intelligent, beautiful, charming and half his age, he understood why Kohl wanted to sell, and left me alone.

Three years have gone by now, and the plant in Tikopia still produces electronic circuit boards more efficiently than any other plant we know of. But this is not its main value to us anymore. After we made sure that the Buru could work well with other ethnic groups with troubled consciences, we started to use the plant to produce more industrial Buru dream-makers. Now we employ sixteen Buru at the plant, and are ready to hire more, if we can find them. We provide a variety of fringe benefits to them; we encourage their reproduction with frequent vacations and feasts in their village, and give them special training to assume dream-making responsibilities in various parts of the world. Seven of them have already been transferred and are making dreams for people at headquarters and the main plant we have in Silicon Valley. We don't know how they do what they do, but we have two research projects probing their ways, and the cognizant scientists think that some day soon they'll have a breakthrough. Till the time comes when we have their secret, we use this limited resource with great care. We assign Buru only to some of our most critical operations and to people who have the most demanding jobs. Bobbo Barkan himself has a Buru dream maker all to himself, and from what I hear he swears by him and doesn't let him out of his sight. All of the transplanted Buru have been received enthusiastically by our top people, and everyone is sure that they would be welcome into symbiotic relationships with employees from every level of the organization. But, Buru don't grow on trees, so we have to be good stewards and conserve this precious resource. When we tell people that a guilty conscience is a requirement for a close dreaming relationship with the Buru, they laugh. "Aren't we all guilty of something or other, after all?" most of them say. I don't argue.

Kohl, unfortunately for us, had the idea of supplying Buru dream-makers to industry first, and is our fiercest competitor. He has managed to place twenty-three of them, by my latest report, in various organizations around the globe, and has more than a dozen getting ready at the village. Fortunately, the Hortons are still reluctant to experiment, but I don't know for how long. Kohl's right to bring visitors to the plant, given to him by the contract I signed, has been a boon for his business, and the most serious flaw to an otherwise superb deal. Alas, "One look is worth ten reasons," as he said. He sold us an assembly plant and got in exchange a demo of a miracle, at no cost. If I had only believed in the value of these people back then, I would have demanded exclusive rights to all the Buru I could lay my hands on, and wouldn't have let Kohl come within…I would do a lot of things differently, but so would he. Would he have agreed to any deal that didn't further his plans?

Well, we do our best with what we know at the time. At least, Bobbo doesn't hold this against me. I've been promoted to executive vice president and as soon as the old man and his Buru retire, I'm a shoe in for the big job. I should add that I'm one of the few top people in our company who has no Buru connection to tailor his dreams. I make do with whatever comes from my own head, and have no one but myself to thank or to blame for whatever happens to me in sleep or wakefulness. That's how I am. There are many realities to explore all right, as Bendyra told me at that first meeting we had, but my dreams will always be of my own making and so will my actions. And, the most significant dream I have these days, besides becoming the CEO, is to buy Kohl out and have the monopoly on Buru dream-makers. Only then can I stop this spreading practice of people delegating their own dream making. It is an abomination that I can only correct by gobbling up Kohl's little operation. I can do this by dropping our fees for the Buru services, squeezing his profit margins in the open market and gaining market share. In any case, by the time I get done with him, no Buru will dream for anyone but a Kogala, period. We'll double, even triple the size of Rakma, but we won't go into the Buru rental business. Humanity cannot afford the expansion of that practice.

Sometimes I wonder what dreams Bendyra makes up for Kohl to dream, but I don't lose sleep over that. Krista still works for us, and I have her husband on a retainer. Matheson tells me that where there is a will, there is a way. Krista says that Bendyra isn't happy having Buru who dream for people competing against each other. They both report that the local Kogala are furious with Kohl, because, against his wife's advice, he tried to increase the Buru population by interbreeding them with the Gonoba tribe "up North," apparently breaking a serious taboo. He is an unscrupulous man, and not much good will come from him. We must stay focused on the goals we have as a business. We have made everybody happy at Rakma by increasing the Buru working at the plant and giving them incentives so they can increase their population in their village. Bendyra appreciates the way we have been treating her people. "A very substantial lady that Bendyra," Matheson never fails to add whenever her name comes up in our discussions. I suppose he knows that it would be hard for an eligible bachelor like me not to have had a dream or two about a woman of such character and charm. He is sure that she would welcome an opportunity to have all the Buru working for us, and she wouldn't hesitate to slip Kohl the right dream to make that happen, when the time comes. That thought is very chilling to me. I didn't think she would do that. When I asked him to tell me how he knew all this, he said, chuckling, that he had a dream after talking with one of the Buru workers. I'm never sure how much I can trust Matheson. I think that Bendyra is an honest person, but who can tell what new things and happenings await us tomorrow? We'll have to wait and see, "which dream loses the shape of mere shadow and takes on the form of fact," as Shakespeare put it.

CHAPTER 10

❁

The Staff Optimist

Sales are down, loans are coming due, bookings are below plan, and overhead is rising, but no matter how desperate our situation may be, my job is to look at the bright side of things and create scenarios of success. And, if there is no bright side within sight, it is my job to create one and express it with enthusiasm. Invariably, it comes down to restoring the faith we all must have in each other and ourselves for business to succeed. My commitment must be absolutely genuine, and my arguments so persuasive that they can slice through all the objections of the doubting Thomases and the Nay Sayers who lurk dispirited in every gathering we have.

People look to me for hope, sunshine and victory when they have lost their bearings and the sky appears to be falling. I am, after all, the staff optimist of the corporation, a job I created out of thin air, despair and the goodwill of our President.

I have no doubt that the time will come when staff optimists will be as indispensable to organizations as controllers and human resource specialists are today. The reason is that the world around us is getting meaner, gloomier, more threatening than any of us imagined only a few years ago. Optimism is the force needed to keep the balance people must have if they are to go on with their lives and embark upon great enterprises. And, people like me, trained to see the light at the end of the tunnel, will have to lead the effort.

Every day is an adventure for me, since I don't know what thicket of negativity we'll hit as we pursue our goals. Yesterday the competition came up with a new product that will render our product obsolete, unless we do something, except that we don't have the slightest idea what to do, and people's faces reflect defeat and resignation. Today we lost a government contract because the budget was slashed by Congress, and it looks like we'll have to lay off a couple of hundred people and revise downward our estimates for growth and profits. Tomorrow—I don't know what kind of snake will crawl from under one of the rocks strewn all around us—it may be a downturn in the economy, the loss of a key technologist to the competition, an error discovered at a manufacturing plant, which results in a recall of thousands of units in the field, or an accounting shenanigan, which will absorb the energies of dozens of lawyers and accountants, and threaten to wipe out our carefully nurtured profits, or land some executives in jail for fraud. Whatever it is, I have to stare it in the face, stare it down, so to speak, and walk over it, or slay it with hope.

Some people think that I have an easy job, and try to dabble in optimism on their own. Because everyone has optimistic thoughts from time to time, some people think that they can provide the services I do. But, just as there is a difference between mere writing and using language to create literature, just as there is a difference between belting out a song in the shower and singing at the Metropolitan Opera, so there is a difference between having an optimistic disposition and creating optimistic scenarios, which persuade people and move them to action.

I don't deny that it helps to be an optimist by nature, but I am inclined to think that the profession of optimism relies on will and skill, rather than natural endowment. I do my job, not because I feel that everything will turn out well, but because I have trained myself to look for favorable outcomes and choose to do so. The proverbial glass is half full, not because I cannot see that it is half empty as well, but because I want to think, as soon as I see it, of ways that it can be filled rather than of all the ways it can be emptied. So, I reject the undesirable scenarios and, by an act of the will, I focus on the favorable ones.

When I was a boy in occupied Europe in the last war, our village was burned down to the ground by the Nazis, and all males between the ages of eighteen and fifty were executed in the square, while the rest of us were left to wonder in the ruins. The old men got together and planned our survival while the women mourned the dead, wailing into the night. The old priest came up to me, took me aside and told me that my job was to keep laughter alive, no matter how many terrors stalked us. He told me to look for little, ordinary things, and point them out and laugh, and not be discouraged if I was thought to be a fool and was treated like a leper and people chased me away. "You've got to train yourself to see the sunlight with your mind's eye, through the black clouds," he said, and gave me his blessing. And, that's how I became the only soul who could laugh in the ruins.

After the war I went to the University and studied philosophy and religion. I remember one of my classmates asked me if I had ever been unhappy, if I had suffered any personal tragedy, because I appeared to be always in an upbeat mood, as if I had never been touched by evil. I laughed so loudly, so contagiously, that I had the whole dormitory in stitches.

In time, I learned how to channel my laughter into arguments, which destroyed negativity and introduced hope into other people's minds. I gradually realized that this ability of mine was rare, and began to think of making a career out of it. I immigrated to the United States and started working in human resources, using my optimistic arguments to convince people around me of the existence of desirable outcomes and showing them ways to achieve them.

Once, I attended a meeting of all the human resources professionals in the company, and heard our President give us his "lean and mean" speech for the future. He wanted us to help management "get rid of the deadwood," and enforce draconian measures to reduce waste, and show people that the lean years were now upon us. I started to laugh. I didn't even know I was laughing until people started staring at me, which, for me, was a sign of effectiveness, and encouraged me to laugh even louder, as I had trained myself to do.

The president stopped talking and pointed to me, wanting to know what the joke was. I stood up and told him and everyone in the room that what he was telling us was the scenario he had chosen to believe, which was his right to do, but I chose to see things differently, and the contrast was funny to me. He wanted to know how exactly I saw things, and I told him. I said that I saw challenges being overcome, people rising to the occasion and creating conditions for success; I saw growth, not shrinkage, synergy and productivity increases, high morale and camaraderie from helping each other, rather than resentment and suspicion from tossing people out in the streets. "Mister president," I concluded, "I choose to believe in you and everyone who works for you, rather than a bunch of facts and figures put together by fainthearted analysts and terrified planners. I may be a fool, but I see a bright future for us."

From the corners of my eyes I could see mouths hanging open in disbelief, and I thought I heard a chuckle or two. "Well, anyway," the President mumbled, "everyone is entitled to have an opinion." Then, after a moment's reflection, he smiled. "You may have something there," he conceded, "though, all I'm saying is let's be cautious, even as we do our best to succeed."

After the speeches and the ritual question-and-answer period, the President found me and told me that he wanted me to work for him and try to bring some sunshine to the gloom he sensed coming down on everyone. He is a great man, but everyone thought that he needed my services more than most. So, I became the staff optimist for the corporation, ready to move into any group in the company, which was gripped by despair, and point them toward hope, and faith, so they could pull themselves out of it, and make their dreams come true.

My job is very trying. At first, most people think that I am a fool, a superficial thinker, who has latched on to a sinecure and will do anything to keep it. But, even after they get to know me, people don't have any great respect for my work. I am often ridiculed for my disdain for facts and figures, which, in their view, tell the whole story no matter what the situation. People have gotten angry with me and called me nasty names for refusing to dwell in the dark abodes they construct out of nightmarish conclusions based on calculations. And, I have been thrown out of meetings, because I have challenged a dozen people at a time to turn away from prophesies of doom and act boldly, self-confidently, even if that means that all may be lost in the end. "Fight the good fight in good cheer!" is my call to action.

Though my arguments, exhortations and enthusiasm sometimes turn things around, and people do succeed where there was nothing but failure predicted, they never thank me, or even admit that I had anything to do with their success. They change their minds and ways after I have left them, and feel entirely responsible for their achievements. This is how my strategy is supposed to work, but just the same, sometimes it's hard on me. There are times when I wish that somebody would come up to me and tell me that I have performed a useful service for the group; that what I said at the meeting made a difference to him; that my laughter gave her a chance to see things more clearly. But, so far it hasn't happened, and, probably, it will never happen. I simply cannot have my cake and eat it too! People want to feel that they are the sole agents of their own conversion; they cannot experience their power if they attribute its discovery to someone else. So, I have learned to live without recognition, without gratitude, without much respect for what I do, and most regrettably without friends at work. Even the President, to whom I have provided many valuable services, keeps me at arm's length, as if the acknowledgment of my value to the company might diminish his.

When I am alone and think of my work, I find solace in the fact that I am doing what is right and needs to be done, regardless of the cost to me. I tell myself that all the people who have been influenced by my work live a better life than they would otherwise. And, the old priest's words ring in my ears again: "You've got to train yourself to see the sun with your mind's eye. Don't be discouraged if they think you are a fool and treat you like a leper." A wonderful feeling comes over me as he gives me his blessing, and I sleep in peace.

CHAPTER 11

❀

An Opportunist's Knocks

One of the executives in the Division—I'll call him Maxwell—became my mentor without any special effort on my part. I'm not going to deny that I was ambitious, or that I didn't do all I possibly could to cultivate the relationship by following his advice and working harder on the tasks he gave me. I did, and I make no apologies for that. What was I supposed to do? Avoid him? Goof off when he asked me to give extra attention to an assignment? I performed my duties and then some. And, Maxwell responded with praise, advice, and, I suppose, though I have no way of knowing this for a fact, with a good word to my boss, now and then. That's how this mentoring game is played, as far as I know. You scratch the right back and your back gets scratched back, somehow.

I got good salary increases, some choice assignments that expanded my capabilities, and two promotions that some people might have called unexpected. But, I wouldn't say that I was the beneficiary of any favors—I took advantage of the opportunities I saw and worked hard for everything that came my way. And, in time, I got used to thinking of myself as a competent manager, who doesn't need mentoring anymore. I felt "empowered," as they say, and it was time for me to give back some of the advice I had received by mentoring others. Besides, Maxwell was at the top of our Division now, and I didn't have many chances to talk things over with him as we had done in the past. When we met at various meetings, he always made a point of asking me how things were going at work, and I always responded with enthusiasm about the progress we were making. He had enough on his mind, and I didn't want to burden him with my problems. Not once did I ask for a favor, but I suppose my boss and my colleagues knew that Maxwell was interested in my career and may have taken that into account when dealing with me. But, I never took advantage of that, and I don't think that I can be held responsible for the attitudes of others or the actions they took. Besides, everyone who works in an organization needs friends, allies and collaborators to get things done. And the higher up one is, the more one can get done.

Business in the Division was good, except for one big program we had with a government contract. Everybody knew that this multi-million-dollar program, which I'll call Program Big Bucks because I don't want to get anyone in trouble, was a mess. Nothing was going well with it technically, financially or managerially. I had nothing to do with it, but I heard complaints from engineers, administrators and human resource professionals, almost on a daily basis. Costs were increasing by leaps and bounds, while no one believed that the products would do what we had told the government they would do. And, the people in the program were working overtime, felt demotivated and were fearful of what would happen next. News of the troubles with Big Bucks must have reached the corporate headquarters, because a Review Board was constituted with executives from other parts of the company to look into the program and come up with recommendations for getting the program back on track.

It was at this time that I got a call from Maxwell, now a vice president and general manager of our Division, and immediately I went to see him in his office. He said he was very glad to see me and, after we went through the usual exchanges of how I was doing and what was my family doing, he got down to business. He said that the Division was in great shape and the "glitches" with Big Bucks could be fixed, "if Corporate left us alone to do our job." But, this Review Board was "a bunch of nervous Nellies," eager to prove to corporate management how smart and dedicated they were, and it could bring disaster to the whole Division, if they came up with "a negative report."

He was upset with the people at corporate headquarters for sending us this "Snoop Board," because it meant that they didn't really trust us. He said that this Board could blow out of proportion the minor problems any big program is bound to have—"make mountains out of molehills," is the way he put it—and that could bring the roof down on all our people. The more he confided in me, the more uncomfortable I became. But, what could I do? I listened and nodded in agreement with him now and then. You can't be stone-faced when the big boss of your organization opens his heart to you. I shook my head in disbelief at the nasty moves of Corporate, I rolled up my eyes in disapproval when I heard about the envy of some people at Corporate and grunted my consent in sympathetic agreement at the right moments.

"That's a disgrace!" I exclaimed, when he talked about the damage the Board could do to our people.

And then, he asked me for a favor: "I want you to assist the Program Manager with his presentations to the Board and act as a liaison person in this difficult process," he said. "I want to have a man I can trust every step of the way, while these people are in our shop," he added, looking me straight in the eye.

I've been around organizations long enough to know exactly what he meant, but I couldn't believe it. I sat there stunned, trying to collect my thoughts, knowing that I was a doomed man. What choice did I have? I could choose to be his helper in a cover-up and stool pigeon rolled into one, or tell the big man of my Division, who also happened to be my mentor, to take a walk. I could choose to do what he was asking and sell myself, or flush my career down the drain. I could go on hoping that all would turn out fine, or begin the nightmare of a life as an outcast, right there and then. This was pay back time all right, but it wasn't as simple as some moralists make it out to be. Not when reality barrels down on you out of the blue like a Mack truck in an alley.

"Will you help me out in this?" Maxwell asked.

I don't know what I expected to hear, but I asked feebly what exactly this liaison role entailed.

"Just keep track of what's going on with the Board, help them get the right idea about the program, see what are they coming up with, help the program manager make his presentations Division-friendly, and keep me posted," Maxwell said bluntly. Then, as if he was adding some detail, he said: "I'd like this to stay between us. You know Davenport, the program manager? He's good with the nitty-gritty of running a program, but he doesn't get the big picture. Let's keep this between us. He would get pretty nervous if he found out that you and I had any kind of special relationship."

So would the Review Board, I thought, but said nothing. Instead, I lifted my ten-ton body up from the chair and said that I would do what I could. I wanted to reassure myself with this somewhat ambiguous response that I would still be free to choose a course of action that didn't tear up my guts and didn't wipe out my career. But, I knew, something in me knew, that there was no such course of action. It was time for one of those dreaded "either, or" choices, with no chance for doing "neither, or both." That was the moment of decision, and I chose to go along with Maxwell's request.

This is not a long story. What happened next was bound to happen; it was unavoidable. My boss assigned me to Davenport, ostensibly to help with all the extra work the Board presentations would require, and I was present whenever significant information about the program was exchanged. Davenport was no dummy and worked hard to present the program in the best possible light for the Division. But, the Board members fanned out in all directions and talked to people from all functions and at all levels of the organization. We couldn't keep track of everything they were finding out. Every evening, after we had wined and dined them, the Board members met in private and pieced together all the bits and pieces of information they were gathering. Next day, they had more questions, and we had to provide the best answers we could devise, which left even more questions to be answered.

I kept Maxwell informed of all that I knew, but he kept pushing me every step of the way for more. He didn't think that the board needed all the data Davenport and I were providing to them; he wanted to emphasize the "bright side of things" and play down the existing problems. He wanted to know names of people who "spewed venom" to the "snoops," as he put it. He kept after me to "manage Davenport's output," because I had "an innate sense of organizational realities," whereas he was "a babe in the woods." He was furious that one of the board members had taken it upon herself to gather together a randomly selected group of engineers and pump them for information. Why weren't we controlling the process? Why didn't we choose this engineer to talk to the board, rather than that one, who was disgruntled with his career progress? He knew so many details about the organization that I began to wonder whether I was one of a whole flock of stool pigeons he had running around the place.

And, my gut was churning every step of the way. I started waking up at dawn and thinking of all the dodges, the mental maneuvers and the lies I would have to concoct and serve that day. I kept thinking of the mortgage in the house, the college tuition for my daughter, the orthodontist's bill for my son…I saw myself out of a job, walking the streets with the Want Ad section of the newspaper underarm. Who would want to hire a middle-aged middle manager of a failed program in the defense industry? I would stare at the ceiling and plan another day's deceptions, because the alternatives were even more distasteful. Fraud still had more benefits than costs. There were a few times when I forgot all about ethics and legality and found relief in the maneuvers of the cover-up and the intricacies of a stoolpigeon's game. It was probably the most challenging job I had ever done, and I was doing it well. I felt like expressing to myself congratulations and condolences with a single pat on the back.

After a week's stay at the Division, the board was coming to the conclusion that there were a lot of things wrong with the Big Bucks Program, and so was I. It appeared that the program was underbid at Maxwell's insistence, because he felt that was the only way to win it. He was heard saying at the meeting for the BAFO (Best and Final Offer) for the Big Bucks contract that the Company would get its due when the overruns kick in. Davenport and I admitted that the bid was based on "an optimistic scenario," but the board wasn't happy with the "success oriented" approach management had taken. Big Bucks was going to production before anyone had proven that it would work, and no engineer could be found to vouch even for its feasibility. Davenport and I attributed this to the engineers' "low risk taking mentality," as if we were a couple of social scientists who had made the engineers thought processes our life's work. And, to make matters worse, the hoped for infusion of additional government funds, which is precisely what all "success oriented" bidders count on to make a profit, were not forthcoming. We, of course, remained "optimistic," as far as the board was concerned, but we weren't very convincing. And, to make my life even more difficult, Jane Farber, one of the board members, kept asking me why was I assigned to the program just before the arrival of the board; what exactly were my responsibilities; and what was my reporting chain. I found myself lying outright and hating it more every time.

Some people, I suppose, can stifle their feelings, mute their conscience, soothe their gut, tell lies that are hard to discredit and do whatever unpleasant things they have to do to succeed. But, I'm not put together that way. I told myself that my reasons for committing fraud were not greed, but self-sacrifice. I did it for my family, that's all. Can you believe that? I couldn't. So, one evening after dinner with the board, I got Jane Farber aside, and told her why I had been assigned to Davenport by Maxwell, and what I had been doing behind everybody's back. She wasn't surprised. She had been around organizations a long time and knew how to listen and what to say. "You're in a tough spot," she said with understanding, "but I'm glad you decided to level with me."

"I'm afraid I did it because I can't stand it anymore. Now, I feel like a traitor, which isn't much better than feeling like a stool pigeon and a cover-up perpetrator. I guess the only thing left is to get out," the words came out of my mouth without previous deliberation.

Her eyes flashed. "No way!" she burst out without hesitation. "I want you to sit tight. No reason to do such a thing now. We need people with distaste for deception in this Company. Maxwell is in trouble without you doing anything about it, but you can help us reel him in," she said, and a smile graced her lips. "Leave it to me. I know how to deal with this." She stood up. "Go home and get a good night's sleep; you look like a zombie," she said affectionately and patted me on the shoulder.

For a while I felt as if a great load had been lifted off my back. But, as I looked myself in the mirror that night I didn't like what I saw. I just wasn't the person I wanted to be. Maxwell didn't do anything to me, nobody did. I was no martyr, just a run-of-the-mill small-time con man posing as a hard-working manager. It was I who maneuvered myself into the quicksand. And, that pitiful confession of mine with the subsequent, conditional absolution was no solution to whatever was wrong with me. I just couldn't go on waiting for the time when my newfound protector would call me in her office and ask me for a favor. Jane Farber probably never would, but I couldn't know that for sure. And, I couldn't trust myself to stand up and be counted next time, knowing that she was aware of my slimy conduct.

I had to put a stop to this sequence of deceptions. If that meant going to jail, I would have to accept that and move on.

So, next morning, I went to Jane Farber's office and told her to call somebody from Legal affairs, so I can give a deposition on what I had done in the program, because after that was done I would quit my job. She tried to dissuade me, but understood my reasons and had a lawyer take down my statement. She seemed pleased with that. Then, I submitted my resignation, asking that the customary two-week notice be waived, if at all possible. My boss was surprised, and so was everybody else who knew me. My boss wanted to know the reason, so I told him that I had come to the sad conclusion that Big Bucks was a dog and I couldn't support its continuation anymore. He didn't want to hear this and said that, as far as he was concerned, I had been an excellent manager and was leaving to pursue my "changed career interests." I said that he could believe anything he wanted, but I knew why I was leaving, and that was that. I thought about telling him of my brief venture in the con-man and stool-pigeon trade, but I was pretty sure that he knew everything about me and was only concerned that my leaving might mean the Board was getting closer to the ugly truth of Big Bucks. Besides, Jane Farber had asked me to say nothing about my role in the program, so no one would be alerted to the latest findings of the investigation. Maxwell's questionable maneuvers, had not been announced yet, but when they became public knowledge, I was afraid that he could easily spread rumors tagging me with a nervous breakdown or worse. I had nothing to say to Maxwell, so I left without contacting him.

Now, by way of an epilogue, I am happy to report that I am at peace with myself, and I have even come to like myself at times. I am in the lawn mower repair business and make a decent living, without owing a thing to anyone. I thought of getting another job in management, but I didn't think anyone would want to hire a manager who had once lost his integrity. Besides, I couldn't bear running into someone who knew of my mistake and tried to use that information to take advantage of me. Anyway, this way, I feel that somehow I'm paying for my mistake. Still, the question plagues me: what could I have done differently? Perhaps, if I knew then what I know now, I might have told Maxwell that I don't do deceptions and cover-ups. Who knows? I might have survived, and might have even become a hero; if not, I would have entered the lawn mower repair business sooner. More important, perhaps, I would have had no need to play this crazy guessing game of bouncing from hero to villain the rest of my life. Friendship with Maxwell, one way or another, did have its costs, and I'll be paying them for quite some time.

Maxwell, by the way, left the Company (some say that he was kicked out) and is managing one of the better shoe stores in Peoria, Illinois. Apparently, the benefits of his fraud had not materialized, because he was counting on the success of Big Bucks to boost him to the top of the bonus scale. People said that Jane Farber tried hard to get him to admit his deception, but she didn't succeed. He had no doubt that he had done the right things to give the Company every possible advantage in the competitive world of business. He said that it was his "fiduciary responsibility to protect the interests of the stockholders." He left unceremoniously, but there were no criminal charges filed against him.

Davenport is totally dedicated to his job as a manager for a sewer cleaning company. He feels that this work has given meaning to his life. "You've got to have working sewers, or you're in deep doo-doo," he said to me when I bumped into him at a shopping mall a couple of months ago. He assured me that no one would think of cheating at this company. "No parasites like Maxwell."

Davenport told me that my old boss was bypassed for a promotion twice, probably because he was associated closely with Maxwell, but is still with the company working on a government contract for gadgets to combat terrorism. He had heard that Jane Farber had Maxwell's job for a while, but then left to become the COO of a Fortune 100 company. "She was a decent sort, I thought," he added, and I agreed wholeheartedly. "But, big fish like Maxwell, always manage to escape from the pincers of the D.A.," Davenport lamented, and I agreed again. I felt that my impotence added to his was doubly unbearable.

He was glad to hear that I was in business for myself and said that he would keep me in mind, if his mower broke down.

"We also repair weed whackers," I added as he was leaving. He smiled knowingly and disappeared behind a kiosk selling plastic flowers.

CHAPTER 12

❀

*The Teleboss Tells it
Like it Is*

The official title of our boss is Telemarketing Overseer, but we call him Teleboss, and, more affectionately, Stewart. We don't see him. We've never seen him, but his voice is ever present in the office and demands attention. It is a deep, calm voice, which comes through our earphones and has something to say on just about everything we do. There is advice, and criticism, and praise, but there is no idle talk. Sometimes I want to escape the constant scrutiny of that voice—yes, that voice *can* and *does* scrutinize—but I have never been able to do it. Though no one has ever said that we have to listen to that voice, most of us don't choose to ignore it or escape from it. We're just not sure of the consequences of such actions. The very last thing I would want right now is to get fired from this job, and have to start looking for another. I can see myself sweating over resumes, pouring over want ad pages, calling to beg for an interview, shuttling around the city like a bouncing pin ball, waiting outside some personnel clerk's office to be probed, checking the mail for the favorable response that never comes—these snatches of a humdrum nightmare keep me fixed to my post, earphones snugly driven into my ears, and speaker phone affixed two inches from my mouth without a chance of ever biting it off in a fit of anger. But, I think, there is another reason that keeps us from rejecting Stewart's intrusions: we need to be connected to someone who seems to understand as much about people and the world out there as he does about the Catalogue.

I'm Chester to him, or Number Three (the number of my cubicle) when he is angry with me and wants me to shape up. And, he is Stewart to me, whether I feel warm or ice-cold about him. But, he is more, much more than Stewart. His "attaboy" for the way I handled a difficult customer can make my day, and his criticism of my inadequacies and foibles, which spoiled an order, can ruin my sleep. Everybody agrees that he can make the sun shine bright in the sky, or roll a lid of lead clouds over us, with equal ease. We tell ourselves that we've given him too much power and resolve to cut him down to size next time we step up to the plate. But, it's all talk. No matter what we do, Stewart does what he's always done, without fear of any power plays that we may come up with.

He knows what each one of us wants and, when we work effectively, he responds to our needs. My good work, for example, is rewarded with his permission to work overtime. Anyone who understands the calculus of low paying jobs would understand why good work is rewarded with more work. The overtime determines whether I can continue my studies at the university or be consigned to this grind forever. Most of us don't plan to be telemarketers, or order takers for life. We have hopes and dream of a better life. And, Stewart wants us to achieve more. He cares not only about the work we do today, but also about our well being in the future. His help and his advice on how to succeed in a "real career," as he puts it, make the hassles of each day more bearable.

And, this isn't unique with me. All of us recognize that Stewart understands us and wants to help us. But he needs our cooperation. Laverne, in Number Seven, wants extra time off when her children are sick or in some kind of trouble, and Stewart allows her to take off without risking her job. She can hardly believe it when he tells her it's OK to leave without worrying about the work. Laverne thanks him and can't say enough good things about him next day. Of course, when Stewart shows his generosity to Laverne, the rest of us go into an anxiety drill. For me, the question is overtime: will I have some extra time to take Laverne's calls, or, will I have to scramble to do it, without relief, on regular time?

Travis of the Mellow Tongue, from Number One, worries that he will be asked to come at hours he has scheduled for his Yoga class at the Community Center, or his Poetry class at Barnes and Noble, or one of the other self improvement activities which some day will propel him to a career in the arts. Stewart isn't always sympathetic to his pleas. And, Sylvia, our Little Sparrow, in Number Six, who frets at the slightest change of any routine, throws a fit, because she works at her maximum speed when all of us are there and Laverne's departure will cause her to stumble and make mistakes in taking orders, or get flustered by what she calls "some super aggressive individual" and make a fool of herself. Won't Stewart view this as a serious failing with repercussions for her job? Stewart offers her some solace: "If you make mistakes with some super aggressive individual, Sylvia, I won't hold it against you; but, don't mess up with soft spoken customers who have been ordering from us for thirty years, OK?" I can hear Sylvia's delicate fingernails drumming fear and trepidation onto her desktop; smoke rises up from her place as if her cubicle is on fire. She sighs in panic and pleads with Stewart to bring in a temp to sub for Laverne. What is he telling her? Be strong, Sylvia! I hired you for this job because you can do it well, no matter who calls. You need to build your confidence and open up that boutique you've been telling me about. I don't know now what he's telling her, but I'll hear it in great detail tomorrow morning when we gather for our coffee klatch, before we put on our harnesses. I poke my head past my cubicle partition, having become a contortionist here, and catch Sylvia's eye. "One person less out of eight isn't going to bring a deluge of work,

Sylvia," I say. I motion her with my hands to calm down. Sylvia's fears are being converted into rage against Stewart. "How much punishment can a person take?" she asks, and shakes her fist above her head, her eyes flashing at the ceiling and beyond.

We are on the fourth floor and Stewart, we are sure, is on one of the floors above us, but we have no idea how high above us. He could be on the fifth or the twenty-fifth floor. We simply haven't been able to find out, in spite of our many efforts to locate him. Company regulations prohibit any meetings between Stewart and the troops in the pits, but it would be nice to at least fantasize going up to his office and having a heart to heart talk with him once in a while; or, barging in there and having it out with him, if that's what fits the situation. But, we don't know. We have theories, given the department we are in, the position he has, the kind of accommodations of each floor, as we know them from our own hurried inspections and from whatever information we can get pumping janitors and mailroom clerks. But we don't really know. Some of us like to think that Stewart's office is up in the tower, right on top of the building, with nothing but blue sky above him. This image, somehow, gives us great comfort. We want him to be on top of our work, on top of our problems, on top of the world.

Harold from Number Two, a retired schoolteacher with patience a mile long, says that we have a tendency to elevate Stewart just to increase our own status. He thinks that Stewart's office may be right on this floor, or even down in the basement of the building, and we wouldn't know it. Who knows if we haven't met him in one of the elevators, or smiled and said good morning to him, as one does with pleasant looking strangers in the hallways or down at the lobby? Regretfully, Sylvia admits that she never says anything to anyone she doesn't know and like. Could this be the reason he is so hard on her? We console her by telling her that he is hard on everybody, and tell her stories from our dealings with him. She doesn't feel alone anymore.

The more I think about this matter of Stewart's whereabouts the more convinced I become that I have seen him. Perhaps I've even had a conversation with him at one of the large meetings we all attend to hear the good news about the company's progress and get motivated to do even better. As I survey the hall, I always find a face, which fits the image I have of him. He appears aloof, far from the babble and the fray of the gathering, but his deep-set black eyes see everything. I smile at him, hoping for a smile of recognition from him. Sometimes he smiles back, and I think that I have finally located him. I feel as if I have reached an oasis after wandering for years in the desert. I would like to start a face-to-face conversation, which will reveal forever Stewart's identity. But, as I approach him, ready with a warm greeting, I realize that he is smiling at someone else, or that he has struck a conversation with people I don't know, or I see someone waving at him and calling him Brown, Penkowski, Charlie, not that the name makes any difference. I feel drained of emotion. I am alone in the crowded room. At least on those occasions, when I smile and get a blank stare in return, I don't have to subject myself to this emotional roller coaster. I just pretend that I'm addressing someone else in the crowd, and wave at no one in particular to cover up my foolish error. But, what if he knows me and is, in fact, Stewart, and chooses to ignore me? I compose myself as if nothing has happened. The company regulations are always a comfort against these very personal matters: Stewart and the troops don't meet in person.

And, who knows what his real name is? Travis has heard from one of his friends who used to work here, that back in the early days of the Catalogue, the overseer of the order takers was called a steward. People never knew the name of each steward they had, but with the passage of time they called him Stewart, perhaps, to make him more real, more personal. According to Travis' friend, when they used to say "Stewart" in the old days, it was like saying "the overseer." Discussing this name transition among ourselves we came up with another explanation as well: management may have implemented this clever little change to assure that none of the troops knew the name of the person who had the job and spoil with some face-to-face chitchat whatever "professional" relationship existed through the wire. So, even now, everybody calls the occupant of the teleboss' position "Stewart," even though we have no idea what his real name is. I don't know what to make of all this lore, but my search for Stewart will go on, I expect, as long as he and I have a working relationship, perhaps, even after I leave here and start a "real career."

Taking orders from the Catalogue is a job that requires us to respond with alertness and a welcoming attitude. The phone rings, the customer's number and name appear on the computer screen, and we are at his or her service. The conversations are recorded to make sure that any future misunderstandings can be cleared up. Some of us think that the recordings are also used to assess our performance and adjust our rewards, though no one has been able to correlate the two. The job can become taxing or boring, a constant ducking of demands and moods, or an adventure full of learning experiences through uncharted territories. It is Stewart's job to give us encouragement when things get rough, and hope that this will not be the way it'll be forever. But, for now, we are in the pits, and we have to do the best we can. And he knows so well what everyone is capable of doing that there's no chance of fooling him. I know that I cannot resist a shortcut now and then myself, even at the risk of being found out and being reprimanded for doing less than I'm capable of doing.

Some of us have come to believe that our work enhances the life of our customers; others, however, cannot see themselves as anything other than bag boys of electronic consumerism. The reality is that all of us hold both views at different times, and it is only thanks to Stewart that we don't turn to cynicism altogether. His commentaries on our orders, transmitted to each one of us in private, are told and retold among us to keep us going: "This sweater, Laverne, was a Christmas present, ordered by a woman for her husband, after many years of searching for just this style. Or, she may have had to scrape to buy for him what he has wanted for a long time. Or, she just glanced at the catalogue and ordered something for a man, without caring very much what, but when he gets it, he may like it so much that he'll change his attitude about her forever."

"I don't think I made any mistakes in taking the order," Laverne tells us next day at lunch, "but he asked me to think of these things and see in my mind's eye the people who talk to me."

Sometimes it is Marcella who has a significant encounter with Stewart: "That was a grandfather who ordered the best bike we carry. He wanted *you*, Marcella, to make sure it was red and had a bell ringer and a light, powered by a generator on the rear wheel. Did you understand why? That was the kind of bike the old man rode back in Oklahoma some fifty years ago. It was the most precious possession he ever had, and wants to give his grandson the same pleasure on his twelfth birthday. That's why he kept asking for it to be delivered before the fifth of June. Don't ask how I know, because it doesn't really matter whether I know or just make it up. Can you see the face of the old man as he presents it to the boy? Don't you want to pray that the boy receives it with joy and has fun with it for a long time? If you don't agree with my scenario, Marcella, make up your own; but don't ever make a fool out of an old man again. You knew very well we don't carry yellow bikes when you tried to get the old man to change his mind. It doesn't become a bright woman like you. I would like you to find a way to show me, not tell me, how you have changed."

We brainstormed solutions to Marcella's problem over lunch. "You have to change your attitude, Marcella, if you want to keep your job," Harold said. I told her to listen to Harold and do her best next time she got a whiff of emotion wafting through the wire.

Once in a while, I report one of my unsolicited feedback sessions with Stewart for the group's edification: "Do you know what you just sold, Chester? A new career, Chester! A brand new career! This man has finally decided to spend the money to buy our best table saw now that he is retired and will have time to build the China cabinet he's dreamed about for thirty two years. And you know what else? It is the very same China cabinet his wife has wanted to have in her house ever since her father sold their family furniture during the depression. She has described it to her husband dozens of times, and he has drawn up plans for it. That table saw, Chester, is the tool for putting together a dream; not a great dream, but a precious little dream, anyway. It'll sustain the love these two old folks feel for each other for the rest of their lives. Aren't you excited, Chester?" I say "of course" but cannot make it stick. "Studying all night is making you stone deaf to the important things happening in the world around you. What will you do to come alive?" I spent that night thinking of ways to come alive, instead of studying Nineteenth Century Political History of Europe. I didn't make much progress.

"Some girl ordered two dozen bird houses, yesterday," Sylvia said one morning as we munched on jelly doughnuts and drank coffee by the ten-ounce mug. "I took it down—no problem. And then, Stewart cuts in and asks me why would anybody order two dozen bird houses in one fell swoop. I told him that I wondered about that myself, but I didn't want to intrude, and so I didn't ask. 'You did fine, Sylvia,' he says, 'but tell me what you think, anyway.' I told him that I get paid to take orders, not to make up stories. I guess he was pretty upset, because he switched me off. I felt real bad, didn't know what to do. And, then, there he is back, talking to me as nicely as he has ever done: 'The young woman ordered two dozen bird houses for her backyard, because she's in love. She has so much love for her husband and the baby she just brought back from the hospital that she just couldn't contain it. It spilled out and landed on the birds she saw perched on her backyard trees. The catalogue happened to be on the coffee table and she called you.' He said I will be a happier person if I make a habit out of 'feeling the feelings.' I don't know anymore what he wants from us: to feel, to see, to listen, to smell, to make up stories…What will he ask next? How can we do all this through one lousy wire? Do I have to get published in the *New Yorker* to keep this lousy job?"

We let the silence linger. If we get lucky, it could hatch some answers. The fact is, however, that we all know what he is asking for. We don't need answers. We need a change in attitude.

Stewart wants us to become ambassadors of goodwill. He believes that even three minutes spent on the phone with strangers, letting them know that we care, may do more good for them than years of relating to people who never gave them their full attention. "There's more to this job than peddling our wares and getting the numbers on the plastic down correctly," he instructs. "This is the training ground for your future undertakings," he reminds us every chance he gets. "If you don't greet the customer who wants just a pair of pliers with good cheer, and are not patient with him as he makes up his mind which one he wants out of the seven brands we carry," he lectures with fervor, "what makes you think that you'll care about your clients tomorrow, when you are a lawyer, a social worker, a politician or a beautician?" He has a lot of patience with our present limitations, but won't put up with any defeatist talk about limits for tomorrow.

So, we try to give our customers everything we have, not only because we want to keep working here, but also because we want Stewart's approval. He is meddlesome and sometimes sounds too grandiose to cynics like us, but we never doubt his sincerity in helping us. We know that it is impossible to please him for long, but we keep trying because he seems to value not only the results of our efforts, but also our stamina in the process. Nobody knows why he gives so much of himself to a bunch of people who just want a temporary day job to make a few bucks so they can support themselves

for a while. We are here today, gone tomorrow, we gripe among ourselves, and, sometimes, even pity poor Stewart, who must have nothing better to do with his life than look after eight temporary order
takers and their clientele of minute made telecom pals. And when we
ask Stewart why does he take his job and ours so seriously, he says
that caring is in his nature. This explains nothing to us whose
natures are tangles of fears and desires. But, whether we pity him, or
like him, whether we laugh at him, or shout at him, or say what we
feel to him, Stewart cannot be ignored or removed from our lives as
long as we work here. His voice echoes in my mind as I try to put
together an essay on the settlers who went west to build a better life
for themselves. "What you do in this least of jobs, will serve you well
later in life, when your dreams come true," Stewart says with sincerity and conviction. I try, but cannot detect even a hint of doubt in his
voice.

"Number Three, I'm going to have a talk with you, later," he said
to me the other day, just as I got rid of a customer. There were only
six of us working and I was rushed. Some shrill sounding woman
wanted an extra large leather jacket for her man, and the computer
screen showed that we were out of them. I didn't bother to check
with the warehouse, and told her, with some satisfaction, I admit,
that she was out of luck. She called me a name, called the company
another name and slammed down the phone, hammering my ear-
drums. I thought Stewart might be busy himself with orders—he's
never reluctant to pitch in and help when we are short-handed—and
I would sneak by him this time. I should have known better. He
caught me on the spot and I could tell that he was very distraught.
When Harold and Laverne showed up and the calls thinned out, his
voice came back and drilled its way into my ears. "How could you lie
to a customer with a straight face like that, Number Three? Didn't
you hear her anticipation when she asked you? Were you deaf to her
disappointment, when you brushed her off like a fleck of dust from

your coat? She may have saved up for that jacket for months, to surprise..."

"The computer shows we're out of extra large," I said to cover myself, sticking to the facts.

There was a long silence. Was he checking to see if I was telling the truth? Was he looking up the latest shipments to the warehouse? I waited anxiously, preparing my next line of defense. "I'm disappointed in you, Chester," came his tired voice like an echo from afar. "You know that when we're out of stock we owe it to our customers to check with the warehouse. You have done that so many times...Why are you compounding a lie with a lie?"

I should have said, "I'm human. That's why." But, because I'm human, I said, instead, "Out of a hundred times I've checked with the warehouse, maybe five times, no more, have I had a different answer than what's on the screen. I was swamped and played the odds. Is that a crime you can't forgive?" I was indignant. I found a little crack on the wall of proper conduct and tried to squeeze through at all costs. My mind was racing; I was laying out arguments like a fish lays eggs; I had probabilities working for me, and epistemology, if he wanted to get fancy on how we know what we know; and I could expound on the necessity of making decisions with incomplete information by taking risks, sure that utilitarian ethics would support an argument that serving many customers adequately is more ethical than serving one perfectly and the rest unsatisfactorily. Oh, I was ready for him, all right! I wasn't going to let myself be called a liar. That was a horrible accusation, demanding a defense. But the more arguments I started presenting, the less I believed them.

I had mentioned to him that some day I might try for a dog-catcher. So, he asked: "You want to run for public office some day, don't you, Chester?" I said nothing. "The good news for you is that with your gift of getting around the truth, you can't miss. The bad news is that you'll never help the people who buy leather jackets, garden hoses, umbrellas and birdhouses when you lie to them. And that's a whole lot of people, Chester!"

I protested vigorously at his branding me a liar. I was enraged and told him that he had no right to criticize from his remote perch; that he should pick somebody at his own level to fight with, and leave us poor bastards alone. "We've put up with you because we need the job, but we're afraid of you and your constant intrusions into our lives," I fired back.

"You're angry with yourself, Chester," he said softly, his voice a whisper now. "You can become powerful, rich and famous with your talents, skills and tricks; but, Number Three, you are a liar and you won't find peace."

I had a lot more to say, but he switched me off. The soft whisper calling me a "liar," was lodged like an arrow into my side. I closed my eyes in my little box and felt the silence stuffed all around me like wads of black cotton.

When I came back, Travis was carrying out a conversation about his favorite place for a summer vacation in the vineyard country of Southern France. I wondered whether he was trying to pick up the woman who was ordering a backpack and a sleeping bag. Stewart must have sent him a message on his screen, because he turned off his charm abruptly and took the order in a hurry. What harsh message did Stewart send to him? What name did he call him? Was he as hard on him as he had been on me? A liar! I could not muffle the sound.

All night long I defended myself against his accusations as if he was in my room, standing at the foot of the bed, a tall scrawny figure, staring at me with sad but unyielding black eyes. "Leave me alone!" I cried in desperation. There are worse things happening in the order room than lying to some hag about a leather jacket. How does he know that she wasn't buying a leather jacket for her lover with the hard earned money of her husband? If you want scenarios, I'll give you scenarios! All of them lead to the conclusion that the lie served a higher good: fidelity, frugality, postponement of gratification—take your pick!

It was long after midnight when I finally fell asleep. Snatches of life and death were turned to dreams. I was a speck, lost on the surface of the map of Flatland City. I was on the map, but couldn't rise above it and see where I was and how I should proceed. When I was found, Harold stood on a pedestal staring down at me. He didn't recognize me. Marcella pointed a finger at me and laughed with a hand cupped around her mouth. The eye of the storm was coming right at me. A soft, steady moaning kept intruding from the edges of the dream. In the morning I couldn't put together the fragmented images, but I felt like a survivor. I saw the sun come up and smiled at my face in the mirror. "You always take things to heart," I repeated my mother's words. It was an unpleasant little incident and it'll be forgotten. Part of the wear and tear we must suffer on the job. All I have to do is be more careful from now on, and Stewart will be happy. I have, after all, the second highest volume of orders after Sly, in Number Eight. Stewart knows that the company needs order takers who can sell, and he'll come around. I'll sell snow shovels in July, bird houses to lumber jacks, outboard motors to mountain climbers, and fire extinguishers to firebugs. I'll sell what people need and what they'll never use. I'll push items the company is stuck with, and items that have the highest profit margins. We'll rebuild our relationship, and forget about this problem we had. Stewart is not a fool. And, I'm not a liar, for heavens sake!

I took a deep breath outside the building and grabbed the handle of the revolving door and pushed mightily to convince myself that I had every right to enter. I was in the lobby. It's the building where I work. I belong here. I looked around, challenging anyone to say otherwise. People went by me in a hurry. We are all making a living here. We belong here. Sometimes we have to scratch and claw, but we don't mean to maim anyone. I was about to head for the elevator, when, right there, leaning against the information desk, I saw Stewart, the tall scrawny figure staring at me with sad but unyielding black eyes, just as he had done last night in my room. I was stunned. What are the odds of that happening? Never mind the odds. What have I got to lose, anyway? I had to talk to him and have it out with him right here, right now. I waited to see if he would recognize me. We always suspected that he has video cameras trained on us. He may be waiting here so he can talk to me. Privately, before we start the grind. Had I ever seen the man before? There are hundreds, thousands working in this building.

I went up to him. "Are you Stewart by any chance?" I asked.

He was startled. "I beg your pardon?"

Several people cast quick glances toward us. People don't disclose their identities to strangers, I thought, as I tried to read him. He may have no idea what I look like, I reasoned: we don't have any proof of video cameras spying on us. "Are you Stewart, the telemarketing supervisor for the people up on the fourth floor?" I explained, still hoping that he was my boss.

"I'm sorry," the man said with regret. "Do I know you?" he added, his voice sounding to me very similar to Stewart's.

"That's a tough question," I said, realizing that it was no use pushing him.

"I hate to disappoint you, but you must be looking for someone else," he said quietly.

I apologized and took off for the elevator.

I got to my cubicle, put on my harness, turned on the computer, and stared at the screen. "Chester, this is the first day of the rest of your life," I read. "How do you want to begin it?" Uneventfully, I thought, cheered by the message. It was still too early for action. The others were probably gossiping around the coffee pot. I pushed the button to connect with Stewart.

"Good morning, Chester. What's up?"

"I thought I saw you today, down at the lobby."

"How would you know me?"

"You were in my mind all night last night." He said nothing, but I knew he was listening to me. The others would be trickling back any moment now. "I feel bad about what happened between us yesterday," I said.

"You needn't worry about your job. You'll have it until it's time for you to do something better."

"I wasn't thinking about that," I rushed to explain. "I just didn't want any bad feelings between us."

"Needn't worry about bad feelings from me, Chester."

He wasn't angry anymore. He was sad, like the visitor in my room; like the man in the lobby. And I was a wretch. I knew right then that I had nowhere to hide because the enemy was within me. "I lied yesterday. No excuses anymore…I've had it with them. I lied, and I'm sorry." I got the words quickly out of my mouth, before I could think about what I'd done.

I let out a sigh of relief, and a sigh of relief came through the earphone.

"I was hoping you wouldn't stay angry at yourself," Stewart said. "Do your best, Chester; you're one of my favorite people."

Now that I felt close to him again, I couldn't resist asking him once more, if we had spoken to each other at the lobby this morning.

"Why are you looking for me, Chester?"

I protested that I wasn't looking for him. It just happened. "Was it you?" I cried out, afraid that he would switch me off before an answer.

"Answer my question first," he said.

"We're always looking for you, Stewart. We've all been looking for you ever since we got here, if you want to know. We want to put a face to your voice. It would be so much easier to carry out a conversation with you, if we could see you. You don't know how hard it is working down here for a boss you have a strong relationship with and want to see, but cannot. You count a lot down here in the pits, Stewart," I said, and meant it with all my heart.

There was a prolonged silence, as if he was pondering my answer. Even if he didn't choose to answer me, I felt good to have told him what was in my mind. "I was down at the lobby this morning, Chester. I saw you talking to someone." He hesitated again. "We've met each other many times in many places, even bumped into each other a couple times. We've even talked to each other on a couple of occasions. I know how hard it is down there. I've been there."

"You've been down here? We've actually talked to each other down here?" I had already begun a mental checklist of people who came to our room for various reasons: janitors, mail clerks, administrators from purchasing...but I had to hurry—the others were returning from their coffee klatch and customers were calling.

"You know the rules, Chester: no face-to-face contact between the telemarketing overseer and his people. Stripped of visuals, the mind can focus better on the words. And, words is our business here, right?" He stopped abruptly, as if he had already said more than he had intended. "I see you got customers waiting to be served, so I'll leave you to do your job. Deal with them straight from the heart, like you dealt with me today."

I had so much to say to him, but he was right: Harold and Laverne were casting frowning looks at me for not getting busy. I thanked him for being tough with me and listening without anger. "No problem. Anytime. That's what I'm here for," he said in that upbeat way of his that could make a cripple want to rise up from his wheelchair and run a mile. And, then, as if he sensed my lingering disappointment that I would never get to meet him face-to-face, he added: "Who can tell, Chester...when you're out of the pits and you start your true vocation, we'll get together and have a long talk over a cup of coffee."

"I'd like that very much," I said wistfully.

"In the meantime serve as many people as you can, as well as you can," he said and switched off his mike.

"The Teleguru of the Catalogue has spoken well," I mumbled to myself, and smiled with satisfaction.

My next caller wanted to know if we sold wigs made with human hair. She didn't have the Catalogue, but she heard that we carry quality merchandise and thought we might have wigs. I was in no mood to cater to anyone's vanity, but I was there to serve, and did a search of the inventory. I found what she was looking for. "At least, I won't look like death warmed over when the chemo gets hold of me," she said, as if she too had no stomach for frills. It took me a few moments to make the transition from a flighty woman looking for some action to a human being of substance trying to cope with one of life's harshest blows. "I suppose you have one for a brunette?"

"We have anything you want," I snapped back into action. "The SilkSoft Premium brand has the top of the line wigs in the market. Long, medium, short and cut to order for a small extra charge. Let's see...yes, they are on sale this week..."

I stayed with her and listened to her story for a few minutes. The chemo will work. She'll beat this monster, and she'll have some good stories to tell about her ordeal. I told her not to side with the enemy, and defeat herself. And, she'll look sharp and sassy in her short brunette SilkSoft masterpiece. Her husband will love it, because he loves her. Hope is a good medicine. I listen. As far as I am concerned, Stewart is the company, and that's what Stewart would want me to do. I am more than an order taker; I provide a service the best way I can. "Pray for me," she says, "I'm afraid of the cancer." I promise to do so. She is excited that she will get her package by overnight mail. "No sense wasting time by waiting right now," she muses, and says "Goodbye" with a playful chuckle. She is already Dorothy Hamill in her short and sassy hairdo, gliding on the thin ice of life. I look up, beyond the ceiling, past the walls of the building, way up, and wonder what Stewart thinks of my service down here.

❀

CHAPTER 13

The Congenial Colleague[1]

The new director of Strategic Planning burst into the conference room one Monday afternoon and sat next to the director of marketing. All the directors around the table were stunned seeing that their new colleague was a hippopotamus. He stared lustily at the chrysanthemums that were arranged in a Chinese vase at the table, and then he trained his beady eyes at the people around him. Everyone at the staff meeting was horrified. They glared at each other and accused each other with their knitted eyebrows and pursed mouths of a distorted sense of humor and worse. The new director sat quietly and listened to the ensuing discussion with his mouth slightly open.

The director of Human Resources reminded everybody that this was their new colleague, a person upon whose ability to formulate a corporate vision and a purpose they would depend, and a director they had so carefully selected from a multitude of applicants' *curricula vitae*. They all lashed out at the director of Human Resources for her poor judgment in allowing a hiring process to go forward with-

---

1. This story parodies Franz Kafka's parable "Leopards in the Temple," in *Parables and Paradoxes* (Schocken Books, New York, Sixth Printing, 1970) 93

out interviews, the poor selection criteria that were used and for her lack of common sense. She reminded them that they were involved every step of the way, and approved every aspect of the selection process. Their directive to her had been to hire the best strategic planner she could find, and that's exactly what she had done. She paused and looked proudly at the new director. Then, her eyebrows arched upward, her shoulders were thrust backward and her eyes challenged everyone to disagree with her. Was it her fault that the most qualified employee for the position happened to be a hippo? They remembered who had proposed what selection criterion, who had opposed which aspect of the process, and they blamed each other for disinterest or lack of follow up. The team members who supported the idea of hiring without wasting time for interviews could not be identified. They argued about many different issues, and grew very angry at each other. Finally, out of frustration, they decided that nothing could be done without further study and called it a day. With nods and signals, they vowed to give the cold shoulder to their new colleague, until he got fed up and left.

The new director, however, shook his huge head slightly from side to side, but remained calm at his place on the floor. He paid no attention to their resentment and their unfriendly attitude. Instead of being offended he came well prepared again and again every Monday afternoon, lusted after the chrysanthemums without ever taking a bite out of them, and participated with enthusiasm in the meetings in his own amicable but unique ways. The directors understood that he had a vision of unity, and his purpose was to get everybody pulling in the same direction. He was kind and considerate, but became angry and threatened to devour the chrysanthemums, if anyone so much as hinted that the company couldn't be the best in its sector unless it laid off people, or made itself attractive enough to be gobbled up by its biggest competitor. The directors learned fast that these were a couple of his few hot buttons and stopped even hinting

about layoffs or acquisitions or the company's "third quartile performance," which was the wound at the CEO's soul.

At first, the new director's contributions were ignored. People
were not willing to admit that they had learned anything new from a
hippo. But the hippo had a thick skin and didn't mind. He kept on
plugging, undeterred. After three months, the directors had to admit
that he made sense, and argued with him only on details of implementation. In time, it was acknowledged that their unsightly, mal-
odorous colleague, encouraged by the team's waning rudeness, was
adding a lot of depth to the discussions of the team. When he chose
to grunt, twitch or yawn, wiggle his ears, arch his eyebrows, or do
one of the many things he could do with his coiled tail to communicate his suggestions to the team, all of them grasped the significance
of his signs and valued his contributions.

In six months, the team had created a vision and a purpose for the
company with the hippo's help, and they were on their way to first
class sector performance and "second quartile" status as a corporation. The company was growing some and there was some talk of
buying out one of the weaker competitors to gain market share easily. To thank him for his dedication to excellence, the team flooded
the conference room with chrysanthemums one Monday afternoon,
and let their friend alone to enjoy them after the meeting. These staff
meetings by now had become so effective and so full of camaraderie
that everybody looked forward to them. And no one would have ever
thought of holding a staff meeting of the team without the presence
of the hippo.

CHAPTER 14

❀

A Genius for All Seasons

There was a strange young man in our Research Center who dreamed of great feats and let it be known that his dreams were not like anybody else's. His dreams were of revolution in the state of the art of robots, wild, drastic innovations, not improvements, not steps but leaps, not advances but breakthroughs into hitherto unexplored domains of humanoid splendor. When he expounded on his beloved subject no one understood exactly what he meant and no one could tell whether he was a pioneer or a flake, no matter how many times he presented his visionary ideas. But he didn't waver; he knew that his dreams were beyond the grasp of others, and didn't feel the need to convince anyone of their worth. And, as it becomes of dreamers, he came to work in torn blue jeans, sneakers, a red bandanna and a sash to match. He worked sitting on the carpeted floor of his office, papers strewn all around and leaning on black silk pillows with dragons painted on them. Incense was burning in the dim candlelight, as he stared for hours on end at mandalas hanging from the walls.

Some people thought he was a genius and waited anxiously for him to give birth to a great theory, a novel concept or a fantastic new product, while others resented the freedom he enjoyed and wanted proof of his greatness today. The director of the Center was patient, open minded, and only stopped by the genius' den to ask if he needed any resources that might ease his labors and speed the delivery of the gift to mankind he most certainly was nurturing in his ultra-convoluted brain.

One day, the genius solved a problem that no one had even identified before. It was a difficult problem that would make robots capable of sensing substances by taste, texture and tenderness. Other researchers in robotic sensing said that he had come up with an uncanny algorithm that correlated the "three Ts of substances" almost as well as human beings could. There was no immediate application for such innovation, but the director was beside himself with joy. He talked about pure research, about the applications that the future will bring to us, and about the sheer joy of creation, He viewed the solution as the beginning of even greater things to come from this free spirit, and convinced the company's Ace Awards Committee to honor him with one of its Ten Blockbuster Innovations, which comes with a golden lapel pin, ten grand, and a month-long trip to any place in the world for a scientific conference of his choice. Everyone congratulated the Ace inventor, some feeling that their faith in him had been justified, and others, sure that the company had been taken for a ride once again.

At the Ace Awards dinner, with all the bosses in their blue pin stripes arrayed at the front of the hotel Alana Grand Ballroom, the employees of the Research Center drank wine with their filet mignons and cracked jokes about the bosses, the winners, and the world of work they loved and hated at the same time, when they felt anything at all about work. They looked for the "Taste Man," as the freedom loving genius had come to be known, but he was nowhere to be found in the circle of the Blockbuster Innovators or anywhere else in the great hall. Then, they examined the bosses at the front, and seeing them enjoying themselves, they relaxed, sure that bosses had everything under control. They posed for the photographers, drank some champagne, and told stories of victories and defeats in battles they fought against competitors for research contracts in markets all over the world from the New York Island to Paris, Frankfurt, Japan and Silicon Valley. The atmosphere was festive, the petty disagreements forgotten, the wisdom of the bosses accepted, the grind of work lost in the glaze of the wine.

The awards ceremony begun with the CEO extolling the virtues of the people whose imagination, knowledge and hard work makes the company win, thanking all the people there and especially the Ten Blockbuster Innovators they were honoring that night. Then, one after another, vice presidents and directors from Centers, Divisions, Facilities and Operations around the world, from the Halls of Montezuma to the Hills of Tripoli, captains of corporate fiefdoms from sea to shining sea stood at the podium, introduced their own winners and sang their praises as becomes all heroes.

And, then came the turn of our Center director, who had the great fortune to have the Taste Man work for him. "The next award belongs to a dreamer who made one of his dreams come true by inventing an algorithm for Robotic Taste, Texture and Tenderness Recognition," he waxed and gave the name of the Taste Man.

Tense moments passed as the Director's eyes searched the Grand Ballroom looking for his man. More moments trickled by with anticipation, as people turned their heads expecting to see the Taste Man rise up from one of the tables and claim his prize. Eyes searched other eyes without getting any clues as to the whereabouts of the man of the moment.

Then, there was a commotion at the side of the great hall, and the Taste Man made his entrance, dressed in a tuxedo with tails and wearing his bandanna and his sneakers as he had always done ever since anyone could remember.

He made his way to the podium amid the flashing cameras and the embarrassed giggles and cackles of his stunned colleagues. Someone clapped and the entire hall broke out into a thundering applause to make the Taste Man's entrance triumphant. He smiled at the bosses and waived his arms high up in the air, making victory signs with both hands and tossing back his long black hair. He reached the podium and waited for the applause to subside. There was silence again, a break in the excitement that had taken over the gathering.

"I sure can use ten grand," he began and the bosses applauded for his honesty, and his colleagues cheered for his boldness, his irreverence and his guts. He put his arms out to quiet the audience. "I want to thank everyone who helped me bring this thing about, those who believe in dreams and those who don't but put up with dreamers." He received his plaque and an envelope from the Director, shook his hand and made his exit shaking the hands of people who offered them to him, letting them pat him on the back, touch him, as if he was used to such things, smiling contented as he had always done in his dreams.

For days afterward the Center was buzzing with details of the Ace Awards Dinner, people telling those who had missed it what happened and how, arguing about who said what, and how the Taste Man had crossed the great hall oblivious to bosses and decorum, or defiantly in the splendor of a free spirit, or in whatever way one saw the entrance, and reporting on what he said to the CEO when he shook his hand, or if he said anything at all to him, and claiming that the CEO was moved, though some said he was gritting his teeth, all guessing, interpreting clues, since no one really knew and no one could ask the Taste Man himself because he had already left for a conference on Robotic Sensing in New Guinea with stopovers in Japan, Katmandu and Australia.

The director was beside himself with praise for the Taste Man's bravado, and every chance he got he told his managers that it was this kind of creative freedom he had been trying to instill in his people all along, and they should not pass up the opportunity to learn from such an example and spread the learning around. He hung the entire front page of the company paper outside his office so that everyone would know he was all for tuxedos, bandannas and sneakers when they were part and parcel of creativity on the job. And he ordered a set of color transparencies for overhead projection to use in presentations with customers, and demonstrate in a tangible way that his Research Center encourages creativity through irreverence, humor and independence of thought and action. His refrain after every showing of the tuxedoed researcher was that "freedom, not necessity, is the mother of all innovation."

Upon his return, the Taste Man said that he had a great time at the Conference, but talked mostly about Buddhist monks, the Dalai Lama, the chief of a tribe in New Guinea, and the Aborigines of Australia, who can sense the approaching death of a loved one hundreds of miles away, and no one knows yet how they do it. And when all the excitement died out, the Taste Man went back to work on robotic smell, suspecting that there was a neat algorithm that could be devised to give robots another sense yet and bring them even closer to their humanoid destiny.

I suppose that if this story was going to end here, it would be just a commentary on creativity—how a genius level IQ is often associated with eccentricity, off the wall thinking and other such unusual traits. The story would just affirm the stereotypes people devise to make life more suitable to their wishes. But, this story goes on awhile longer, and its message changes as the world changes. The Taste Man's future is in process...

The Company, you see, wasn't doing well, its research projects notwithstanding. A mammoth conglomerate, hungry for acquisitions and focused on short-term earnings growth sniffed the Company out and bought it on the spot. The New Company changed the structure, the businesses, the people and the culture on very short notice. Basic research projects were dropped, and only businesses with "synergistic potential" were retained. Research in taste algorithms was judged to be "of protracted maturation," but some of the fallout benefits of the project were seen as valuable assets. It was this creative thinking which was responsible for the use of the taste algorithm in pet food products that were produced in one of the other acquisitions of the New Company. It didn't take long to construct a functional taste sensor by adapting the crude instrument used for the Taste Man's research project. The sensor was used to taste an enormous amount of different types of dog food and isolate the taste parameters that were most desirable to dogs of different breeds. After that was done, there was no longer any need to try different dog food on different dogs, since it was known from the start what taste, texture and tenderness were pleasing to various breeds of dogs and they could be mixed in by design. But, the most valuable aspect of the research, according to the VP who was present when the taste algorithm was developed, was the picture of the tuxedoed Taste Man. The picture, properly doctored so that he could hold a cuddly beagle and lovingly look at it, appeared on the box of the "Algorithmic Kiblets Unlimited" with a little note on the side that gave the particulars on the Taste Man and his algorithm. In describing the power of basic research, the VP reported that "the new management found the colors of red, black and brown surrounding the beagle and the smiley face of our Taste Man an irresistible ensemble."

The Taste Man, along with many other researchers, was laid off in the restructuring that took place after the takeover. One of his research colleagues said that he had found a job in a small high tech company, which was working on better smoke detectors and alarm systems. Even before 9/11/01, the colleague went on to say, the Taste Man had been gradually moving toward the development of an algorithm for detecting smells. "But after that infamous day, he had become a kind of a prophet and folk hero, changing fast into a veritable Smell Man." His new goal, if funding could be found for his idea, was to develop a machine that could sniff explosives in airport luggage more reliably than trained dogs and CAT scanners. "If anyone can do it, the Smell Man is the one," another colleague mused. And then as an afterthought, he added, "What would the world do without its weirdoes?"

CHAPTER 15

❁

A Regular Samaritan

Borg was a tiger; everyone was afraid of him. He was known in the Department as a tough manager, an autocrat who worked his people to the bone. The director didn't care for him either, but he had hired him on the spot because he needed one such manager to keep the place lean and mean, and to unleash him in the marketplace whenever the situation demanded predatory actions to win. Sometimes the director said that he felt compassion for the people who had to work for Borg, but he bore this burden for the good of the entire organization, believing that such was the lot of a good executive. The director was a quiet, gentle man, liked by the people for caring and respecting them, especially when compared with that beast, Borg.

Borg had not disappointed the director. His insensitivity was useful in handling unpleasant situations, which the Director preferred to avoid, like squeezing suppliers, manipulating customers by taking advantage of their weaknesses, cracking the whip with employees who had given less than he demanded for whatever reason, and firing anyone who broke the rules to gain an advantage.

Borg thought of himself as a tough but fair boss, and was often heard saying that he didn't get his job because he had charisma, but because he worked hard and got things done. His answer to the do-gooders and humanistic consultants who tried to soften his management style was that he wasn't interested in winning popularity contests. Besides, he would point out, participative management, industrial democracy, interlocking teams and other such schemes had no place at work. When the experts expressed disbelief at such medieval views, Borg would ask them to reflect upon the fact that the great wall of China, which stands as a great monument to human achievement and can be seen from outer space, was built with slave labor; ditto for the pyramids in Egypt; and, if that wasn't enough proof of the efficacy of dictatorial rule in the work place, they could ponder on the success of the Catholic Church, which has endured adversity for two thousand years and thrives to this very day, being ruled by one man. As long as he could produce results, he felt that he was doing the right thing, because, in his view, it was results not congeniality and pats on the back and phony smiles that kept people employed.

But, unbeknown to anyone, Borg was in the habit of doing one kind, unselfish, caring deed every day, before plunging into his managerial duties. Some mornings he picked up hitchhikers and even went out of his way to drop them off where they wanted to go, or where they could get another ride easily; sometimes he stopped to lend a hand to a driver with a stalled car; other times he would drop off his neighbor to his job, if he needed a ride. And, if nothing else had happened on the way to work, he would give a few dollars to the old man on the wheel chair who sold flowers outside the plant gates. He had been doing his kind deed every day since he started working, and wouldn't think of beginning his workday without the warm feeling he got from it.

One particular morning, he started for work, thinking of his first appointment with Harris, one of his subordinates. Before leaving work the previous evening, the director had stopped by his office and told him that Harris had to go, because the work he was doing for an important customer was unsatisfactory. The director was surprised that Borg hadn't already fired the man, since this wasn't the first time Harris had failed to perform acceptably. Harris hadn't been himself since his wife left him for another man, but that wasn't an excuse. Borg wasn't in the habit of presenting all the sad stories of his people to his boss. He was there to make sad stories disappear. Only this time he was a little slow. The director was right: he cared for the good of all the people under him, and if the Harrises of the world were allowed to slough off because of their personal problems, losing customers as a result, everyone would be out in the streets looking for work. He apologized, and promised to take care of the matter right away. It was a very unpleasant task he had to do, and was trying to prepare himself. He had to start the day with a warm feeling inside.

But, there were no hitchhikers looking for rides; no favors asked of him by a neighbor; no motorists in distress; no women struggling to fix flat tires on the road, and no accidents on the way to work. And, when he arrived at the plant, the old man on the wheel chair selling flowers was nowhere to be seen. Borg hesitated at the gate, looking around, glancing at his watch, but there was no sign of him. It was a bright, sunny day, and everything seemed to be right with the world. If he had known that, he would have stopped for breakfast and given the waitress a generous tip; he might have taken the River Road and gone down, under the Carpenter Bridge, to give a few dollars to one of the homeless people gathered under it. But, he was thinking of the meeting with Harris and counting on the old man and his flowers at the gate, if nothing else came up. He felt anxious, uncertain about what to do next. Breaking the routine he had followed all his working life was painful.

He went in, unsure of himself, looking around for a chance to discharge the tiny dose of daily goodness he harbored inside him. The guard was busy with visitors and didn't even smile at him. He remembered that there was a blind computer operator working at the plant, and people sometimes helped him at the elevator or at the

Xerox machine, but he was nowhere to be seen. He walked hesitantly toward his office, looking for a chance to be of assistance to somebody, but people went about their business in a hurry, as if to show him how hard they were working. He met his secretary as she was bringing him his morning coffee, and felt a sense of loss because it had occurred to him that this was the morning that *he* would bring coffee to her instead.

"Harris is waiting for your appointment with him," she said in the businesslike manner which was precisely what he had required of her all along, but which he wished she would drop this morning and ask him for a favor, that she had to leave early because her child was sick at home, or because she had to pick up her mother from the hospital, or anything at all.

"Ask him to come in," he said and then regretted it, thinking that if he took a little time to go around the plant, he might have found someone to help with some little thing. Now it was done, and besides the problem with Harris had to be taken care of first thing. He knew the director meant business. He wanted to know as soon as Harris was told that he no longer had a job.

"Come in," Borg said when Harris appeared at his office. "Close the door, please." He asked him to sit across the desk from him. He knows, Borg thought, looking at his trembling subordinate. He knows and he can do nothing to change the situation. And, Borg's insides churned as he started to recount the problems with the customers, his inability to provide adequate service, his wallowing in self pity and anger for too long...But as he rattled out all that was wrong with Harris' performance, he felt a strange warmth inside him. Harris was silent, looking down at the floor. When he finally looked up at his boss, his eyes were filled with sadness.

Borg could stand it no longer. "I'm going to save your ass this one last time," he heard himself saying. "You've got to pull yourself together and stop screwing up; no more excuses!" he shouted at the stunned Harris.

A tear trickled down Harris' cheek. Clearly he hadn't expected mercy from Borg, the man-eating tiger. "You won't regret it; I promise," he said quietly.

"All right, then!" Borg said with enthusiasm, venting the good feeling inside him. "Let me know if you need help, but don't let me down."

"I won't," Harris reassured him.

The director had been keeping an eye on Borg's office and, as soon as Harris was gone, he appeared at Borg's door. "How did he take it?" he asked with a conspiratorial tone of voice.

"I decided to give him another chance," Borg said. "He's had some serious problems at home and deserves a break."

"You decided what?" the director pounced on him, shutting the door behind him. "What do you mean you decided? Last night..."

"Like I said: I gave him another chance," Borg cut in.

"Well, I promised the customer that Harris would be gone, and he will be. Otherwise he'll pull his business out, and you know damn well what that means, don't you?" he lashed out at Borg.

"I'll talk to the customer myself," Borg persisted.

"No! You'll go and tell Harris he's fired, or else...or else, *you* are," he shouted unable to restrain himself. He was furious not only because Borg had reneged on his promise to get rid of Harris, but also because Borg was forcing him to be a harsh and uncaring boss, and that was precisely what he had hired Borg to be.

Borg looked the director straight in the eye. "I don't want to fire Harris," came Borg's soft-spoken but firm reply. "I believe that now he can make it with a little help." The director stared at him dumbfounded. "I guess that's that; I'll be leaving right away," he added, and started collecting his personal things from the top of his desk.

"Some tough guy of a manager you are, Borg!" the Director sneered as he opened the door. "I would have never guessed that you are such a soft touch." And shaking his head, he added: "I'll be damned!"

"You may well be!" Borg mused as he took down the poster of a snarling tiger, a gift from the director, which had been hanging on the wall behind his chair for years. He tossed it in the wastebasket and watched the glass break and splinter. He smiled, thinking, "man-eating tiger, no more…paper-tiger, not quite…a human being, perhaps…" He took one last look at his cage, and walked out of it, carrying his personal things in a hardboard box under his arm.

"Goodbye, Laura," he said to his secretary. "You did a great job for me, and I thank you for it." Then, unable to hold back a thought that lodged in his mind, he added, "I'll miss you."

She stared at him in disbelief. "Goodbye, Mr. Borg. Are you leaving us?" she managed to say.

"Jonathan," he said softly. "Call me Jonathan. I've done all I can here. Time to move on," he said, slowing down for a moment in front of her desk.

Her eyes clouded and her voice faltered. "Goodbye, Jonathan. You've been a very fair-minded boss," she said hurriedly.

He said no more. "I've paid dearly for this lousy job," he thought with regret. He just shrugged his shoulders, bowed his head and gave her the warmest smile he had ever given anyone at the office.

He never realized that he had just done his good deed for the day.

Leading with Heart, Brains and Backbone

❀

CHAPTER 1

Kratylus Automates His Urnworks[1]

Little did Kratylus know, when he contracted in Corinth to buy some foot-operated potter's wheels for his workshop, that his capital investment would become the subject of a spirited discussion among four Athenians touching on such topics as olive harvesting, burial mound building, input-output measurement, and participative management. Formerly, 20 workers in Kratylus' operation turned out 200 urns a day; now, with the new pulley-equipped devices, 12 employees can do the job.

What is productivity? How can you measure an individual's contribution toward a goal? How can an employer further human productiveness? These are the difficult questions that arise from the sacking of Nikias and seven others. Besides him, those airing the issues are Ipponikos, a rich landowner; Kallias, a politician and member of the Assembly; and Socrates, the philosopher.

---

1. Reprinted by permission of *Harvard Business Review.* "Kratylus Automates his Urnworks," by Tolly Kizilos, *May–June 1984.* Copyright © 1984 by the Harvard Business School Publishing Corporation; all rights reserved.

Kallias: Here comes Nikias, troubled as usual about some social injustice or other.

Socrates: Good morning, Nikias. Isn't it a bit early in the day to be looking so troubled?

Nikias: Good morning, my friends, if you can call good a morning on which you lose your job.

Ipponikos: Sit down Nikias, and tell us what happened. Remember what Socrates always says: "Nothing bad in this world is uncontaminated by good."

Nikias: I know what Socrates says, but it doesn't make sense to me just now. I don't know what will happen. I showed up for work at Kratylus Urnworks this morning, as I've done for three years, and he told me and seven others that we were no longer needed. He's installed some new foot-operated potter's wheels with pulleys, so he doesn't need as many people to do the work. Just like that I'm unemployed.

Kallias: It wasn't all that sudden, though, was it, Nikias? I heard Kratylus almost a month ago talking openly at the agora about the new wheels he was buying from Corinth. It was no secret that he was going to install them to raise productivity. He had to do it, he told me, or he'd go out of business. I realize that you and a few others will suffer for a while, but he had to increase the productivity of his business or everyone working for him could end up without a job. And if he and others don't become more productive, Athens itself will take a back seat to Corinth and other cities, and all its citizens will suffer the consequences.

Nikias: We knew about it, all right, but we were hoping there would be other jobs we could do. Is it more productive to have people out of work, doing nothing, than to have them gainfully employed? How can the city's productivity grow if a lot of people are out of work? As far as I'm concerned, that kind of narrow-minded productivity increase helps no one but Kratylus; it just feeds his greed.

Kallias: Come now, Nikias; you can't possibly mean that! Productivity gains, no matter where, benefit everyone in the long run. You'll find another job soon, or Kratylus' business will expand and he'll need more workers to operate the faster wheels.

Socrates: Is productivity then both good and evil? Is it both the requirement for the workers' prosperity and the cause of their misfortunes?

Ipponikos: Ah, Socrates, how cleverly you always pose your questions—so pregnant with answers of your choosing! Why don't you go on and say that this is impossible, therefore productivity is either good or evil and, consequently, only one of our friends here can be right?

Socrates: Because, my dear Ipponikos, there is always a chance that a pregnant question will deliver a revealing answer. I find that I always discover new things, as I grow older.

Kallias: Well, I'm always suspicious about ambiguous concepts. Productivity is either good or evil, and only one of us is right. Otherwise the concept is meaningless.

Ipponikos: People can always stretch the meaning of words enough to understand and agree with each other. All it takes is a common culture and goodwill.

Kallias: You aren't so bad at clever arguments yourself, Ipponikos. You imply that if we can't understand and agree with each other, it doesn't mean that some of us are wrong but that some are barbarians or rascals, or both. But perhaps you didn't mean that?

Nikias: If this is going to be a battle of wits, count me out.

Socrates: Nikias is right. Let's abandon generalities, which make philosophy irrelevant, and search for the meaning of productivity. Perhaps productivity is such an elusive concept that we can reach only a partial understanding of it, which, however, is acceptable to all of us. Let us be hopeful.

Ipponikos: With an ideologue like Kallias in the discussion, I'm afraid it'll be a waste of time.

Nikias: So is what we're doing right now. Let's discuss the issues instead of arguing over trivia.

Wages and outputs

Kallias: I'll tell you what productivity is, Socrates, or at least what it means to me—take it as you like. It's not such a difficult concept. It is simply the ratio of useful work output for a given valuable input. The higher the output for the same input, the higher the productivity is.

Take for example, Kratylus' Urnworks. I know something about his business because occasionally he asks for my opinion. Kratylus produces about 200 urns a day and used to employ about 20 workers. If he can produce the same number of urns with half the work force, then he doubles his shop's productivity. It's as simple as that.

Ipponikos: It's so simple, it's idiotic. Whose productivity has he increased? Nikias isn't productive anymore. He worked hard and still got laid off. Kratylus' productivity gain is Nikias' productivity loss.

Nikias: More productivity for Kratylus means more satisfaction of his greed.

Kallias: I don't understand what's happening to us. If we are here to denigrate Kratylus, I want no part of it.

Socrates: The path to the truth is often obscured by thorny bushes, Kallias.

Kallias: I know it's hard to be objective right now, but the facts are irrefutable. When you were working for Kratylus—I'm sure very hard—you weren't very productive because you were using a slow wheel to shape the urns. You were paid wages to produce something that cost so much it couldn't be sold easily. Activity isn't productivity, Nikias.

What's needed is more output for a given input; what's needed is more drachmas from the sale of urns per drachma of wages. Now you produce nothing, but your wages are also nothing; so, it makes no sense to talk about your productivity. Only when you get paid to produce something of value, that is, when there's an input and an output, can we talk meaningfully about productivity.

Ipponikos: This input-output stuff may be useful when talking about machines or oxen, but it makes no sense when we're discussing human beings. Productivity means productive activity. Human beings can be very productive even when they're supported by hand-outs. Why, only two weeks ago I heard that the geometer Diomedes, a pauper, mind you, if there ever was one, invented an instrument for measuring angles he calls a theodolite. I heard Telemachus say it will save thousands of workdays for his surveying crew when they're setting the boundaries of farmers' fields all around Attica. Diomedes received no wages—no input, as you would say, Kallias—but does that mean we can't talk about his productivity? He *is* productive, *very* productive.

Kallias: Of course he is, my dear Ipponikos. Your example of Diomedes is precisely what I've been looking for to make my point. Maximum output with minimum possible input yields the highest productivity.

Nikias: So, productivity according to you is using up people. Humanity subordinated to the goddess of productivity. Perhaps you'd like to add another goddess to the 12 Olympians? It wouldn't surprise me.

Kallias: I said minimum *possible* input, not minimum input. Possible is the essential…

Ipponikos: I don't understand why you keep using inputs and outputs when you talk about human beings, Kallias. We could never define such things for humans, capable of an infinite variety and an infinite number of possible inputs and outputs, none of them exactly predictable. No man can be bound by defining him in terms of input and output. "Man is the measure of all things," as Protagoras said—he cannot himself be measured.

Nikias: But to Kratylus and others who own shops, Ipponikos, there's little difference among men, beasts, or machines. A person at work is told exactly what input he'll have (that is, what wages he'll be paid), exactly what he has to do, and what he is expected to produce. That's what happens when you work for someone else; you're dehumanized.

Kallias: You're too angry to contribute to this discussion, Nikias.

Ipponikos: Since when has anger been proven to be an obstacle in the search for truth?

Socrates: Nikias agrees with you, Ipponikos, that man is fundamentally different from the machine, and one of the reasons is that only machines have finite and measurable inputs and outputs by design.

Ipponikos: It's even more fundamental than that: Kallias talks about wages as inputs, but that's so narrow-minded it is absurd. People can get more than wages for doing their jobs; they can get satisfaction, learning, enjoyment; they can be frightened or encouraged by what happens around them; they can be made to feel stronger or weaker by the actions of others. Their productive activity is often the result of all these impressions shaped by thinking, feeling and judgment. And as for their output, sometimes it's so unpredictable as to instill awe, admiration and delight.

Kallias: I'm really surprised by your views, Ipponikos. It seems that Protagoras and the other sophists have clouded your thoughts.

Ipponikos: I can do without your sarcasm, Kallias. Do me the courtesy of treating me like a person who can think for himself. If you have something to say about my views, say it without insinuations.

Kallias: I will, my friend, I most certainly will. You are espousing a very irresponsible view and I couldn't possibly avoid commenting on it. According to you, a workshop owner should hire workers and pay them wages, but demand nothing specific of them. Some of them may want to loaf; others may decide to take up playwriting or singing instead of making urns; and some of them may even choose to work and produce urns once in a while. Now and then, perhaps, a worker will invent a new tool that improves the quality of urns or the productivity of the shop, but there will be no guarantees. And the wages have to keep coming steadily, guaranteed.

Is this a responsible way to run a business? Could the workshop owner entrust his future to the whims of his workers? The workers have no stake in the business and, if the shop went broke, they could leave at a moment's notice to take jobs elsewhere. And what about those who really work hard to produce urns and urns alone? Wouldn't this irresponsible approach be unfair to them?

Ipponikos: You talk as if the workers want to loaf and behave irresponsibly toward the owner and their fellow workers. You don't trust them.

Kallias: Not everyone is responsible and trustworthy.

Ipponikos: Perhaps not. But if the owner trusts his people and rewards them fairly, I believe that the workers will strive to do their best for the business. Some will be less productive than others, but the productivity of the whole place will be higher when people feel free to use all their talents and skills. As for fairness, the workers themselves will set standards and require that everyone pull his weight.

Socrates: I hear a lot of views being expressed, but no conclusions. If this were a workshop, its productivity would be very low, and some of us, I fear, would have to be replaced by more productive philosophers, probably from Sparta. Can't we first agree on what productivity means?

Kallias: It's apparent to me, Socrates, that this isn't possible with Ipponikos and Nikias present. If you and I were alone, we could be more productive than the whole city of Sparta discussing the issue.

Socrates: You and I, Kallias, might come up with conclusions very fast, but the quality of our conclusions might not be as high as it can be with our friends here contributing their ideas.

Kallias: Sooner or later, I suppose, we'll have to talk about effectiveness and efficiency. I believe that productivity is high only when both efficiency and effectiveness are high.

Socrates: All right, Let's see what you mean. Suppose you hire me for a drachma a day to pick olives fallen from your olive trees in Eleusis. While I'm working, I notice that the fence protecting your property from the wild pigs is down. Pigs can get into your fields and devour the ripe olives that have fallen on the ground. Because I think this is more urgent and because I'm much better at repairing fences than gathering olives, I decide to fix your fence instead.

I work hard all day long and by sunset I'm done and I'm sitting on a rock admiring the good work I did. You return from your day's debates at the Assembly and find me in this contemplative pose. You see that I have picked no olives but have fixed your fence. The question is, will you pay me as we agreed or not?

Kallias: Of course not. You changed our contract arbitrarily. I could suffer losses because of that. You shouldn't have changed the output.

Nikias: He means he didn't want you to think; do only what you were told. Be a machine or a mindless ox.

Socrates: But a contract is a contract, Nikias. What if he was counting on me to pick the olives so he could deliver them to someone who had a contract with him to buy them that same evening? I was productive, all right, but not productive doing what we agreed on. In that, my productivity was zero. So isn't it true that productivity has meaning only when there's an agreement on the inputs or wages, and the outputs or goals?

Kallias: Of course it is.

Ipponikos: And if someone produces something very valuable without any agreement?

Socrates: It appears that it doesn't make sense to talk about productivity when there's no agreement, explicit or implicit.

Kallias: Exactly. Productivity pertains to work toward a goal. There must be expectation of output and fulfillment of that expectation.

The story-telling slave

Socrates: I'm glad you agree with what I said. But I have some difficulty with it, and you may be able to help me. It has to do with something that happened when they were building the mound commemorating the glorious dead who fell at the battle of Marathon.

Kallias: I can't for the life of me imagine what Marathon has to do with productivity. Are you serious?

Ipponikos: Perhaps you've hit on your problem, Kallias—lack of imagination.

Socrates: Please, allow me to continue. Everything is related to everything else, say some philosophers, and I'll be happy to explain what I mean, if you let me.

Nikias: You are the last person on earth I would want to stop, Socrates. You're usually able to deliver what you promise, but even if you weren't, you're too stubborn to be stopped.

Socrates: I'll take that as praise, Nikias, and go on. After Pericles gave his marvelous funeral oration on that hallowed ground, he left behind General Meno from Orchomenos in charge of 100 slaves and ordered him to build the mound in 30 days. Meno was determined to obey the order even though he estimated that the project would take twice that time. It is said that General Meno became a tyrant with the slaves, driving them ruthlessly to work.

One day, during an inspection of the project, he discovered a slave who sat on the nearby edge of the marsh in blissful repose. Furious, he ordered his lieutenants to flog him until he was hardly alive. General Meno wanted to make this laggard an example for the other slaves, demonstrating to them that because the slave didn't produce, he made everyone else work harder. "He is a weight upon the earth!" he shouted for all to hear, using Homer's words.

Kallias: I still don't see...

Socrates: Then one of the most productive slaves stepped forward and asked to speak. General Meno could hardly hold back his anger, but because he valued this slave greatly he allowed him to say his piece. "This man, sir," the slave said, pointing to his doomed comrade, "is one of the most productive slaves you have. It is true that he neither sweats nor strains his back digging and shoveling earth, but he contributes to the building of the mound more than anyone else."

"And how does he do this? Gazing at his belly button while you and the others break your backs?" the general demanded.

"You see, General," the slave said with conviction, "he is a story-teller, not a digger. If he was shoveling dirt with all his might, he couldn't do in a day more than I do in an hour. But after work, when we all return to camp, dog-tired, miserable and hopeless—for what can we expect from the future but more bondage and more mis-ery?—when we are gathered around the campfire at night, this man spins tales of hope for us and makes our lot bearable. We listen to him and dream of a better life after we end this project. He makes our burdens lighter, and we can fall asleep with dreams of freedom in our heads. Next day we are ready for work, believing that if our work pleases you and the Athenians, we may some day gain our freedom."

Kallias: I think I'm beginning…

Socrates: Please let me finish. "So," the slave went on, "this man does his part. If you beat him senseless, or cripple him, or—worst of fates!—kill him, who will keep us hoping, dreaming, and working? If hope vanishes, punishment and death hold no fear, General. We may not be able to build your mound. Think of that, sir, and allow this man to go on producing what he is best able to produce: tales of hope. You need him as much as, if not more, than we do."

So spoke the valued slave, and General Meno listened. He ordered his lieutenants to release the man, who went on to tell tales until the project was finished—exactly on time. The question, dear Kallias, is this: Was the storytelling slave productive or not?

Kallias: Of course he was productive, probably the most produc-tive of all. He contributed to the achievement of the goal, didn't he?

Whether he knew it or not, he worked toward the same goal as all the other slaves.

Setting the Goal

Socrates: So, you say, productivity is work toward a goal. You wouldn't pay me for fixing your fence because you had set the goal as gathering fallen olives. What about here? Here the goal was to build a mound, just as Kratylus' goal is to produce urns, and ours is to come up with the truth. But this slave wasn't building the mound, I wasn't gathering olives, and some workers at Kratylus' Urnworks may not be producing as many urns as their fellows.

Yet, you just told us that this slave was probably the most productive slave working on the mound. Could I have been more productive to you by fixing your fence? Could Nikias, who wasn't producing as much with his old wheel, and I, bumbling now on my way to the truth, be more productive than others who achieve stated goals? Could it be, Kallias, that Nikias, now that he is searching for the truth with us, is more productive to our city (and of course to Kratylus) than when he was making urns?

Kallias: I thought you would twist things sooner or later, Socrates, and I've been alert to it.

Ipponikos: It won't help you much, Kallias. You're too efficient to be effective. If you're sure you know the truth and you're sitting here searching for it, you are obviously wasting your time, and your productivity has to be nil.

Kallias: Leave your sophistry for later, Ipponikos, and let me respond to Socrates. It seems to me, Socrates, that you are mixing two kinds of productivity. Yes, Nikias is more productive to our city when he's searching for the truth with us than he would be if he were doing nothing. To the extent that Kratylus is a citizen of Athens, he benefits from Nikias' philosophizing, as does every other citizen. But Nikias is not productive to Kratylus because he simply isn't making urns any more.

Socrates: But if our city is more productive, doesn't Kratylus have a better chance to sell his wares? And if that is so, isn't it fair to say that Kratylus, as the owner of the workshop, is benefiting from Nikias' philosophizing?

Kallias: Productivity loses all meaning if you put it that way. Humanity benefits from anything productive anyone does. But I still say that productivity is a useful concept only when it's limited to specific goals achieved by specific persons.

Ipponikos: Come on Kallias; use your imagination! Think of all the ways the workers, even at Kratylus' workshop, can contribute to the production and sale of urns even when they're not actually making or selling urns. No one can say whether a person is productive by just looking at him or by measuring only specific inputs and outputs.

Kallias: Use your reason, Ipponikos.

Socrates: But Kallias, how can you tell when a person is doing something or nothing? And how can you say that a person can be productive to the city but not to Kratylus' workshop, which is, after all, a part of the city? And how can you tell if a person is productive when the goals set for that person are different from the goals toward which a person works? One can still contribute to the goals if one interprets goals more broadly.

Kallias: All I know is that somehow or other using a new wheel makes Kratylus' workshop more productive because he can lay off Nikias and some other workers and still produce the same number of urns. Then Nikias, as Kratylus had thought, finds something else to do—philosophize, in this case—and he becomes productive again to the city and to Kratylus, because he is also a citizen.

Socrates: That's well put, Kallias. But if Nikias is now productive to the city, he must be paid for his productivity. Yet I haven't heard of anyone willing to put philosophers on the public payroll. Would you propose that the Assembly pass a law to do that? It certainly would help us all, Nikias and me in particular, since we are not influential politicians like you or wealthy landowners like Ipponikos.

Ipponikos: It's not only philosophers who are productive and should be compensated but also geometers, poets, musicians, and all kinds of other people, who work with their minds.

Kallias: Everyone would become a freeloader.

Nikias: Are you saying that all thinkers are freeloaders?

Kallias: Don't be absurd, Nikias. I'm saying that people with no talent for geometry or music or bent for philosophical search would claim to be geometers, musicians, and philosophers in order to collect money from the city and avoid sweating in workshops and fields. Since there is no way to measure their output, no one could tell whether Socrates was more productive than the man who sweeps the steps leading up to the Parthenon. The sweeper could claim, for example, that gazing at the blue sky was helpful in proving the Pythagorean theorem in a new way.

Socrates: And so we have arrived at a point where we must make distinctions: there is productivity and there is productivity, and unless we sort these out we will never come to any conclusions. There is productivity of persons who perform manual work with a physical output; productivity of persons whose output is thoughts, poems, songs, inventions, proofs, and so on; and productivity of groups, such as ours, organizations or institutions, such as Kratylus' workshop or our beloved city of Athens. These are the entities to which we have attached potential for productivity.

Nikias: I'll start by defining the productivity of manual workers.

Kallias: Their productivity depends simply on their output, be it urns made, olives picked, marble slabs quarried, or what have you, divided by the cost of production, which is mostly wages.

Nikias: You may think it's that simple, but I don't. Even a manual worker has a mind that he can use when he does his work. His productivity can be defined your way only if you rob him of his mind. If one does that by rigidly defining the input and the output, that is, if one dehumanizes him, then one can define his productivity accurately—so many urns per drachma of wages, so much earth moved to build a mound per loaf of bread, so many olives gathered per day's wage.

One can go even further and define the productivity of those workers who work with their intellect that way—so many plays written, or songs composed, or theorems proved, or philosophical conclusions reached per drachma. But remember, the only way this can be done is if you set rigid, unalterable inputs and outputs. If a philosopher wrote a poem and an urnmaker proved a theorem of geometry their productivity would be nothing.

Ipponikos: In other words, Kallias, you have to choose between having a precise definition of productivity and missing a lot of good work, or having at best a sloppy definition and allowing other, unanticipated but valuable work to be encouraged.

Kallias: I can't believe this! You argue with the same cunning as some unscrupulous colleagues of mine in the Assembly. I will give you a precise definition that at the same time encourages all valuable work to proceed: set outputs that are to be met unless more valuable outputs are produced. General Meno set goals, but when a slave produced stories that helped the goal indirectly, the general recognized that his output was more valuable than his manual output would have been in furthering the goal directly. This way the worker whose output is supposed to be the production of urns will be rewarded when he produces urns or something else, a new potter's wheel or a great poem perhaps, which the person who set the goals and must pay for their accomplishment finds equally valuable or even more valuable than the production of urns. This is my position, and I challenge you to find fault with it!

Achieving the Goal

Socrates: It is indeed an excellent position, Kallias. You have said that productivity for an individual worker is his valuable output per given input. It is a good definition, but you haven't told us how the value of the output is determined or whether the person who evaluated it is competent to do so.

Ipponikos: I would hate to have Kratylus decide the relative value of ten urns versus Sophocles' *Antigone*.

Kallias: Again, your way of arguing is to ridicule. I'm getting annoyed with you, Ipponikos, and unless you change your ways I will have to bid you farewell and seek a more congenial discussion elsewhere.

Ipponikos: I apologize for my sarcasm, Kallias. But please, do respond to Socrates.

Kallias: I don't believe that shop owners are any less competent to evaluate the relative worth of urns and plays than anyone else. Judgment, after all, is one of the most important attributes one must have to succeed in business.

Socrates: Wouldn't it perhaps be better if the employer and the wage earner could discuss the value of the work or the productivity of the wage earner and agree on it? After all, the person who produces something may be the only one who can explain the purpose for which he produced that thing and judge its value from his perspective.

Kallias: That process might work in Socrates' ideal state, but I don't think it has a chance in Athens. The wage earner can discuss all you like him to discuss, but when the time comes to decide how productive he is, when it comes to making a decision on how much he should be paid, the one who has the power, who pays the wages, will have the final word.

Ipponikos: You say that those who have the power set the standards and you accuse *me* of arguing like the sophists? Why, what you just said is exactly what Thrasymachus teaches.

Kallias: Then I have to admit that even a sophist can be right, once.

Nikias: I've had enough of the sophists. I want to hear Socrates on what workers have to say about the value of their work.

Socrates: Even if we assume that power is what one needs to set standards, what I said still stands. The wage earner also has power because the employer needs him to be as productive as possible, not be a mere machine executing set goals. If the employer doesn't evaluate him correctly, the wage earner will cease coming up with new products, new methods or new ideas, and the productivity of the organization will suffer. Since the employer cannot *make* the wage earner be creative or take the initiative, or modify goals to suit changed situations, he must ensure that the wage earner stays motivated. And the best way for the employer to achieve that is not to be arbitrary or authoritarian but to share his power of evaluation with him.

I see you're shaking your head, Kallias. When you reflect on these thoughts you may become less skeptical. In any case, it is an alternative way of settling the issue we were discussing. Productivity increases come not only from getting faster wheels in the workshop but also from workers such as Nikias who feel in a way like owners of the workshop. Isn't it then correct to say that productivity is defined by whatever reasonable input and output both wage earner and employee agree on?

Kallias: Though I don't believe that this process will work, I agree that it is worth an experiment to find out. But I don't think we have really defined productivity.

Nikias: If we have arrived at a conclusion...

Socrates: Definitions can get us only so far. It's the dialogue between well-meaning people that gains our ends. This is the process, it seems to me, that will also determine the productivity of organizations such as Kratylus' workshop or our beloved city of Athens. Plato may not agree entirely with me on this, but I believe that the productivity of Athens is great because we all partake in making the decisions that govern our lives. Democracy is a form of participation, and it's surprising that it hasn't been applied to our workshops in some appropriate form.

Kallias: Well, I have always felt that productivity was of great concern to both politics and business. If we set goals and compile a list of all the services our city provides for its citizens, then measure them...

Socrates: I doubt that it would be either possible or meaningful, Kallias. The evaluation of our city's productivity is in the hands of future generations. Whether we sink to oblivion or history remembers us is not predictable or determined by a list of services or the Assembly's definition of goals. Athens and other cities and states will live on if they encourage their citizens to excel in what they do best.

Nikias: Before you go any further with an encomium to our city, Socrates, I would like to know if anyone here intends to inform Kratylus of my contributions to our discourse and ask him whether he would reconsider his decision to lay me off. If this isn't anyone's intention, I'd like to move on and look for another job before my family has to beg for food.

Kallias: I can certainly talk to him about it. But would you be willing to moderate your demands on wages? At least until his workshop begins to make profits again?

Nikias: I'll do anything reasonable to keep my job, of course. But if the job could be a little more satisfying than what I used to do, or if

I have some say on what I do and how I am evaluated, then I'll bear the load more comfortably and I may even turn out more urns than ever before.

Socrates: I'm sure, Nikias, that you're speaking the truth.

Kallias: Can anyone venture a guess as to our productivity in this discussion?

Socrates: We've done our best, and I believe we've reached some agreements. If we didn't answer all the questions and didn't solve all the problems, it isn't because we were unproductive but because some problems are beyond our reach. Sisyphus, who rolls his stone up the mountain only to have it roll back down, is not unproductive; he works as hard as he possibly can, doing everything a human being can do. If he isn't as productive as he could be, it's because the gods have chosen it to be that way. So with us; we have done as well as we can. The gods may allow others in the future to do better.

Nikias: If one could only eat the truth he produces…

Ipponikos: Of course one can, Nikias. All one has to do is make the truth wanted by many.

Kallias: Next time I'll ask Kratylus to join us. We should have more businessmen-philosophers around.

Socrates: It would be a wonderful thing to do. I pray for your success.

⚙

CHAPTER 2

Polydor: A Socratic Dialogue on Participative Management[1]

Participative management: It sounds so simple, so easy to define. But its true meaning may be buried beneath a pile of assumptions about it. Like many management concepts participative management has a tendency of becoming all things to all people.

What would Socrates, known for his method of systematic search for answers make of this term? In this fanciful dialogue with the Greek manager Polydor, Socrates flails away at some false assumptions surrounding participative management and reaches some tentative but useful conclusions.

Socrates: What does "participative management" mean to you, Polydor? A lot of people would like to know, because it seems to be a helpful method and they would like to practice it.

---

1. Originally Published in *Management Review* with the title, "A Socratic dialogue on participative management," by Apostolos P. [Tolly] Kizilos, *September 1982*, and printed by permission.

Polydor: Participative management, Socrates, is what the words say: management by involving others in the process. It is better than any other management style because it makes my job easier, my work more satisfying, and my organization more effective.

Socrates: You consider yourself a participative manager because you practice participative management and have a good reason for doing so. Well said, Polydor. But tell me; do your people, with whom you practice participative management, like it as much as you do?

Polydor: I thought that it was obvious, Socrates. People like to be asked what they think, how they like this or that decision, what they value and so on. Communication is good for managers because they know what their people think and feel, and because people realize that managers care enough to ask.

Socrates: Again, I want to congratulate you, Polydor, for the knowledge gained from your experience, but I am still a bit confused. I am led to believe that a manager is participative if he involves his people in the affairs of his organization, if they participate in the process, if he communicates with them and shows that he cares about what they think and feel. But I still don't understand exactly what activities people are involved in doing. Let me give you an example of my confusion: Suppose that I am in the market for an oxcart. If I am to manage my affairs participatively, should I go around and ask some people what kind of cart they think I should buy?

Polydor: I don't think that is a very good example, Socrates, because your buying a particular kind of cart doesn't affect anybody but you. However, it wouldn't do you any harm to ask people you trust, and who care about you, their opinions about different kinds of carts. You'll learn more than you know now and make a better decision; also, those who were asked will feel good because they had a chance to help.

Socrates: You seem to say that participative management is not only management of things, but also management of people. Since, in my example, the only problem I had was how to manage my money, that wasn't a particularly good example.

Polydor: I feel you are trying to apply Participative Management to a situation that is not related to management at all.

Socrates: I'm only trying to scoop a few basic concepts from the gushing fountain of your knowledge, hoping that I can more fully satisfy my thirst for it later on. Now, you said that asking for the participation of others whom I trust will give me more information and that this will also be helpful to others and me. This means, then, that participation and involvement in participative management are desirable only when the person who has to make the decision can trust the participants.

Polydor: This is so.

Socrates: It may be so, Polydor, but you didn't say so, at first.

Polydor: It seemed too obvious to mention.

Socrates: If you introduce trust as a condition for participation, you limit the number of people that the manager chooses to involve. Since trust is not something one can see or measure, the implication is that participation and involvement of others is left to the manager's discretion.

Polydor: It makes sense. Participative management is not exactly a substitute for democracy—one person, one vote. Participative management is discretionary management. The boss tries to involve people he trusts in the process.

Socrates: If a boss has 10,000 people in his organization but he only trusts two people, and involves only them in his management process, can we say that this boss is a participative manager?

Polydor: There are many things in this world that are transformed in quality by quantitative change. For example, how many seeds of wheat make a pile? Would you say a million, one hundred or ten? Surely ten seeds are not a pile, but a million are. A pile stops being a pile at some point, even though no one defines that point exactly. If one trusts and involves two out of 10,000 people, I wouldn't call him a participative manager; I'd call him a misanthrope. But exactly how many people he has to trust before becoming a participative manager, I couldn't tell you.

Socrates: Your explanation is indeed enlightening, Polydor; but, if we cannot determine the nature of involvement, or the constituency and number of those involved, what exactly can we determine about participative management?

Polydor: Participative management is a continuum of styles. One can be more or less participative, by including more or less people, in many or in few matters, and so on. It is not necessary for something to be clear in order to be real. Love, hatred, trust, power and so on are not clearly defined or quantifiable, but they do exist.

Socrates: I couldn't agree with you more. But there is a difference. People know what love and hate are, but when it comes to participative management, it seems to me, it is anything one wants it to be.

Polydor: That's unfair! One cannot be a participative manager unless he involves people whom he trusts, communicates with them, cares for them, and so on.

Socrates: Let me ask you something, Polydor: Would you say that a dictator could also be a democrat?

Polydor: Of course not! One is a dictator because he makes all decisions himself. When he does that, he cannot be a democrat, because a democrat shares decision-making with many others.

Socrates: Precisely. But I can say to you that one can be a dictator and a participative manager—or a democrat and a participative manager—and still satisfy all the conditions you yourself laid down in defining participative management.

Polydor: There's no such thing as a participative dictator, Socrates, and you know it.

Socrates: I agree, but not because of what you have said thus far. When you made the distinction between a dictator and a democrat you didn't say anything about involvement, trust, caring and such things. You relied entirely on one dimension of their total behavior: the manner by which they make decisions. Since you did not define participative management on the basis of decision-making, I was perfectly within your definition when I said there could be a participative dictator.

Polydor: Dictators don't trust people and care for them. Their only concern is to acquire power and hold on to it.

Socrates: I must disagree: I see no such inherent qualities in dictators. I can imagine a benevolent dictator, whose only motivation for acquiring and holding power is to make the world better for his people. In doing this, I can see him asking a lot of people what they think, delegating power to many people, and trusting them. The only things he doesn't do is let anyone else have anything to do with the final decisions, or set up a procedure defining how decisions are made. To put it bluntly, the issues that define Participative Management are not involvement, trust, participation and caring for others; the issue is power to make decisions by one or many, and the acceptance of a procedure, regardless of the kinds of decisions made. Had you defined participative management on this basis, I would have understood and kept my silence; but since you didn't, I remain confused and quite talkative.

Polydor: Confused, indeed! You have known all along that participative management means sharing decision-making power.

Socrates: Yes, it is true that I have had some thoughts along these lines. But if I am the only one who has these thoughts and everyone else has different thoughts, communication is difficult at best, and implementation of participative management will result in confusion.

Polydor: You are saying that you know what participative management is, if you can define it yourself, but you are confused because others define it differently.

Socrates: Precisely. When we use terms to describe complex concepts, we must be careful to set boundaries on their meaning, to ensure that the concepts don't also mean their opposites.

Polydor: Like "participative dictator."

Socrates: Exactly. Now, I think that participative management and Participative Management are two different things. The first meaning is generic: management that allows any reasonable amount of participation by some people in some decision-making. Participation may mean some sort of power in the final decision or just opinion giving, consulting, suggesting—any involvement without power to actually decide. In short, in this generic sense, "participative management" means whatever the speaker and the listener choose.

But the second meaning of Participative Management, which we can think of in a capitalized form, is specific and particular. In this sense Participative Management means that some decisions, at least, are made with the participation of subordinates in the decision-making process. The decisions to be made participatively the people who will participate, and the method by which the decisions will be made are defined in advance. This, I believe, is the minimum requirement for meaningful Participative Management.

Polydor: It's a good try, Socrates, but your definition with this clever capitalized form is no different from the first, generic meaning. I think that any kind of Participative Management in a hierarchical organization is a contradiction in terms, just like "participative dictator." Participative Management would smack of double talk in any hierarchy.

Socrates: We certainly have come a long way from our initial positions, Polydor. But, let me respond to your remark that "we cannot have Participative Management in a hierarchy." This, I take it, means that participation in decisions by subordinates doesn't make sense in a hierarchy, because there is always a boss who has all the power he wants in making decisions. And, even if the boss encourages his subordinates to oppose him on his decisions, why should they do so? The boss can always pull back, cancel his Participative

Management approach and revert to absolute autocracy. Is this why you think Participative Management won't work in a hierarchy?

Polydor: It most certainly is! As long as the boss is the source of livelihood, job assignments, career progress, peace of mind on the job and whatever else matters at work, his subordinates would be fools to believe that they have any real power to make decisions that oppose the boss's will.

Socrates: You certainly are correct in general, and this is how the world of organizations would be if it weren't for one bit of missing reality: From the outside, it looks like a hierarchy, and is organized from top to bottom in order of decreasing power and authority. But the organization charts of hierarchies don't tell the whole story. The boss can give orders, but subordinates can implement them brilliantly or poorly, speedily or slowly, literally or imaginatively. If the job is complex enough, or if it requires mental rather than physical activity, there is little chance that the boss can accurately assess either the quality or the quantity of the output even after a considerable passage of time. So, Participative Management can work because it is not only the boss, who can withhold sharing his power, but also the subordinates who can control their power of implementation. In this way, a kind of work contract exists: "You give me some power to decide, and I'll give us more power to implement what *we* decide." Or, from the boss's point of view: "I'll let you participate meaningfully in the decisions, and expect that our organization will perform its objectives better. This way, all of us will be more powerful and effective."

Polydor: If what you say is true, everyone would practice Participative Management; but, in fact, few managers do. Perhaps, this is the problem: You said the manager shares his power and then becomes more powerful, somehow. This doesn't make sense.

Socrates: Suppose that I know the solution to a problem and you don't. If knowledge is power, then I am more powerful than you in this situation.

Polydor: That you are.

Socrates: Now, suppose that I systematically teach you everything I know, and you, being an intelligent, motivated person, absorb it. Now I ask you, did I share my knowledge, and therefore, my power with you?

Polydor: You did.

Socrates: Am I less knowledgeable and less powerful than I was before I taught you all these things?

Polydor: I suppose not, but only because I don't wish you any harm. If I were your enemy, you might regret that you taught me so much. Making me more powerful, then, might make it more difficult for you to be the teacher.

Socrates: I agree that teaching an enemy is foolish. But teaching a trusted individual is different. Am I less powerful because Plato learned a few things from me? And will he be less knowledgeable or less powerful because others will learn from him?

Polydor: All right, Socrates; I get the point.

Socrates: So, we have arrived at the conclusion of our search, I think. Sharing power (and one might add, other feelings and capacities such as love, joy, leadership, and so on) with those one trusts—those who share one's own basic goals, as members of an organization or any other entity—doesn't diminish one's power. Furthermore, if one gets in return greater commitment to implement decisions, everybody will feel and be more powerful, and the organization will be more enabled to perform its mission. Is that agreed upon, then?

Polydor: Oh, I suppose so…

Socrates: Why such a halfhearted response, Polydor? We came to a consensus, did we not?

Polydor: Your example of sharing power by sharing knowledge isn't exactly analogous to sharing decision-making power. I don't have any difficulty accepting teaching those one trusts and sharing the power of knowledge, but sharing one's power with subordinates to make decisions affecting the livelihood of hundreds or thousands bothers me. Why will the many make wiser decisions than one man, if that man is smarter, more experienced or more caring than the rest? And, there is the problem of time.

Socrates: Hold on, Polydor. I feel that the tapestry we have so carefully woven is unraveling. Let's take one thread at a time and examine it in the hope that we can weave it back in and prevent a mess. You say that sharing knowledge is not similar to sharing decision-making power. I didn't say whether it was or wasn't. All I was trying to show is that power based on knowledge doesn't diminish when shared. Isn't that so?

Polydor: Yes; when it is shared with those one trusts.

Socrates: Precisely. And, I also said that there are other feelings that do not diminish when shared. The more love one gives, for example, the more love he experiences; and if love is another feeling which makes one feel more powerful, then sharing this kind of power makes one more powerful. I thought then that I could rightly say that power increases when shared. Am I wrong? Can you think of any kind of power that decreases when shared with people one trusts?

Polydor: Decision-making power, of course. That's what we're interested in here, isn't it?

Socrates: Perhaps, then, one should not talk about decision-making power so abstractly. Let's talk about the decision makers, the managers. Is a manager who shares his decision-making power less powerful because of that?

Polydor: I don't mind looking at our problem this way, but I don't think it makes any difference.

Socrates: I don't know, Polydor; but let us be hopeful and try: What does a manager use his decision-making power for?

Polydor: To solve problems; to lead; to achieve personal and organizational goals.

Socrates: I think that summarizes everything. The hierarchy gives managers decision-making power so that they can achieve the organization's goals.

Polydor: And, their own, personal goals.

Socrates: I don't believe so. Organizations don't recognize individual goals apart from organizational goals. If my goal, for example, is to write a tragedy that will win a prize at our city's festival, but the organization that gives me decision-making power has nothing to do with producing prize-winning tragedies, my goal is of no concern to the organization. And, if I use any of that power to attain my goal, I would be misusing that power and I would be unethical. Do you agree?

Polydor: I see what you mean. I meant to say that the organization gives a manager power so that he can accomplish the organization's goals and…

Socrates: That is all. If the managers do that, then their own goals that are related to the organization will also be furthered. That is what managers have to do; nothing more, nothing less. But, if any managers try to further their own goals apart from the organization's goals, then these managers are unethical.

Polydor: Correct—if there is no coincidence between personal and organizational goals.

Socrates: Now then, if the organization's and the managers' success depends on achieving the organization's goals, the only reason managers could possibly have for not sharing their decision-making power is that they feel the organization's goals will be achieved better if they decide by themselves.

Polydor: Especially if the boss happens to be bright, experienced, wise, hardworking, and so on.

Socrates: Most managers are, my dear Polydor, especially in their own opinion of themselves.

Polydor: It seems reasonable, though. They are managers of others because they have something more than their subordinates in what is important to the organization.

Socrates: Every time you answer me, Polydor, you open up a new subject. We were saying that a manager would decide without sharing his power, if he felt that the organization's goals would be achieved better in this way. But, even if he is brilliant, skillful, experienced, wise, caring, and hardworking, he cannot achieve his organization's goals best, unless he shares his decision-making power.

There are two reasons for making this claim: First, it has been shown time and again that people working as a team make better decisions. This is what we call synergism. Something happens when people pool their energy, when they trust and respect each other, when they have the same commitment to the team's goals—something, which allows them to reach higher than any one member of that team could.

My second reason for the manager's sharing power concerns implementation. Decisions are only a step toward achieving goals; others must implement them. Even the best decisions are worthless if they are implemented halfheartedly. So, if a manager cares to achieve goals, he has to make the best decisions and implement them in the best way. This means sharing his decision-making power to improve the quality of decisions through synergy, and the quality of implementation by unleashing the discretionary, but real, energy of subordinates. So, sharing decision-making power, even if it decreases the boss's decision-making power, will increase his overall power to achieve the organization's goals. Since this is the manager's job, I say that the boss is more powerful when he shares his decision-making power. This holds true even if the "ideal" manager is making decisions; if a manager is less than that, there is no question that he will be more powerful when he shares his decision-making power.

Polydor: There is a problem with all of this. You said that you would talk about managers as decision-makers not in the abstract; but, thus far, you have forgotten that managers are human beings.

They certainly want to achieve the organization's goals, but they don't want to kill themselves doing it. Do you realize how much more frustrating it is to reach decisions in a team, than decide on one's own? And what about the time it takes to decide? Why should a boss work more hours trying to reach a consensus when he can do his job without it? Subordinates may be happy to put in more time in exchange for more power, but why should the boss make *his* life more difficult? Isn't it a matter of balance between personal and organizational goals here?

Socrates: I take it that you agree that the manager's overall power can only increase, if he shares his decision-making power. You recognize that the quality of decisions is higher, if team members work well together, and the quality of implementation is better, because people feel more powerful and more committed to goals when they have some decision-making power. But, you don't see how the boss can afford to do this.

Polydor: I see why he *should* share his power, but I don't see why he should *want* to.

Socrates: We haven't really talked about the mode of decision making very much, and I think it is time we did so.

Polydor: I don't see how this will answer the objection I just made: Why should a manager give up some of his decision-making power and make it difficult for himself? What has this got to do with the mode of decision making? Let's stick to what managers want and forget about modes and other such abstractions.

Socrates: First of all, I don't believe that a manager's work, which includes making decisions and finding ways to implement them, is more difficult if he shares his decision-making power. But mostly I wanted to talk about the mode of decision making to show you that decisions made with the participation of others may take longer, but they don't have to be more difficult for the manager, if he chooses the right mode.

Polydor: I'm all ears, Socrates. Show me how a manager can have fun haggling for hours on end over decisions with a bunch of people who don't feel the responsibility of management weighing down their shoulders.

Socrates: All right. You know that, in a hierarchy, there are many different modes of decision-making; but none is more suitable for sharing power without giving up control than consensus.

Polydor: But, Socrates, consensus means that anyone in a team has the power of frustrating the will of others. If that is the case, the boss will have a harder time making decisions and will be more frustrated. The organization charges him with the responsibility of making decisions, but his subordinates can prevent him from doing precisely that. Do you want to put managers in the position of having to ask subordinates permission for doing their jobs?

Socrates: Once again, Polydor, you look at the surface of things. If a group of strangers who don't share a common goal were to try to make decisions by consensus, the process could be very frustrating, indeed. But in a hierarchical organization, there is a common goal—at least nominally—among the members, and there is a leader, by definition.

If we had chosen majority vote, instead of consensus, for decision-making, the boss could, on occasion, find himself in the minority, and he could lose. But in decision-making by consensus, no team can decide to do something he doesn't want done. The boss has the power to block any decision he doesn't like, just like any other member of the team. And because he is the boss, and his subordinates recognize that those above him hold him responsible for any decisions his team may make, they will refuse to go along with his views only if they have very good reasons for doing so.

Also, the culture endows the leader with a certain authority, which, no matter what mode of decision making is agreed upon, cannot be totally overlooked. Lastly, team members know that if they resist without good reasons, they are breaching the boss's trust, and the boss may punish them or even rescind his decision to make decisions by consensus. For these reasons, the boss retains the position of "first among equals" in consensus decision-making, and his opinion counts more, even in this mode of ostensibly equal power sharing between manager and subordinates.

Polydor: We have come full circle: Participative Management with consensus is actually generic participative management with mere involvement, which is not different from autocratic decision-making. It seems that we wasted a lot of time.

Socrates: Not quite. There is a difference when the boss and his team decide to make decisions by consensus. It is true that the boss can prevent a decision from being made if he doesn't agree with it; but, if he does this often, his team members will recognize that team consensus is meaningless and will withhold their power for quality implementation of the decisions. So the boss must be reluctant to exercise this blocking power, or he will be working against his own rationale for allowing team decisions by consensus in the first place. If he is a wise leader, he will not object strenuously when a decision is not always his preferred decision; he will go along sometimes, just as others will go along, trusting the expertise or the enthusiasm of other team members. His implicit primacy will serve as a last resort, not as his first and final word on each decision. When someone holds his ground and refuses to go along with the prevailing solution to a problem, everyone will know that this must be a very important matter to that team member, and they will listen and try to understand why their prevailing opinion might harm the team or the organization. The boss will know that the subordinate is taking a risk in going against his fellow team members and against his boss, and will not overrule him arbitrarily. In trying to reach consensus, everyone will try to present good reasons and examine this issue from every viewpoint possible, until the subject is exhausted.

Polydor: And what then? What if everyone has had his say and the team is still unable to reach consensus?

Socrates: When all reasons have been exhausted and still no decision can be reached, the members have to begin examining their feelings. You'll be surprised to learn, Polydor, how often people disagree because of feelings rather than good reasons. When someone puts up enough resistance to hold a team of his peers off, he must have some very strong feelings about that decision. Fear is usually lurking underneath resistance. It is at this point that team members must be skilled in discussing matters as whole human beings, rather than mere organizational functionaries. It helps if they know one another as human beings—if they have knowledge of each other's hopes, fears, preferences, skills and abilities. And, it is at these difficult times that the boss must know how to lead his team—not by ordering what must be done, but by guiding his subordinates through the reefs of conflict to the calm seas of collaboration. The leader becomes a facilitator of the process, the midwife, who gives birth to the decision of the team.

Polydor: When reasons cannot prove your case, Socrates, you resort to your favorite poetic metaphors.

Socrates: My dear Polydor, there is wisdom to be derived from metaphors. We need metaphors to help us understand our context and ourselves, and we should never hesitate to use them for our enlightenment.

Polydor: I would be a fool to argue against that, but I'm not sure that managers and leaders will pay much attention to these arguments.

Socrates: Don't be so skeptical, Polydor. Remember: managers are leaders, and they are chosen because they possess exceptional skills; they can grasp more than mere facts and logic, and deal with tangled feelings and even metaphors better than most of us. Give them credit and be hopeful.

CHAPTER 3

❀

Tom Sawyer's Management Philosophy

Doug Hawkins, a manager at Microtronics Corporation, in the mid-nineteen-fifties, wrote the memo presented below. It was recently found in the corporate archives of the company, during a search for noteworthy documents prior to the compilation of a corporate history for Silicon Products Inc., which acquired Microtronics in the mid-sixties. It is worth noting that research into the personnel files of Silicon Products Inc., shows that Hawkins was repeatedly criticized for not working hard, but was given high ratings, nevertheless, for meeting or exceeding his departmental goals.

Hawkins, unfortunately, does not give a reference for the article from which he has excerpted the "new" version of the whitewashing episode of Mark Twain's *Tom Sawyer*. My literature search of magazines on literary criticism could not unearth any such "article." Whether Hawkins found such an article is uncertain but irrelevant to our purpose here. The most probable explanation for writing this memo is Hawkins' desire to defend his managerial conduct without appearing to be defensive or self-serving. Using Tom Sawyer instead of himself, and Aunt Polly instead of his boss, Larry Winter, he was able to say what he wanted to say about his work habits, without focusing attention to his own situation. "Working smart, not hard, means success," became one of the best known and most cherished slogans at Microtronics, and Hawkins' memo may have been its origin. It is worth noting that, no matter how rational this slogan may appear to be, connotations of laziness will always taint the good intentions it attempts to convey. At Silicon Products, Inc., the slogan was modified to read, "Working hard and smart means excellence."

Robert Stambolland
Editor, *The Record of Silicon Products, Inc., Cupertino, CA 1995*

ॐ

Microtronics Corp.   10/17/55

From: Doug Hawkins
To: Larry Winter and his Staff
Subject: Management Performance Appraisals

I recently came across an article that, I believe, contains some important clarifications on the subject of management performance appraisals, which we discussed at our last two staff meetings. This article presents an unpublished version of the famous episode in Mark Twain's novel *Tom Sawyer*, where Tom manages the whitewashing of the thirty-yard-long fence in front of his Aunt Polly's house. The author of the article is primarily concerned with the literary aspects of this version, but I am reproducing it in part below, because the issues it deals with pertain to our management appraisals.

As everyone knows, Tom Sawyer, having been given by his Aunt Polly the task of painting her house fence on a beautiful summer Saturday morning, comes up with a way to get the job done through other people, while accumulating all sorts of interesting odds and ends, which represent "wealth" to him. When the fence is painted, he reports to his Aunt Polly the result, and gets rewarded with "a choice apple" from her closet. Now, this version is technically flawed: it suits Mark Twain, but it doesn't make sense. How could Aunt Polly, who doesn't trust Tom as far as she can throw him, sit all day "by an open window in a pleasant rearward apartment" without checking up on Tom's work progress? Apparently the author recognized this deficiency and wrote another version of the episode, which, however, never saw the light of publication until now. In this later version, Aunt Polly looked out a window and saw Tom having "a nice, idle time," sitting on a barrel in the shade close by, dangling his legs and munching an apple. She watched indignantly for a while to discover how this state of affairs had come about and saw a boy offer Tom the contents of his pockets and "a dilapidated old window sash." Unable to hold back her anger, she shouted for Tom to get right back in the house.

So, here is the extract, which, I believe, is relevant to our present concerns, because it is essentially a manager's performance appraisal:

"What you doing loafing out there, Tom?"

On his way in, Tom had decided to defend his actions, finding nothing to feel bad about. Seeing his Aunt's eyes flashing, he responded in a low voice but without the slightest hint of contrition, "I've been gettin' the paintin' done," he said.

"And how are you doing that? Sitting on your duff and collecting your friends' possessions while they do your work? Don't you have any sense to know that's doing wrong to your friends?"

"No," said Tom quietly, but with absolute certainty. "Jes' because I don't do no paintin' it don't mean I don't do no work. Look for yerself! They do good work, honest they do——I've been watchin', and they have fun doing it. I plan the work, I watch them, and keep'em goin'. I'm like a sorta headman, see?"

"Headman, my foot! Yer' lazy, and make excuses for it. How you done that? There ain't no value in settin' there havin' fun, boy!"

"That ain't the way I see it," said Tom stubbornly. "You tol' me you want the fence painted and that's what's gettin' done. How I done it, that's another thing."

"How?" his Aunt demanded menacingly.

"I got this idea that I make the job look like it were fun to do; and plenty difficult too, so they think it ain't nothing everybody can do, jes' a few. And, the idea works. They even buy me to let them have a turn with the brush."

Aunt Polly covered her face with both hands in despair.

"I didn't even ask them for help. They come to me and pestered me to let'em have a go at it. If I hadn't done it, they'd have felt bad. They like what they're doing," he insisted. "And, there ain't nothin' bad in what I done," he added.

"You go to your room and stay there until you figure things out in a proper way," she said without equivocation.

Tom spread himself on his bed and tried to think of a way out of his fix. This time, however, he couldn't think creatively because he felt he was right, and his mind was stuck on that thought. He had discovered a great law of leadership, it seemed to him, namely that by making work difficult to attain, work can be made attractive; and when work is attractive, people want to do it; and when people want to do something, instead of being obliged to do something, that something is "Play," not "Work" anymore. But, how can I explain that to Aunt Polly? To her, "Play" is always useless and unproductive, because it don't need no suffering, no sweat, no tiredness and grief. How can I make her understand that those who can get the work done by organizing, attracting people, setting high standards and looking over everything do at least as much work as anybody else?

He got up and looked out the window at Billy Fisher, still working hard on the fence and concluded that his Aunt, angry as she was, nevertheless had not stopped the boys from working. Johnny Miller was hurrying Billy up, anxious to have at it, especially now that Tom wasn't there to ask for his honey-butter-streaked marble for letting him work. But, before he had time to enjoy the result of his genius, Aunt Polly came out of the house and told Billy to stop what he was doing. That was easier said than done, however. Billy Fisher had bought his chance at whitewashing with a kite in good repair and wasn't about to quit. "Stop right this minute, Billy Fisher!" ordered Aunt Polly.

"That ain't no fair," Billy protested. "I gave Tom my kite to have some fun with paint," he protested, sneaking in a few more brush strokes.

"You *like* to paint the fence?" Aunt Polly asked with astonishment.

"Tom didn't want to give us a chance. He wanted all the fun for hisself, so I traded him for some," Billy explained.

"I'm next," chimed in Johnny Miller.

Aunt Polly shook her head and went back inside the house. She was sure that no good would come out of that boy, Tom, but she didn't know exactly why. It seemed to her sinful that anyone could earn his bread without the sweat of his brow, but that boy Tom had found a way. And, what was to be done with him?

When she opened the door to Tom's room, she found him praying on his knees. She naturally assumed that the boy had repented for his sin and her heart softened. It never occurred to her that Tom might be asking the Lord for inspiration on how to make his Aunt Polly understand that he was right and deserved her respect rather than her disapproval.

"Go and finish up," she said. "I dunno how you done it, but you done it like you said. Them boys must be touched in the head and that's no fault of yourn."

Tom got up and went out quietly. "But, give back what you took from those boys, hear?" she called out after him.

"I will Aunt," Tom said, and in his head made a solemn promise to return everything he took, sometime in the future—sometime, like six months from now, or maybe six years hence—he hadn't promised when, and wasn't about to. And, he thanked the Almighty for giving a measure of wisdom to his Aunt.

It seems to me, that this passage demonstrates better than any theory of management, the essence of our profession. We are here to get the job done, and how we achieve that should be totally irrelevant, as long as our people remain motivated and feel challenged. Managers must work smart, but whether they work hard or not should be up to them. Working hard cannot be the primary criterion for evaluating a manager's or anyone else's work for that matter. I hope that we can all agree on these matters and finalize our system for the Performance Appraisal of Managers at our next meeting.

CHAPTER 4

❀

A Machiavellian Gambit

The two letters that follow were preserved in the files of the company Nuova Cristalleria of Venice, and were donated to the corporate library of Megatech Inc., when the latter acquired the former in 1907. The first letter, addressed to Niccolo Machiavelli (1469–1527)[1] by Luigi Quirini, one of the owners of Nuova Cristalleria, is a request for help in applying certain principles to the management of his company. The second letter by Giacomo Lorendano, an employee of the company, shows the unexpected effects management actions can have upon some subordinates. It is worth pointing out at the start that eventually Nuova Cristalleria became an example of a well-managed company, becoming finally a jewel in the crown of Silicon Valley's Megatech Empire.

As far as we know, Machiavelli, was never aware of the existence of any Quirini or anyone from that man's business establishment, even though Luigi Quirini was his contemporary, nor is there any evidence that he was ever involved in the business affairs of that man.

---

1. Niccolo Machiavelli was the author of *The Prince,* a literary classic, which was written in 1513, but published in 1532, five years after the author's death.

However, the correspondence presented, historically validated and accessible through the archives of Megatech, Inc. in the Internet reveals how leaders of various kinds, to achieve their own selfish ends, have misused Machiavelli's writings.

Machiavelli is considered by many scholars to be a humanist writer, whose guiding principle of "the end justifies the means" was meant to further the advancement of human beings by steering toward a noble end. However, his belief that political expediency should be placed above morality, and that the leader must use craft and deceit to maintain his authority and achieve his goals are difficult to justify on the grounds of either effectiveness or human growth. Managers, who accept *manipulation* as one of the dictionary definitions of management, ought to be on the alert that manipulation, which is not always avoidable or undesirable, does not mean *Machiavellianism*, which is always avoidable and undesirable.

A Letter to Signor Machiavelli

ॐ

Luigi Quirini
Master of Nuova Cristalleria
Ramo Beroviero 155
Venezia

March 8, 1521

Signor Niccolo Machiavelli
Master of Arts and Letters
Villa di San Casciano
Firenze

Dear Signor Machiavelli:

I trust in Providence and the Grace of our Lord that your days in your peaceful estate of San Casciano, where you have been making your home, are most pleasing to you and conducive to the pursuit of your intellectual projects. Your absence from the public affairs of Florence is indeed a great loss, but I have faith that in good time your contributions to human understanding will be the gain of mankind.

Our mutual friend Signor Giovanni Gondalvo, aware of my great admiration of your contributions, has done me the great honor of showing me the passage from your work titled *The Prince*, examining leadership in state affairs—a magnificent opus to which, I am told, you have devoted your energies for some time now. I believe that leaders in all spheres of human endeavor will benefit from the guidance you provide. I consider it my good fortune to be one of the earliest recipients of your insights and I have applied whatever knowledge I could glean from the few pages I read of *The Prince* to my own circumstances.

Though you do not know me, I trust that the name of Quirini is not unfamiliar to you. I am now the managing owner of the famous Nuova Cristalleria in Venice, established many years ago by my grandfather, and known throughout the civilized world today for its magnificent crystal products. We employ over one thousand people in our factories, and leadership is, I believe, essential to the maintenance of our success. I recognize that your work addresses leadership in the affairs of state, but I am certain that it applies to commercial enterprises and factories as well. I have, therefore, taken steps to judiciously implement throughout my commercial domain the advice you offer in *The Prince*.

There are, however, certain difficulties that have arisen as a result of this, and I appeal to you for help in resolving them. I take the liberty of asking for your counsel on the basis of the friendship we both share with Signor Gondalvo, and my great respect for your work. I am, of course, prepared to offer you generous remuneration for your valued services, should you decide to extend to me your consultation.

Here, then, is a brief account of the origins of our enterprise and the situation in which I find myself at this time. My grandfather, Luigi Quirini, was a superb glassblower and founded our company with help from Signor Skolas and other notables, in response to the great demand for his manufactures. He taught his craft to others and the quality of our Company's products was maintained. He resisted all advice to expand beyond what he, himself, could oversee, and remained to the end a friendly, trustworthy, merciful and generous man of humble birth. These, I recognize are not the qualities of a great leader, according to your manuscript, but in those times and under those circumstances they must have been adequate for his small enterprise to survive. Our enterprise attained the reputation it has today when my father Pierro Quirini took over the leadership. Unfortunately, I do not know much about my father's qualities of leadership, as I was sent to Pizza at an early age to attend to my basic education at my uncle's school, and later to the University of Padua, to further my scientific interests. I have heard, however, that my father devoted his talents to expanding our markets in Italy and abroad and, obviously, was quite successful in this. The factory was managed by my older brother, Cesare, in what I believe was a tolerant manner. Being a mild-mannered, friendly man, not unlike my grandfather, but lacking the knowledge of glass making, Cesare was able to succeed for a time. The problems of his lack of leadership became manifest to me upon my return to Venice almost two years ago. Though production had been greatly expanded and quality had been maintained, it was apparent to me that the workers were becoming ever more demanding. They had even started a secret guild and were planning rebellious actions, if Cesare did not accede to their demands. It was at that time my father departed from this earth—God have mercy on his soul—and I decided to take over our company, thus preventing Cesare from bankrupting us, through his foolish generosity. Also, I didn't want Cesare's tender-heartedness to result in throwing thousands of people out of work by his lack of courage to keep wages low.

I believe that I possess "the characteristics of beasts…those of the lion and the fox" as you put it, Signor Machiavelli, and I was able to outfox my brother for the greater good. In accord with your advice that "the wise leader cannot and should not keep his word when keeping it is not to his advantage," I made my brother think that I was in total agreement with what he was planning to do and pretended to leave everything in his hands while I traveled to see the world and expand my education. Poor Cesare was so trusting and generous! He felt sad to lose my counsel even for a short while and loaded me up with treasures and letters of credit throughout Italy and France, so that I would lack no comforts whatsoever.

Of course I used my resources to plan for the demise of that faint-hearted, pushover. If I, his own brother, had no respect for him, I was certain that none of our workers could possibly have any either. So, I organized a force of 200 workers, trained them to fear and respect me, as you advise, and after four months I returned to Venice and wrested the reigns of power from Cesare. For awhile I thought that I should execute Cesare to show the workers at the factory that from that time on they would have to deal with a new master; but, I decided against it, because I could not kill him and make my deed exemplary, lacking the power of the prince to use the law to achieve his ends, as you suggest. Instead, I sent Cesare to a monastery in France, where he will spend the rest of his life in comfortable isolation. Since I assumed leadership, I have done my utmost to place people I trust in all essential positions and to eliminate those who deceive themselves with idealistic views of the nature of human beings, thus inflicting untold suffering upon humanity. For it is clear to me now more than ever before, Signor Machiavelli, that men are exactly as you describe them: "ungrateful, fickle, and deceitful, eager to avoid dangers, and avid for gain. And while you are useful to them they are all with you, offering you their blood, their property, their lives, and their sons so long as danger is remote…but when danger approaches they turn on you." In this way, I have restored discipline through fear and I agree with you "men have less hesitation in offending a man who is loved than one who is feared. For love is held by a bond of obligation which, as men are wicked, is broken whenever personal advantage suggests it, but fear is accompanied by the dread of punishment which never relaxes." As a result, I have broken the back of all organized resistance in the fledgling Glassblowers Guild, which I decided not to disband but, rather, to control with my own people at its helm. This way, the workers think that they have a forum for expressing their grievances, while in fact they have nothing.

I have used a variety of ways to justify my actions against Cesare, my rejection of the workers' extravagant wage demands, the strict discipline I have imposed throughout the factories and the ever-expanding wealth I am accumulating. You couldn't be more right when you wrote, "it is necessary to know how to disguise this [deceitful] nature well and how to pretend and dissemble. Men are so simple and so ready to follow the needs of the moment that the deceiver will always find someone to deceive." A prince or a manager of a large commercial enterprise such as ours, must "appear to have" qualities which he does not have, as you put it. I know that few people will appreciate the courage and intelligence it takes to do this, but I certainly do. I am one of the few people who believe fully that "it is good to appear clement, trustworthy, humane, religious, and honest, and also to be so, but always with the mind so disposed that, when occasion arises, not to be so [to be in fact]…the opposite." But since I am not any of these things, I have trained my spirit "to adapt itself as the varying winds of fortune command." Indeed, when the survival and growth of our enterprise is at stake, I "know how to follow evil," as you bluntly state.

Let me give you two brief examples of the ways I have used to create the image of a caring and humane owner, while in fact I am nothing of the sort: Cesare's removal was presented to the workers as an act of supreme sacrifice on my part. They believe that Cesare abandoned them for a life of luxury and profligacy, and I had to come to the factory to save it from ruin, giving up my only desire in life, the pursuit of the sciences. Because I am a miserly man—one of the qualities of the prince, I am happy to say, I do possess—they accept all kinds of deprivations in working conditions and wages, thinking that this is the way to save the factory. This is the only way their savior can accomplish his noble goals, even though they know our products are sought everywhere and our enterprise is as great as it has ever been.

And my second way of giving the appearance that I do care for them, relates to what I said previously: I have instituted all sorts of awards and contests with prizes and make quite a splendid show of these. The most productive worker, the most creative worker, the most caring worker, the most aggressive salesman, the most resourceful manager, the most cost-conscious manager, and many others are rewarded every month with a few flimsy prizes—a medallion here, a vase there, a few ducats now, a dinner with the boss at the Ristorante di Gondola sometimes—and they appreciate these immensely. They never seem to stop and think that these awards and the recognition they are given cost me but a minuscule fraction of what it would cost me to improve the working conditions and pay them higher wages. And, my image is as esteemed as any mortal would wish it to be. The power of pomp and ceremony, as you point out, is truly incalculable.

These and other deceptions have made it possible for me "to avoid being hated or despised" which, as you write, is essential for any leader's survival and prosperity. If the situation is as I have described it (and I assure you that I have been most faithful to the facts, not being a man who values imagination) you may ask, "Then what is the problem?" Why have I bothered to write you this letter appealing to you for assistance?

Perhaps your completed manuscript addresses my concern, but the few pages I have seen, though they make reference to it, do not provide a solution. My problem, to put it simply, is that even though human beings are wicked, cunning, mean, and fickle, as you say, there are many of them who are intelligent and quite capable of learning from their betters, and can appear to be dullards and ignorant. I am of course constantly on the lookout for those who have learned the princely art of deceit and I have discovered and banished several of them; but I suspect there are others who are masters in the art and cannot be detected. There are times, Signor Machiavelli, when I seriously consider subjecting to torture anyone who displays any sign of intelligence, that I may discover the contents of his mind. But, even if I do this, what could I gain? If I eliminate all those who think and create at the factory, all those who receive the miserable awards I offer them, how will our Company prosper? I, of course, follow your advice to befriend certain people, but how can I trust what I see, when I know how skillful deception can be? I believe that there are seemingly loyal, obedient, hard-working craftsmen in our factories who, sooner or later, will penetrate my image and discover my true nature and will conspire against me and destroy me and my domain before I have a chance to foil their dark designs.

And, to make matters worse, the publication of your manuscript will reveal to everyone all the arts and crafts of leadership, giving them equal understanding of these matters and even giving them ideas they might not have thought of previously. How can this treasure be entrusted to swine? But, perhaps, you have some answers to the problem I am facing; perhaps there is a key to unlocking this storehouse of knowledge, which you don't intend to give to everyone. As I said, I am willing to pay for this key. But, if no such key exists, I am prepared to rent the exclusive rights to your manuscript, at a price that will make you a wealthy man. If you are not in any hurry to publish, I will contract with you that your great work will be published after my death. Then, I will have no need of earthly power and, having no heirs, I will leave my fortune to a fund, dedicated to the perpetuation of the greatness of my leadership. I want Quirinism to become synonymous with excellence in leadership. I will be known from now to the end of time as a man who knew how to harness the skills of little people to achieve great feats at minimum cost.

I am waiting anxiously for your reply. Giacomo Lorendano, the bearer of this sealed correspondence, can be trusted absolutely to deliver to me your sealed response, because he knows that the welfare of his family is under my complete control.

Your friend and admirer,

Luigi Quirini
Master of Nuova Cristalleria

An Unexpected Response

ॐ
Giacomo Lorendano
Glassblower Second Class of Nuova Cristalleria
Via di Passato Potenze 248
Venezia

July 9, 1521, Padua

My Dear Signor Quirini,

I now have your letter to Signor Machiavelli and I have you in my power. I am not so good with words, but I can read. You are right; some of the swine are clever! I knew this letter was important or you wouldn't have troubled yourself with my family and me. The house you gave us and the promotion you gave me made me suspicious that you wanted something in return. I thought at first it was my wife you were after, but that didn't make sense, because you could have found other ways to get rid of me. Then, when you asked me to deliver this letter and sent your henchmen to be servants in my house, because you didn't want my family "to be inconvenienced in any way," I knew that this letter was very important and my loved ones were your hostages. Not bad thinking for an ex-glassblower and now a half-witted overseer, you must admit!

Anyway, I have thought the matter over and I have decided that now I am the lion and the fox and you are nothing more than a flea-bitten dog. You do as I tell you and all will be well! First of all, I want my wife and my children delivered safely and with a generous treasure—I will leave the amount to your newly found generosity—to the bearer of this letter, who is a friend of mine. After that, if I am pleased, I will send you instructions regarding the ways and means by which we will operate your "domain," as you put it.

By the way, I know that I am not an educated man and not capable to tell you all that needs to be done for our Company to prosper; therefore, I have retained the services of Signor Machiavelli, whom you respect so greatly, and he will be advising me. He knows all about our understandings and believes that you have failed to demonstrate adequate cunning for leadership, and I am now, therefore, the person who has gained his respect. Signor Machiavelli has, unfortunately, distributed pages of his manuscript to several of his friends to solicit their comments, and so there will be others who know of the qualities the prince must have. However, he assures me, that he has no intention of publishing his manuscript unless and until the circumstances are such as to permit him to incur the favors of the Medici and return to public service. Politics is really his first and only love, and he has agreed to advise me instead of Prince Lorenzo De Medici, only as an experiment to test his theories in the present context of affairs. He believes that our Company can be the model for the enlightened state. It seems to me that Signor Machiavelli was happy to learn that his methods will continue to be applied by someone who will strive for betterment of the human condition, rather than by someone like you.

He told me that *The Prince* is like a musket: it can be used by a good man to defend his life, or by an evil man to commit crimes. I take it that he finds you to be an evil man.

Your first instruction from us is to bring back your brother Cesare, who, in our opinion, is a caring man and an enlightened leader, and install him as the Master of the Company. You are to obey him, not to reveal to him our understandings, and to allow him to manage as he sees fit. This may also be the last instruction I will send you, but we must wait and see. If any further instructions are to be issued, I am confident that a man with your talents will find a way to implement them, even though Cesare will hold the reigns of power.

In any case it all comes down to the fact that I see things pretty much the way Cesare saw them, and that would make things easy for everyone. The challenge for you, Signor Luigi, will be to learn how to do good, since you are an expert already on how to do evil. Signor Machiavelli, in my humble opinion, was addressing leaders who usually do good and for lack of knowing how to also do evil to attain good ends, lose their power; he wasn't writing advice to leaders who want to attain evil ends, as you seem to think.

Giacomo Lorendano

PS If you disagree with any of my proposals, Signor Machiavelli will expose you. He has already written a chapter to be included in *The Prince* with you as an example of misapplication of his methods, and will publish it along with the rest of his book immediately, and, I suspect, you will be infamous from now to the end of time. But, if you behave as instructed, that chapter will be destroyed, and the publication of the book postponed. You don't really have a choice.

G.L.

CHAPTER 5

❊

Fear Factor

Morale at our company went down for no apparent reason. People didn't seem to care about their work anymore. Managers demanded an explanation and instructed the Human Resources people to pinpoint the source of the problem. Communications specialists went to work sampling the workforce about the cause of such disinterest in their work. The people said that there was a fear factor in the company. When pressed to explain the origin of such a thing, they remained silent, looking past the faces of their bosses, beyond the confines of their cubicles. The managers examined the company policies and procedures, reviewed their plans, recalculated their sales projections and called staff meetings to tell people what they found. "Everything is in order," they said, and asked people to either come up with reasons for this fear factor or get rid of it. The people, however, chose to affirm the reality of the fear factor, without feeling any obligation to give reasons for it.

The quality of the products made by the company started to slide, and customers complained of shoddy workmanship. It was a disgrace for a company, known all over the world for more than a century as the model for others to imitate, to start peddling second-rate products. The managers, of course, found many reasons to explain

the decline in quality, but they didn't even consider telling the customers that there was a fear factor loose among their employees.
They offered apologies and promised prompt changes. They said
that they had vendors who had been slipping in their work; that they
were in the midst of plant modernization and process improvements, which, everyone knows, require a period of adjustment
before excellence is restored. But, in their own hearts, they knew that
it was the fear factor and nothing else that was the cause of all their
troubles, and unless they could wipe it out it would be the company's
undoing.

Lloyd Jones, the CEO of Southern Ultima Corporation, was very
troubled by this turn of events and wanted to find the cause of the
problem and eliminate it. So, he authorized the hiring of Organization Development consultants to conduct surveys and interview the
people with guaranteed anonymity. When the consultants were done
with their work, they held a meeting with all the managers present
and announced with gravity that there was indeed a fear factor of
indeterminate origin, rampant in the company. They proposed a
second phase study of the problem to test several promising hypotheses they had formulated on the basis of their preliminary confiden-
tial results. They wanted to conduct a systematic investigation to
determine whether the fear factor had its origin in a person, animal
or plant life, a mineral, a gas, or a conceptual entity of some kind.
Once this was done they believed that zeroing into the actual origin
of the fear factor would be a piece of cake. The managers huddled
together and decided that they had no time for research, or analysis,
or systematic anything. They paid the consultants and told them
they were done with them.

Lloyd Jones gathered his managers together in the corporate conference room and asked them to get close to their people and open
up a dialogue because the company could not long endure this pro-
gressive slide into paralysis. In the discussion that followed, he even
urged any managers who felt that they might have contributed to the

unpleasantness in any way to make amends for their wrongdoing. After he left, the managers did a lot of soul searching and started pointing fingers, accusing each other of misdeeds and improprieties that might have caused the condition known by now as Double F. Finally they agreed among themselves that they were men of action and would get to the bottom of this, each in his or her own way.

Then, production dropped precipitously, waste went up and the near perfect safety record the company had enjoyed for many years was marred by a series of industrial accidents. People were looking worried, their eyes darting uneasily around, searching the very space they occupied, suspecting it for harboring a living, stalking, ugly Double F. Managers fired some people who looked particularly distraught and acted out their gloom destructively, but no one changed. One of the more caring managers suggested environmental poisoning as the origin of the problem, and there was testing of the water for pollutants, examination of the walls and ceilings for asbestos and lead, and analysis of the air in the ventilation system, all in the hope of detecting some insidious bacteria, a fungus, a mold or a substance of some kind that was affecting the mind and soul of the people. But, their hopes were dashed when every test turned out negative.

The managers imposed new rules to control inertia, goldbricking, malingering, spreading destructive rumors and the like. They pressed their people for a clue, a hint, even a guess about this disease that threatened to put them all out of business. They could not believe that the people who affirmed the existence of the fear factor were ignorant of its origin, its nature and its course. They suspected a conspiracy. They started looking for its leaders, but there was no sign of any leaders or followers. They came to believe that the problem was "systemic," but no one would venture to define it any further, or even explain what this word meant in this context.

A sense of impotence spread among the managers. They no longer tried to project confidence that they would take care of all the little problems at work in their own time, as they had done in the past.

They stayed in their offices, staring blankly out the windows at the parking lot, no longer interested in reprimanding people who came to work late, or left for lunch and didn't return. They even stopped talking about the fear factor as if they expected it to lose its potency through this studied forgetfulness. And, when they confided in each other in hushed voices, they talked vaguely about the days before "that thing," recalling with fondness little victories and satisfying encounters. Lloyd Jones lost his pleasant smile; his voice grew faint and his usually empowering gaze went out of focus and turned dark and indifferent. The CEO felt sad and incompetent because he couldn't heal his people.

The company was now in decline, its stock dropping, its customers bolting to the competition, and the community around it going through hard times. Layoffs were announced, and talk of going out of business was the main topic of conversation at the endless coffee breaks. People seemed defeated, resigned to the inevitable. It was clear to everyone now that the fear factor would run its course with the closing down of plants and offices; there was no doubt anymore that the disease would be terminal for the company.

Lloyd Jones spent many hours alone in his office staring at charts with projections of increased bookings, and sales, and profits, which seemed forever unattainable now. He hated having to tell his board of directors that the company was failing and there was nothing he could do to turn it around. Sometimes he thought that failure had the smell of decay, and other times he thought it sounded like rain beating down on the steel of a cheap car's rooftop; but the most persistent manifestation of failure was an unspecified discomfort in his gut, which he invariably attributed to "the thing." He realized that there had always been some things he had dreaded—aggressive people, regimentation, yes-men and "going by the book"—things he had found stunting to human growth. In every position he had occupied on his way to the top of the organization there had been obstacles to overcome—autocratic bosses, ornery customers, unscrupulous competitors, dishonest Wall Street analysts, unprincipled do-gooders and focused evildoers. But, "the thing" that clawed now at his gut and his mind, could not be defeated without sacrifice, some yet-to-be-defined loss. He folded the charts he had been studying, stacked the computer printouts in a neat pile and decided to call it a night. It was just as he was about to leave his office that the janitor appeared at the door.

"I'm sorry," he said, realizing that he had intruded upon the top executive's privacy. Looking at him with concern, he added, "I didn't know you were still here."

"Just leaving," Lloyd Jones said, and, as if the janitor's presence had triggered a thought in his mind, he added, "I see you're still working hard. Haven't you heard we're about to shut down the place?"

"Sure," the janitor said, "but that's got nothing to do with me. I work the same way, regardless."

Lloyd Jones smiled. "Fear factor hasn't got you down yet?"

"Fear factor gets those that don't do what's the right thing; it's they that becomes afraid," he said as he went about the business of emptying the wastebasket. "People's got to stand up for their self sometime...do the right thing."

"That's a good way to think about it," Lloyd Jones mumbled. A couple of minutes later, still pondering the words of this broom-totting philosopher, he bid him goodnight and left his office.

On the way home Lloyd Jones' mind kept circling around the janitor's words, looking for a door to enter and unlock their meaning. He thought about "doing the right thing for oneself" during dinner at home, lying awake in bed, trying to fathom the meaning of it, whatever it was that gave the janitor immunity from "the thing;" but whatever that was, it remained just beyond his awareness. Only at dawn, still suspended between dreams and troubles, an answer hit him with the force of a thunderclap. He hurried through breakfast and drove to the office, ready for action.

"Good morning, Lloyd," someone greeted him on the way to his office.

He didn't smile as he had always done. He dismissed the greeting with a sneer and moved on.

Before his secretary could greet him, he told her that he wanted a cup of coffee and his mail right away, as if she hadn't done these very things every morning for years on end. She put her head down and with an obedient "Yes, sir" started for the coffee machine. "The mail, first," he called out to her. She was flustered and stopped dead on her tracks.

"Of course," she said, barely able to restrain her tears.

He took off his jacket and sat down. She brought him the mail and some phone messages. "Only one of the messages seems urgent," she said, "the one on top." He thanked her without looking at her. Then, as she turned to leave, he told her to forget about coffee and get him a doughnut from the cafeteria instead. "I'll get the coffee myself," he said. She paused for a moment. In all the years she had worked for him he had never asked her for a doughnut, never been so abrupt, so inconsiderate. He waited for her to say something, but he knew she wouldn't. She just bent down her shoulders and hurried out. Jones shook his head in frustration.

Half a dozen people were waiting in line at the coffee machine. Lloyd Jones went ahead of everybody, and jingled his change as he waited for a man to get his cup filled. "I'm in a hurry," he announced in a gruff tone. "I got an important appointment." The man behind him stared at him dumbfounded. "You don't mind; do you?" Jones sneered.

"No problem," the man said in a flat, bored tone of voice. He had no interest in claiming his spot. He just didn't seem to care.

Lloyd Jones stared at him with contempt. He felt like shoving him down to shake him up, but he controlled his anger.

And, then, something happened. "Wait a minute, Mr. Jones," a young woman down the line called out to him, tossing back her short black hair. "Just because you are the Big Boss, it doesn't mean that you can push your way to the front of the line like that!" she protested. Everyone's eyes were upon her, and she, fully aware that she had made a decision from which there was no turning back, fully erect like a warrior with feet planted on the earth for battle, stared at the Big Boss and said in an instructive manner, "You've got to take your place on the line, sir!"

Now, the others around her trained their eyes on him. "Yeah!" they blurted out in unison like a chorus in some ancient play, suddenly come to life. "You can't shove people around like that! We got some rights."

"I'm sorry," mumbled Lloyd Jones. And, shoving his change back into his pocket, moved to the end of the line to wait his turn. The man at the head of the line, who had been pushed back, shook his head and, reclaiming his position, dropped his coins in the machine's slot. "Creeps…they don't give a damn about you," he mumbled as he retreated with his hard earned cup of coffee.

The news spread like wildfire on dry grass. Rose Parker, the accountant who had told Mr. Big where to get off at the coffee machine, when asked what she had done, replied with modesty, "I just did what I thought was the right thing, that's all."

Her words were repeated many times from cubicle to cubicle, in corridors and shop floors and wherever people worked: "she did what was right," they echoed her words. "She just didn't want to be pushed around by the Big Boss."

That afternoon, Lloyd Jones's secretary marched into his office and, without any introduction, told him that she didn't appreciate the way he had treated her that morning. "And there have been a couple other times," she complained, "when I wanted to tell you how terribly you made me feel, but I kept it to myself."

Lloyd Jones raised his head sheepishly and looked at her. "Why didn't you speak up?" he asked.

"Because..." she hesitated, as if she needed time to figure out a difficult calculation, too taxing to do now in her head. "Because I was afraid," she said defiantly at last.

"You're right," Lloyd Jones said. "I won't treat you that way anymore. You must not let me." He shifted his weight on his chair, as if that would ease his discomfort, and added with well-timed hesitation, "I'm sorry."

She stood still for a while, reluctant to leave the spot on which she had stood up and defended her dignity. Then, she turned around and strolled out of his office, tall and light on her feet.

All day long people were getting things off their chests, coming to grips with fears that were lurking for a long time in their guts. "Sometimes, you've got to stand up and be counted," people were saying to one another. Professionals, clerks, shop floor workers, people who had been around for a long time and newcomers to the company found the people who had kept them awake nights, people who had made them hate, and people to whom they had surrendered chunks of their souls, and leveled with them without shouts or angry words, but with firm unwavering voices, conveying faith in what was "the right thing to do."

Several of Jones' direct reports went to see him and tell him what they believed was a nasty turn of events, a widespread rebellion, started, no doubt, from a misunderstanding of whatever he had said or done that morning while getting his coffee. Jones listened to their anxious comments and suggestions for "regaining control of the situation," as they put it, and told them that the first person who tried to put down any "rebellion," or did anything at all to stop what was happening, would be fired on the spot. They looked at each other as if they had seen their boss morphing into the Mad-Hatter and Dracula rolled into one. Lloyd Jones told them to think about the situation and do the right thing, or he would get others managers who will. It took them a couple of hours to figure out what he meant, and they did respond, a couple of them forcefully, by telling him how lousy they felt when he played games with people. Lloyd Jones took it all in without arguing, without any sign of defensiveness. He felt that, at least on this day, he had served his people well.

That evening, Lloyd Jones waited for the janitor to show up. He wanted to thank him for saving the company, and offer to help him get a better job, if he wanted one. The man's advice was sure worth more than what he had got from his communication specialists and the consultants. But the janitor who always tried to do the right thing never showed up. The next day, he found out from the foreman that the janitor had been fired. "He called up and said he couldn't come to work last night because his little girl was in a school play and he had to be there," the foreman said, not without sadness. "He was a hard worker, and I hated to lose him, but I can't afford to have a guy like that around." And, pensively, he added, "If he could have, at least, reported sick…"

Jones smiled. "But, he wasn't," he said, as if talking to himself. "He was probably the healthiest person we're going to see for a long while."

The foreman looked puzzled, but said nothing. "Try to get him back," Jones told him. "We need people like that."

"I don't think that's possible," the foreman said with some apprehension. "He called this morning and told me not to worry about him because he had just answered an ad and was hired on the spot."

Lloyd Jones burst out into a roaring laughter. The foreman watched dumbfounded as the Big Boss laughed, holding his belly. Lloyd Jones was now sure that he had done the right thing, and this insight would sustain him for a long time.

CHAPTER 6

❀

Slim's Edge

The electricians who installed the high voltage lines between the power plant and the mills of Steelcraft's Indiana Harbor Works were skillful and worked hard. They crawled into pits under mammoth presses and climbed high up on ladders and steel structures to lay cable and mount transformers and power up rolling mills and cranes. They never complained about "the conditions," or safety, or the bosses, or anything else they had to put up with. They worked as a team, knowing what the job required, and what each one of them expected from the others, before it was even asked. There was danger all around them, but they took their work in stride and prided themselves in overcoming challenges. A pat on the back, a smile and a touch of a hat, a couple of words of thanks—that was the extent of their acknowledgment of success.

But, there was one man who didn't work hard at all and kept pretty much to himself. It seemed that the group norms didn't apply to Slim. He read the paper from cover to cover behind the cable spools in out of the way places, and found the quiet nooks and crannies at the plant to sleep on top of piles of rugs. His fellow workers knew exactly what Slim was doing but didn't seem to mind him at all. Their spirits were high, their work first rate, and their safety record the envy of the trades. And when Slim would get bored and saunter back in the midst of things, not only did they greet him with smiles and crack jokes with him, but they made sure he didn't start helping with the work they were handling so well.

Barney Torvig, a college boy, who had just joined the group as an apprentice electrician for the summer, was puzzled by the odd arrangement and asked some of the guys what was wrong with Slim. The young man didn't think that there was anything really wrong with him, but he surely thought that there was plenty wrong with all the others who put up with such blatant goldbricking by a fellow worker. He was in the process of bonding with the group and wanted to protect them from such an unfair practice. His textbooks told him that every group has norms that the members find very hard to break. Why wasn't this group, his group, conforming to the Group Dynamics research like the rest of the world's work groups do? Why weren't sanctions being imposed upon the norm-breaker?

One day at lunchtime, while Slim was out of sight, Barney asked his teammates why they put up with a loafer like Slim. The electricians laughed and said with good humor that Slim was Slim, and one must accept other people the way they are and not try to change them. Barney thought about their answer but, no matter how hard he tried, he found it totally inadequate. He was a little angry that his friends were being taken advantage of and wanted an opportunity to restore fairness to this little world where fate had placed him that summer. He was always on the lookout for some other reason that might explain the peculiar arrangement, or some insidious explanation that would give him a chance to raise the issue with upper management and show his friends how much he cared for them. But, what made matters even more difficult for him to understand, was what appeared to him to be a total acceptance of the situation by the foreman and the other bosses who happened by. They appeared to be delighted to meet up with Slim and get a chance to exchange a few words with him. He figured that Slim was either well connected to someone at the top of the company, or was a damn clever actor with a terrific act of some kind. Or, worse yet, all of them, managers and workers, were involved in conspiracy, and Slim was its mastermind.

One day, an order came to lay cable between two towers between the power plant and the new rolling mill building. The towers were two hundred feet apart, and there was a two-foot-wide "bridge" connecting them, fifty feet up in the air. This excuse of a bridge was made up of two angle iron rails two feet apart, with slanted flat cross bars now and then between them, for strength. Regularly spaced every few feet there were one-foot high vertical posts with guide holes on them for threading the cable through them. While Barney was wondering how anyone could stand, let alone walk and work up on that flimsy structure made up of a couple of steel rails and lots of thin air, Slim appeared from nowhere and started climbing up the spiral steel stairway on one of the towers. He had one of the cable ends hanging from a loop on his belt and was dragging the cable behind him. He reached the rail bridge and stood up, erect and alone for a moment, fifty feet up in the air, and surveyed the bleak landscape of tin plant roofs, smokestacks, blast furnaces with sludge piles next to them, mammoth trucks, and mountains of iron ore and coal around him, as if to get the feel of the place. Barney couldn't help but imagine that he was in the presence of a creature ready to touch the heavens with his hand and the earth with his tail. He looked furtively around him. No one was staring at him. Slim took a few steps, testing his footing on the steel. He bent down and started feeding the cable through the first post's guide hole. His boots, pressed against the edge of the angle iron beams, but couldn't quite fit on the slim flat edges, and half the soles could be seen from the ground. The entire crew was gathered below watching Slim string the cable, holding their breaths as if a magician was performing his final and most spectacular act of the evening. Or, Barney wondered, they may be so awed by that man's daring that they had to pray for God's forbearance and for life.

When Slim reached the tower at the other end of the bridge, one of the workers looked at Barney's deathly white face and said with a smile, "Hey, Barney, now you know why it's not such a good idea to try and change people, right? Slim is Slim, and thank God for that, or we'd all be out of a job."

Barney Torvig smiled, wanting to hang his head. He felt so stupid, so guilty and so thankful at that particular instant of time.

CHAPTER 7

❋

The Principle of the Thing

Books were disappearing from the Library after hours. A management meeting was held to decide whether the Library should be locked up to stop the losses, or kept open anyway, so that people could study on their own time. It was a meeting without a meeting of minds. Arguments were thrown like spears, and counter-arguments were put up like shields. Reasons were offered, explanations were produced, dire consequences were predicted, benefits and costs were laid out for all to see, and the *principle of the thing* was brandished to prove a point, gain advantage, shore up a position, or win an argument. All the forces that could be marshaled had been marshaled, but the battle raged on, because, as someone said, "one's view of the world is at stake here."

"Lock and lose work, but not books; keep it open and lose books, but not work," someone summarized the issue, only to be opposed by someone else, who put it this way: "Lock and protect company property, or abandon management's fiduciary responsibility to its stockholders and let thieves have their way."

The two brightest systems thinkers in the group produced the most far-reaching formulations of the problem. One said: "Lock to help employees with their moral development, by removing unnecessary temptation, or leave it open and show your total disregard for them." The other said: "Lock and proceed with business as usual, or leave it open and rely on people's ability to find out for themselves the value of right conduct based on their own free will, rather than out of necessity, obligation, fear or lack of opportunity."

The staff accountant, who had been asked to make tradeoffs on the Library pilferage, its use and the financial aspects of the situation, was asked to give her report when a stalemate was reached. She said that a hundred books would have to be stolen every day to offset the benefits accruing to the company as a result of the Library's usage after hours, assuming a mid-level professional employee's salary for the average Library user and the figures on the number of "patrons" given to her by the librarian, who estimated them from records of the automatic entrance counters. "Since only three books are stolen every week, on the average," the staff accountant concluded, "it follows that the company gains two hundred and thirty three times more, if the Library is left open after hours, than if it's locked up."

Practical people with trust in the work of others wanted to leave the Library open and thought that they had won the day. But, they forgot about the practical people who questioned the librarian's counts and the staff accountant's assumptions and calculations, and wanted the Library locked to stop the financial drain. But, most importantly, they didn't take into account the moralists who advocated either freedom or responsibility first and thought the issue should be decided on *the principle of the thing*, rather than benefits and costs of any kind.

After more than two hours of discussion, debate, arguments, accusations and recriminations, the boss decided that he couldn't afford to ever be accused of wantonly accepting theft as part of his efforts to run a productive organization. The Library was locked up after hours, for good.

Somehow, there are still three books, on the average, stolen every week, and no one knows how. So far, no manager has proposed that the Library be locked up permanently, but there are people concerned, both about the theft of books and the Library's existence.

CHAPTER 8

❀

Cover-up 101

1

༄

From: John Podany, Senior Research Scientist
To: Lester McIntire, Fiber Optics Section Head
Subject: Fiber Optic Transmission Line Difficulties

The latest series of experiments, conducted with extra-low impurity glass, show that transmission efficiency is extremely high, approaching the 99% level, but fabrication is difficult as of now. None of the additives tried offer any improvement in the brittleness of the material and, as a result, the operating temperatures for underwater cable cannot be met. Since these experiments have been ongoing for the past six years and no fruitful alternatives appear to exist at this time, I recommend discontinuation of the program.

2

֍

From: Lester McIntire, Fiber Optics Section Head
To: Mario Conti, Optical Materials Manager
Subject: Optical Transmission Lines

Research on ultra-pure-glass fibers is progressing. Though fabrication and brittleness problems continue to be serious, particularly at low temperatures, the program is basically sound, and could be completed with some slippage and the expenditure of additional funds. Details on cost and schedule will be presented at the next progress report.

3

֍

From: Mario Conti, Optical Materials Manager
To: Jake Streep, Director of Materials Research
Subject: Progress on Transmission Lines

Additional funds may be required to carry through to successful completion the preliminary success we have been having with high-grade glass fibers. There remain some concerns about temperature effects upon the material, which can be addressed and hopefully resolved.

4

֍

From: Jake Streep, Director of Materials Research
To: Don Hoyle, VP of Research
Subject: Long Range Fiber Communications Project Nears Completion

The high purity fiber program is progressing satisfactorily and is expected to be available within cost and schedule constraints. Residual temperature corrections can be made prior to making it available for production.

5

From: Don Hoyle, VP of Research
To: Harlan Sutherland, VP and general manager
Subject: Nearing New Fiber Materials Breakthrough

According to the best estimates of our staff, research into new fiber materials for long-range transmission lines is meeting with success and release to production is expected as planned.

CHAPTER 9

❁

Divining the Will of Management

1

ɞ

From: Trevor Bell, Chief Corporate Scientist
To: Stan Talbot, V. P. Dawson Research Center
Subject: President's Visit to Dawson Research

I want to thank you and your staff for the excellent presentations and the tour of the labs at our recent visit to the Center.

The President and I were very impressed by the well thought out portfolio of research projects you have assembled and the businesslike way you are following toward their execution.

We feel particularly good about your recent breakthrough in the development of the inexpensive solar water heater for home use, and would like you to keep us informed of its progress. I ought to add that we have some doubt regarding the efficiency of the gas producer from food wastes, though we understand that the results on the bacterial decomposition efficiency are only preliminary.

2

∾

From: Stan Talbot, V. P. Dawson Research Center
To: Jane Ward, Director of Research, Dawson
Subject: Top Management View of Your Research Efforts

Many thanks to you and your staff for the outstanding job you did at the President's visit.

He was very happy with the directions we are following, and expressed high interest in our Solar Water Heater Project, which needs to be accelerated. There were some concerns expressed regarding the feasibility of the Gas Producer to which we need to be sensitive.

3

∾

From: Jane Ward, Director of Research
To: Dick Perkins, Home Energy Sources Mgr.
Subject: Home Gas Producer Project Assessment

Serious concerns were expressed by the President about the value of the Gas Producer at his recent visit to the Center. As I have pointed out to you, we need to assess its progress and review the funding level for this project.

The Solar Heater Project looks like a winner and we should allocate additional funding to speed it up.

4

∽

From: Dick Perkins, Home Energy Sources Manager
To: Barry Bates, Gas Producer Section Leader
Subject: Concerns About the Gas Producer

It appears that my fears regarding the value of your Section's work on the Gas Producer have been justified. The President, at his recent visit, thought that continuation of work raises too many questions, given its doubtful feasibility, low efficiency and market penetration difficulties, even if we had a technical success. At best, project funding in our next funding cycle should be minimized.

5

∽

From: Barry Bates, Section Leader
To: Tom Chang, Lead Engineer
Subject: Gas Producer Funding

Top Management feels that lack of substantial progress in developing the Gas Producer does not justify further expenditure of funds in this area.

Please, set up a meeting to arrange for reassignment of the staff to other more promising efforts with a potential layoff being the last resort.

CHAPTER 10

❀

Demands Upon One's True Self

Hiroshi was hired to sweep the floor of the jade factory. He worked hard when the floor was dirty and meditated under the shade tree in the yard when he was done cleaning the floor.

The foreman saw him meditating and shouted at him to get back inside and sweep. "The floor is clean," said Hiroshi, "but if you have some other work for me to do, I'll be glad to do it." The foreman wasn't used to such answers, and told him that his job was to sweep the floor, and do it all day long. "If the manager comes by and sees you like this, I'll lose my job," he growled. "Get back to work, or you'll be gone before I am."

Hiroshi didn't want to lose his job and he didn't want anyone else to lose his job on his account; but neither did he want to sweep clean floors just to look busy. When he worked, Hiroshi chose to work hard; and when his work was done Hiroshi chose to meditate. He could have chosen to do otherwise, but then he wouldn't be Hiroshi—he would be Someone Else.

So, from that day on, Hiroshi worked hard at his job, sweeping the dirty floor, and when the floor was clean, he would dump out on the floor all the dirt he had swept into the trash cans and start sweeping all over again. Seeing his job in this new way, Hiroshi was able to satisfy the foreman, his own needs for food and drink and his chosen self.

When someone asked him why he had stopped meditating under the shade tree, Hiroshi replied that he had never stopped. He said that the only thing different was the location of the shade tree under which he meditated. He had transplanted the tree from the yard into his own mind.

CHAPTER 11

❀

Little Things Count

John Harris, a junior administrator at Honeypot Inc., stood by the door of his supervisor's office, discussing a task that had to be completed. Nothing profound was being said, no new knowledge was being created, nothing urgent was being communicated; but, there was something important happening, because these two people were affirming the existence of each other.

It was just then that Doug Marston, Honeypot's vice president of Administration, appeared at the supervisor's door, stood behind the junior administrator and, with a booming voice, urgently and imperiously told the supervisor that he had to talk to him right away about the Jenkins contract.

He was already past the junior administrator, already half a step into the supervisor's office, when that usually compliant subordinate put out his hand, like a traffic cop at a busy intersection, and said with unmistakable determination: "As soon as I'm finished here, Doug."

Marston stopped dead on his tracks, cast a severe glance at this underling of his, and then, seeing the junior administrator next to him for the first time, uttered an inflated "Oh!" and, as an afterthought, a labored, bruised "Sorry!" A few moments went by in awkward silence. "The Jenkins contract needs work. See me right away," he said, returning to his officious tone, which could justify in his mind the making of any demand at any time. Then, with no quaking of the earth and no trembling of any subordinates, he beat a hasty retreat. He was clearly displeased by such disrespect toward leaders, such disinterest in business matters by today's workers.

John Harris had grown wings by now, and was ready to fly toward his supervisor, who had become a tree, driving roots deep into the earth, and growing branches for winged creatures to land upon them, and build nests on them, and dash away from them to wherever they wanted to go.

CHAPTER 12

❀

Making a Dent in the World

The story, which follows, was submitted to the company newspaper, *The Microtek Participant* by a Rudy Barbick, one of the employees of Microtek, Inc., a solar cell manufacturer in California's Silicon Valley. It was published in *The Participant* on 5/8/84 with the following highfaluting editorial commentary:

One of the central problems of modern Western man is that he experiences himself as an insignificant, meaningless, impotent being. His individuality has been reduced to his social security number and his freedom of action is exercised in making choices among TV channels. Without identity, faceless and limited in the institutional factories of education, work, leisure, politics and the rest, modern man cries out for a way to affirm his existence in the world. Sometimes this cry takes the form of rebellion against 'the system': man may not know who he is, but at least he can influence the system and be noticed.

We, here at Microtek, are committed to the proposition that every human being is complex, unique, powerful and worth every effort the organization can expend to enhance his or her self-esteem. We live in a time of transition, where high technology can grind down individuality and produce cogs in the machine of mass culture; but we are not helpless. We possess imagination. We are not only unafraid of the power of imagination, but also encourage its use in whatever context, whenever and however the individual employee chooses to use it. Rudy Barbick's and Calvin Brown's way of making a dent in the world may not be the most constructive or the most satisfying, but it shows the depth of the problem and offers, at least, a solution. We hope that our employees will find their own ways of shaping the organization by impressing upon it their individuality, and publish Barbick's story with minor editorial corrections, to demonstrate in a small way our commitment to fearless and, from our point of view, responsible self-examination."

It says in the paper that you want anybody who has a story from work to write it up and send it to the paper, so this is what I'm doing. My English isn't so very good, and I can get fired telling this story, but I kinda think it's got to be told anyways, because it's something I and Brown did together that gives us a chance to be somebody. I dunno if newspaper people feel sort of lost, and that they don't count anymore, and nobody gives a damn about who they are, who do they work for, or that nobody will remember if they ever worked here or lived here even, but Brown and I sure as hell care about such things. We didn't talk much about it though, only when we got half a dozen beers down after bowling and things didn't look so heavy and black.

So, one evening we got to talking about nobody knows that we are alive or what we do inside the plant or out, except for our families and even they don't know much about us high techs. What's polishing and etching solar cells to them anyway?

I was machine operator once and then that was done and I spent sixteen months looking for work before I got a chance with high tech. Anyway, like I said, even the family don't know. Besides, why upset my wife with these thoughts about being a nobody, when she is a nobody too and don't do one damn thing she likes? Nobody knows me or cares about me like nobody knows a damn thing about the people who put up your pyramids or dug the Panama Canal or put together the tanks during the Big War to beat the hell out of Hitler. The Pharaoh didn't built the damn pyramids; the president didn't sweat in the jungles down there digging dirt and getting malaria; and sure as hell as much as I liked our generals they didn't sweat in the mills to make the steel for tanks and battleships.

So, I tell Brown that this dog's life ain't fair; just ain't worth it to go through it and make no mark, no scratch to last a year after we are goners. I don't mean no gravestone, everybody gets that. I mean something to tell the world that Rudy Barbick was here and worked hard all his life—eight hours a day like a dog. And Brown says we should do something about it, because no one is gonna do it for us.

So, we talk and talk about all kinds of schemes to make a dent in the world like we were a coupla kids getting ready to carve our names on the biggest tree around so as to be remembered for eternity. Only there's no tree at work and those plaques they have to carve your name when you do something big, they are nice but don't last long, what with new managements, new buildings, new decorations, you name it. No sir, this thing's got to last awhile and the only thing I know is the damn solar cells we polish all day long which go into satellites and they whirl around and around the earth for a good long time, dozens of years sometimes, I hear.

It was then that Brown says he'd heard that there was a probe coming up and they would be putting cells on that too. And that baby was going far, I mean very far, like past Saturn and Jupiter and past the whole damn solar system, out of the blasted Galaxy maybe. And Brown says, that's where we oughta get our John Hancocks scratched, if we're really gonna do something big because it wouldn't be not only lasting but also first. The only dudes with their personalized satellite sailing past the stars! The thought was a boost. I mean, I went home that night and the world wasn't so bleak no more. We hadn't done nothing yet, nothing had changed in the world, but I tell you, my head was all new and it felt warm inside me.

From that day on, Brown and I took our jobs real serious. We had our purpose now and wanted to know more than just what to do with the little solar cells we worked with. Like what is it for? Where is it going? How will it fit? There were lots of questions we asked the engineers and more about how they mark the numbers so as to know which piece fits where. It wasn't easy figuring things out, but if a man has a goal that's worth something to him, I mean something important deep down, he learns fast. And with all this interest the work got better and a coupla months later the supervisor says maybe I want to learn how to etch the serial numbers on the cells, since I got motivation and the job pays better. I would have taken the job if it paid less, so I jump at the chance.

Brown and I are like brothers now. We are like a secret society that knows the answer to the secrets of the universe. We have lunch together as always, but because we talk secret things we eat far from the other guys. We practice the signatures we're going to put on the cells, or maybe just paint the names, maybe on more than one cell, three maybe, both names together or maybe separate, with the date next to them, maybe with a USA next to it. And, we try to figure out how to get these fixed up cells past inspection. Like we study each inspector, try to figure out who sloughs off and who is a stickler; who might miss a cell now and then and who will raise the roof if he discovers our names. Maybe we should get the inspector aboard this thing, Brown says. We figure that Halloran is fed up with his job and might go along with the plan. Approach him with the idea like it was a gag, nothing serious, so we can back out of it. We try to figure all the angles, but it's just too damn important to risk blowing the whole thing if the guy disagrees. So as we mull this thing over, weeks go by, months, until the interplanetary probe appears on the schedule, and I tell Brown we got to do it now or never.

Nobody knows the job that's got to be done better than the guy who does it. You know how fast, how much, how many, when and how, and ways to get around all the answers the supervisor gives you. You got to know the system and work it so that you can do your thing day in day out, I mean stay sane, except that now it was more than that. So, I'm working on the probe cells and trying to figure out when to take the chance, but the inspectors are double-checking these cells for flaws—they are going to be up there for thousands of years, may be millions and they got to work for ten, twenty years so there's no taking any chances with putting up a defective one. Brown and I are getting desperate. We are past the halfway point on the job, and we can't figure out how to get them past inspection. Halloran is too tough; we can't risk it with him. The cells would work just fine with or without our little messages to space. I mean it wasn't like we would sabotage anything, that we could never do—we are Americans one hundred percent—but inspectors are there to check what's supposed to be and what's not supposed to be on each cell, no matter whether it's good or bad. They see "Barbick and Brown" strung around the border of some cells and they go ballistic. We'd be on our asses, out in the street, no doubt about that.

And then Jackson one of the inspectors gets into a car accident and will be in the hospital for weeks with a broken pelvis. This was my chance, I figure, and go to the supervisor and tell him I really would like to try my hand at inspecting. He needs me to etch numbers, he says, and besides it takes lots of experience before I can pass probe cells. But, I've been doing a great job etching, so he asks Halloran to show me what to look for on the microscope. My heart is about to bust as I sit there and watch the cells. The first week they give me rejects and Halloran checks my comments and says I'm a natural inspector. He is a swell guy that Halloran, knows how to make you feel good so you can do better every time. The second week I'm inspecting probe cells, and Brown is learning how to etch numbers, as I'm teaching him.

Late one afternoon, I give Brown the signal that we are now ready to do our thing, "implement our plan," like the bosses say. So, I etch our names, Rudy Barbick and Calvin Brown, the date, and a big fat USA and inspect the cell. Under the microscope our names look like they are up on a marquis, all lit up and proper. No one is watching, so we do it again and again, three times total, on real sharp cells, no flaws, marked properly, ready to be installed.

Seven months later the interplanetary probe was launched successfully and started its trip to the stars. Both Brown and I stayed home to see the launch on TV, but they didn't show it. By that time, launches like that were old hat. But it didn't matter because we could see the thing take off and soar in our minds. A proud bird carrying in its belly the immortality of Brown and Barbick. That night we celebrated, the two families together—big dinner of roast duck at the Peking Gardens. We just said it was for doing great on the job and moving ahead. When I told my wife about this some months later, she couldn't understand what the big deal was, but she was happy because I was so fired up. "You are immortal because you live forever in the mind of God," she said and believed it a hundred percent. I know she's right, but Brown and I got a little extra earthy immortality, I figure.

Since that time, there have been pictures of the planets, the rings of Saturn, Jupiter, and messages from beyond the solar system. All systems are go with the probe. It's working perfect, no problems at all. And our names are out there, somewhere in God's space, traveling for eternity. Who knows, maybe on some distant planet this thing will land and alien scientists will analyze the fragments, and—well you know how it goes…

Now, the funny thing is that ever since that probe went up, I don't feel so lost anymore. I get in a scrape and I think, damn it, a guy whose name is traveling past stars ought to be able to figure a way out. Or, I get sick and I think its OK if I die, there will be something out there that marks my passing from earth, something of myself that lives on in time and space. It isn't exactly a statue in a public square or a bust at the Capitol, but it is something, and maybe something more than a bust or a statue. And, it isn't something that I can show my kids like old carpenters or masons could show houses and buildings and such to their kin and be proud, but it is something big, something I can tell my kids and they can tell their kids and all can remember me.

So, this is my story, in case you think it's worth something to you, since I hear that Microtek wants people to use their heads. I sure hope that it's true not just hot air, and I get fired. I hope that everybody can find a way to make a dent in the world somehow, and that the Company help them out to do it. Believe me, it's a good feeling to know that a man's passing through life is not forgotten, that a man's work produced something that lasts in this world for a while. By the way, nobody did nothing with solar cells—there are many parts in any probe that one can sign his name on. And, there ain't nobody by the name of Barbick and Brown around here! These names are aliens, in case you wonder.

See you all in some other world or other some day.

0-595-25827-1

CPSIA information can be obtained
at www.ICGtesting.com
Printed in the USA
FFOW02n1726211216
30562FF